THE INK DRAGON AND THE ART OF FLIGHT

JORDAN RILEY SWAN

EZRA ZABIT

Cover design: James T. Egan, BookflyDesign.com

Managing editor: Diane Callahan, QuotidianWriter.com

Copy editor: Angela Traficante, LambdaEditing.com

Sign up for notifications of upcoming releases by Jordan Riley Swan at JordanRileySwan.com

Comic panel art by Ami Agisi

 Created with Vellum

To every fantasy loving, comic reading, romance adoring nerd. We love you all.

CHAPTER
ONE

The crisp autumn air in New York City was unseasonably cold, and Jade's Flighter jacket wasn't doing much to cut the chill. She was made even colder by the darkness that concealed Night Armor's outstretched wings above their pedestrian target a thousand feet below. Jade leaned close to her dragoncoat's neck as they glided over Central Park West, turning in wide, slow circles. The black metal of his scales not only absorbed any stray light but seemed cool to the touch even through her leather gloves. Jade flexed her fingers and tried to will warmth into them.

The sidewalks were relatively empty at this time of night—verging on three in the morning. The quietest part of the late shift, and well before the early risers could emerge to start their days. The City That Never Sleeps was, at the very least, looking a little weary.

But David Felman certainly wasn't. Even from this precautionary height, Jade could see the briskness in his step as he made his way down the dimly lit street. He was a man with a destination, and wherever he was headed, Jade was going to follow.

Jade and Night Armor had been on this assignment for less than twenty-four hours, and so far, Felman hadn't done anything particularly *interesting*. He'd spent most of the day at a tilted artist's desk in his publisher's office, inking pages that Jade couldn't see from her perch on the opposite building's roof. Nothing suspicious other than an exasperated phone call and a quick trip to a corner store, and then on to his apartment for even more drawing. It had been a challenge to find a rooftop nearby with the proper angle and still keep Night Armor from being seen, but she'd managed.

Drawing, drawing, drawing. Until two in the morning. Jade had almost dozed off, but Night Armor's excited chattering had kept her awake. The black-steel dragoncoat had been thrilled to witness the artist at work on his favorite comic series. All night, while Jade's fingers stiffened around her standard-issue binoculars, Night Armor had alternated between fidgeting restlessly in an attempt to see the pages, and fretting about the possibility that he might spoil the next issue for himself.

Finally, around two-thirty, Felman had gotten up from his desk, donned a coat, and left his apartment. Their target was on the move.

Felman paused at the intersection with West Sixty-Sixth, lifting a hand to glance down at his wristwatch. Around him, a cold wind rustled the husks of dried-out autumn leaves.

"Fly lower," Jade whispered to Night Armor.

The dragon was quiet for a moment, and Jade could feel the hesitation in the tense cords of muscle on Night Armor's neck. Then, in the high-pitched, whistling language of dragoncoats, he said, Lower? Is that... is that a good idea? What if he sees us?

"What's he going to see? Look up. Sky's pitch black. Need I remind you that you're a Blackwing now?"

Night Armor hesitated, banking to the left for another circle. But... if we're lower, won't we be closer to him?

"That's sort of the idea," Jade sighed. "Can you do me a favor and trust me?"

Jade. She could hear the dragoncoat's nerves echoing through the clicks of his voice. I trust *you*. It's just that—

Jade ran a hand down the side of Night Armor's neck. She began to hum softly, hoping to calm him down. His uneasiness seemed to fade, his anxious clicks tapering off.

"Better? Now, do we think we can get a closer look?"

Despite his reluctance, Night Armor chirped in affirmation, angling his wings to dive. The ever-familiar thrill rose in Jade's chest, a weightless rush that waxed and waned with the pitch of the black dragon's plunge. Even on a night like tonight, exhausted as she was from her lack of rest, and with the chill biting at the exposed skin of her face, it was all worth it for *that* feeling.

Night Armor pulled up halfway to the ground, a few hundred feet above the target. From here, Jade could get a better look at him. David Felman cut a striking figure in his worn-out brown overcoat, his dark, wiry hair unruly and stirred into a frenzy by the wind. He kept looking over his shoulder, like he was worried about being followed.

Smart man, Jade thought to herself, with a note of satisfaction. *But not smart enough.*

After a few moments of lingering at the curb, he seemed to make a decision. He turned to the left, down Sixty-Sixth and into Central Park.

"Follow him," Jade breathed.

Night Armor complied, smoothly coasting above the tree-lined street.

It was a little strange, Jade thought, for an elite Flighter to be sent after a comic book artist. She wasn't sure what Felman had done—or planned to do—but was operating on the assumption that he was likely a Tsarosian spy; most targets of the Blackwing Program were, in some capacity. On a surface level, aside from his apparent penchant for late-night walks in the park, there wasn't anything especially suspicious about Felman, but Jade's job didn't end at the surface. And she wasn't the kind of Coat Warden who failed missions.

A few hundred yards down the street, Felman came to a halt next to a parked car. He hesitated, glancing around at the empty park . Then he looked up. Jade's heart jumped, and Night Armor let out a low, quiet hiss as Felman's wary eyes scanned the sky. His gaze swept right past the slowly circling Flighter.

Blackwing is one hell of a project, Jade thought, her heart light with relief. Night Armor wasn't the only one who had to adjust to his new looks. In the beginning of their time together, before their acceptance into the program, he'd been a regular copper, his scales weathered by a verdigris patina. The patchy green-gray of his chemical coating would have stood out starkly against the clear night, but now, he was all but invisible against the darkness.

Apparently satisfied that he was alone, Felman opened the passenger door of the car and slid inside.

Jade bit back a curse. She pressed her torso to Night Armor's neck. "How close do you think we can get without being spotted?"

Night Armor seemed to freeze in midair, his graceful glide faltering. You shouldn't be asking *me,* he exclaimed. You're the Coat Warden. Isn't it your call?

"We're a team. I wanted your input."

What do *you* think we should do?

Jade sighed. So much for prompting him into making some decisions. "I want to hear what's being said, if possible," she murmured, half to herself, "but I don't want to risk him spotting you, Olive, or the jig's up before we can even get a foot in the door."

Night Armor huffed. <u>They didn't give me an ace Blackwing name so that you could keep calling me *Olive, and definitely not the full version.*</u>

"Sorry, *Night Armor*. Can we fly lower? Please?"

<u>How much lower?</u>

"Take it fifty feet above the trees. We'll head back up if there's an issue."

Night Armor drifted downward slowly, keeping his flight in a controlled spiral. <u>Like that scene in issue forty-eight where the Black Dragon Gang heisted those gold bars from the trunk of the Rolls-Royce Phantom while Red Angler wasn't looking, and Pennydart had to keep watch from above!</u>

If he keeps referencing comics all the time, I'm going to stop reading them to him, Jade thought but didn't say—the last thing she wanted was a forlorn fourteen hundred pound dragon on her hands. She kept her eyes on the car, waiting for movement. Even from here, she still couldn't hear any conversation that was going on inside, and she couldn't make out the driver—if there *was* a driver.

After a few minutes, the passenger door opened, and Felman stepped out. A thick manila envelope was tucked under his arm, held to his chest. He closed the door behind himself, and there was a sputtering growl from the car's engine as the vehicle started, pulling off into the street.

Felman watched the car continue down Sixty-Sixth for a few seconds. Then he turned on his heel and walked off in the opposite direction.

Damn. Jade watched from her slow, gliding vantage point in the sky as the distance grew between Felman and his unknown compatriot. Her orders had been to find a way into Felman's life, to figure out what exactly his plans were. She didn't have to follow him solely, and whoever was in this car,

JORDAN RILEY SWAN & EZRA ZABIT

they might prove a valuable source of information in their own right. At the least, her superiors would want to know who he was talking to in such a clandestine manner.

But ultimately, the surest way to know what was in that envelope was to be watching when Felman opened it. Besides, Jade's instructions had been specific about keeping tabs on Felman. She was relatively new to the Blackwing program, and after all of the sacrifice it had taken to get her on the back of a dragoncoat in the first place, she wasn't about to throw her position away on a hunch. Her job wasn't secure enough to start improvising—not yet.

Jade tapped Night Armor on the shoulder and whispered, "Stay on Felman."

Sure thing! Night Armor chirped.

On the sidewalk below, Felman froze. His dark eyes narrowed in suspicion, and he looked over his shoulder, then back up at the sky once more. This time, his gaze lingered longer, searching.

Jade held her breath. Beneath her, she felt Night Armor tense. About a quarter of the whistles and clicks of dragoncoat speech were too high pitched or too low in tone for most people to hear, and the Dragonese equivalent words for "sure thing" fell into the too-high-to-hear range, only audible to those with a Coat Warden's finely-tuned ears. But they had dropped low to eavesdrop and made a classic blunder. It had been in his file when she prepped: he used to be a Coat Warden.

Felman waited on the sidewalk for a few more seconds, his brow furrowed. Eventually, he seemed to come to a decision, continuing on his way—walking faster than before, like he knew he was being followed.

Sorry, sorry! Night Armor bobbed upward in the air to increase their vertical distance, getting out of Felman's earshot. Jade knew her dragon well enough to feel the stress radiating

6

from him; he was kicking himself. <u>I forgot that he was a Flighter. He can hear us. I'm so *stupid*—</u>

"No, you're not," Jade said quietly, soothing him. "Come on, buddy. You just made a mistake. It's okay. We're still in this."

Night Armor took a deep breath, shaking his head as if to clear it. <u>Okay. You're right. You're right.</u>

"Let's keep going."

Night Armor righted himself, gaining some altitude, and continued to follow Felman like a skyward shadow. He turned his head to the left, glancing back at Jade. <u>Do you think he'll sign my comic book?</u>

Apparently his earlier mistake was already forgotten. Along with the concept that they were supposed to be secretly watching him.

"I don't know," Jade said, resisting the urge to roll her eyes. "Maybe. But remember, he can't see you. If he sees you, we're made. You got that, right?"

<u>Of course, of course</u>, Night Armor agreed hastily. <u>But you'll try to get an autograph for me, won't you?</u>

Jade had never been able to understand her dragon's fixation on *The Coated Crusader* stories. Night Armor and many of the other dragoncoats at the base could spend hours discussing the latest issues amongst themselves. Night Armor, like most dragoncoats, couldn't read the stories for himself, which meant that Jade was often forced to relay the ridiculous tales to him. She did so willingly, of course—the comics made him happy, and who didn't want to put their best friend in a good mood? But she still couldn't say she *liked* them. They were childish, full of strange exploits and even stranger outfits.

"I'll see what I can do," Jade said evasively. "Now, can we focus?"

<u>Right. Of course! I'm on it!</u>

As Jade and Night Armor flew low, their view of Felman was periodically eclipsed by the canopies of half-bare elm trees.

Felman had his hands in his pockets, the suspicious folder tucked close to his body, his head down.

A handful of blocks up from his rendezvous point, Felman turned abruptly to the left, traversing Central Park West toward the canyon of the cross street. Jade and Night Armor kept above the buildings, where there was more maneuverability for flight. Jade could make out Felman in the intermittent glow of streetlights.

He passed by a narrow alleyway, and as he did so, three figures slipped out onto the street after him. They kept some distance, but they were close enough that Jade, observing them, surmised that they weren't exactly professionals.

Uh oh, Night Armor said quietly. What do we do?

Jade hesitated, considering. She couldn't drop down to street level and risk Felman spotting Night Armor—one brush with a black-steel dragon, and the game was lost before it had begun. But she also could hardly allow Felman to get jumped. If Felman lost the envelope, then Jade would never be able to figure out what information it contained. Plus, if the information was sensitive to the Blackwing Program, then she couldn't let it fall into the wrong hands.

Often, Jade found herself guessing, trying to determine what course of action her commanding officer would insist upon if he were able to assess the situation. Her orders felt woefully unspecific once she was actually in the field, making a split-second decision from her dragon's back. If they'd been a regular Flighter pair, it might have been easier to make those heat-of-the-moment calls. *Track down jocust beetles. Attack jocust beetles. Sleep. Repeat.* Nowhere near the amount of fine-tuned precision that this would require.

What if they're feds? What if they're with a different division within the FIB, and I mess up their assignment? I haven't exactly been given all of the information. What if I'm supposed to let this happen?

The three men following Felman shuffled along the edges of the storefronts, the shadows disguising them. They quickened their pace with each step, and Jade, looking ahead, saw what they were waiting for: a streetlight with a burned-out bulb. A window of darkness—no witnesses.

Jade's instincts won out over pragmatism. She couldn't watch this man get mugged without intervening, regardless of the risk to her Flighter's cover.

As Felman turned another corner, Jade whispered to Night Armor, "Get down there. We need to cut them off. Quickly."

For once, Night Armor didn't respond with a worried question, as if he sensed the seriousness in Jade's voice. He tucked in his wings and dove, his body streamlined, the cold wind drawing tears from the corners of Jade's eyes.

Night Armor alighted on the sidewalk soundlessly, quite the feat considering the steel and claws. Before any of the would-be muggers could open their mouths to cry out, Night Armor rushed them, slamming into them bodily and knocking them to the concrete.

"Don't move," Jade warned in a low tone. "Stay down, if you know what's good for you."

She glanced behind her at the streetcorner, hoping that she wasn't about to see Felman standing there. But the intersection was empty. If Felman had heard the ambush, he hadn't turned around. He had been on edge enough that he might have even suspected he was being followed and known better than to turn and face his pursuer.

One of the three masked men pushed himself to his feet. Night Armor showed his teeth threateningly, but when he spoke to Jade, he sounded giddy with excitement. Jade! This is just like page twenty of issue two of The Coated Crusader—

"Night Armor, *focus,*" Jade said through gritted teeth. Louder, addressing the men, she added, "If you know what's good for you, you won't make this complicated."

The man still on the ground scrambled away, pale and cowering, but the others stood firm, one's hands reaching for something in the belt behind his back...

Idiot, Jade thought, growing frustrated. *Do you really think a bullet is going to stop a fully armored dragoncoat? Might ruin my hearing though, and we can't have that.*

"Night Armor," she said.

Her dragoncoat took another step forward, flashing fangs. The mugger hesitated, as if reassessing his situation.

"Who are you?" Jade demanded. "Why were you following that man?"

"Why do you think?" The mugger's eyes narrowed.

"Do you know who he is?"

He sniffed. "No. Should I?"

Jade exhaled, unsure whether to be relieved or annoyed. These men weren't FIB or anything of the sort. They were just out for some quick, dirty cash. "Get lost," she snarled. "Don't make me ask again. My dragoncoat is the impatient type. He might act... rashly and *make a meal of you.*"

Given what would happen if Night Armor got human blood in his mouth, it wasn't a real threat, but it usually worked wonders on the rubes and the uneducated.

Night Armor snaked out his head, snapping at the air above him—hamming it up, as usual. But the performance worked. The mugger's fists uncurled. He turned to his partner, reaching out a hand to help him up, and the three of them scurried back down the street, shooting wary looks over their shoulders at the dragon.

How did I do? Night Armor turned his head to look at Jade.

"You did great, bud," Jade said, jumping at the chance to pay her dragon a much-needed compliment. *Could've done without the comic book reference, but on the whole....*

What now?

"Back to the air," Jade said. "We have to try and catch up with Felman."

Night Armor heaved off the ground with powerful hind legs, climbing into the air in a tight spiral. Jade clung to his saddle as he reached the tops of the surrounding buildings, leveling off into normal flight.

She scanned the street. There were a few cars and a couple of scattered, insomniac pedestrians, but no Felman. They'd lost his trail. She cursed under her breath.

"Come on," she said reluctantly. "He's not here, and we have no way of knowing where he is. But odds are, he'll be back at the publisher's or his apartment. Not too many places to look."

That's true, Night Armor mused. And we can get him to sign my comic book!

"Right." Jade sighed, staring out across the almost empty street. "Come on. Let's get back to base and try to get a little bit of shut-eye before tomorrow. We'll want to be well rested."

Sure. Night Armor turned sharply to the side, his tail whipping behind him as he changed course. He flew at full speed over the buildings, toward the tip of Manhattan and the Upper Bay, chirping nonstop as he went. Hey, what issue do you think I should give him? Obviously the first one is the classic, but in issue four, the Coated Crusader fights this villain who tries to steal Blindside's special abilities, and he has to...

CHAPTER
TWO

B y the time David Felman returned to his third-floor loft apartment, his hands were shaking too much for him to get the door open. He fumbled the ring of brass keys, dropped them, then took a deep breath to steady himself before picking them up and trying again.

The apartment was dark, save for the dull glow of street lamps below that always filtered through the large, warehouse-style windows that faced the main drive. David tossed his keys onto the coffee table and collapsed into the patchy couch, with its sagging, threadbare cushions. The manila folder that Margie had handed him in the car dropped to the floor beside him. He left it there, where it seemed to glow in his periphery like a beacon—or a warning.

Everything had gone well back at the park. Why was he still so nervous? There hadn't been any interruptions to the hand-off, and he was pretty sure there had been no witnesses. Margie had assured him there was no trouble on her end, either. He had gotten himself a little too worked up, though. And he could've sworn, as he left the area, he had heard dragon whistles.

With a sigh, David pushed himself upright, then got laboriously to his feet. *Dragon whistles.* He must be more stressed out than he'd thought. Hearing things. Conjuring up Backscatter's voice in his head, like an auditory ghost born out of his own anxieties.

David crossed the apartment to the kitchen, rooting around in the lower cabinets. It was a little late for a nightcap, but his nerves were shot; if he wanted to get a few hours of restful sleep after all this excitement, he needed a drink, Prohibition be damned.

His hand closed on the burlap-wrapped bottle in the back corner, but at the same moment, there was a harsh knock on the door.

David's hand flew back as if the bottle had burned it. He slammed the cabinet shut and glanced over at the door as it rattled in its frame with the force of his visitor's second knock.

"*Felman!* Hey! Open up!"

Inwardly, David groaned. *At this hour? What in the world?* He cast a longing look over at the door to his bedroom before shuffling to open the front door.

Levi, the editor in chief of Freedom Press, blustered into the room like a gale-force hurricane, his tattered coat trailing behind him. He swept his hat from his head, releasing a puff of dark, prematurely graying curls, and whirled around to face David. In his right hand, he clutched an inked comic page, the last page of the latest proof David had sent to press. Levi jabbed an accusatory finger at the lowest panel of the page.

"Felman," he began, the boisterous cadence of New York in his tone, "is this some kind of mean-spirited joke?"

"Levi," David muttered, "it's almost four in the morning."

His friend ignored him, shoving the page under his nose.

David squinted at what Levi was pointing to—the yellow box at the bottom of the last panel, his sign-off for the issue.

"So?" David looked up, frowning. "What's the problem?"

Levi gave him a wide-eyed stare, like he couldn't believe David's audacity. He cleared his throat and held the page out, adjusting his glasses to read the text. "'The adventures of *The Coated Crusader* will conclude in the next two thrilling issues!'"

"Yes?" David raised an eyebrow at him. "Is there a point to this? I always write a sign-off at the end of the issue."

"*Conclude?*"

Ah. "I told you when I started," David said. "This isn't a story that goes on forever. It has to end at some point."

Scoffing, Levi made a show of throwing up his hands and shaking his head. David watched him blankly, unwilling—and unable, at this late hour—to give Levi the satisfaction of an outward reaction.

"You can't do this," Levi insisted. "This is our number one seller. This is Freedom Press's bread and butter."

"I'm not interested in... what is it they say here?" David cast around in his head for the English idiom. English was his second language; he was fluent, but occasionally, the more idiosyncratic turns of phrase slipped his mind. "Beating a dead horse."

Levi was already shaking his head. "No, no, no. This is not a dead horse. This is the most alive horse I've ever seen. This horse is the morning-line favorite at Belmont Park, and Felman, I've got all of my money riding on him."

David exhaled, brushing past Levi and pacing into the living room. "The story has to end."

"Listen to me," Levi said, visibly flustered, "you're the artist. I can't force you to keep making this thing, and if you really want to stop, that's your call. But I've got half a dozen small magazines that don't turn a profit. All that printing, all those writers' salaries, are riding on the back of *your* comic book, because that's what people are buying."

David stooped to pick up the manila folder Margie had given him, adjusting the pages within. He carried it over to his slanted drafting table, letting it rest on the lower tray. "I understand that, Levi."

"Do you? Because people are gonna lose their jobs if this goes under. Ink costs money, paper costs money, wages cost, well, you know... and without *The Coated Crusader,* we aren't making any."

David hesitated, drumming his fingers on the edge of the drafting table. He looked up at the editor. As annoyed as he was by Levi's sudden appearance, he had to admit that the man had a point. He didn't want to be responsible for Freedom Press's financial struggles, even if he hadn't asked to be responsible for its success. "I know," David said finally, with as much empathy as he could muster. "I understand. Once *The Coated Crusader* is done, I—I think I might have more stories in me."

If I'm not in jail, you can have as many stories as you want. As for food and rent, they cost money too, Levi.

Some of the clouds seemed to clear from Levi's face. "Oh, yeah? You got something in mind?" His friend skirted around the couch, approaching David, an eager gleam in his eyes.

"Nothing in particular," David said evasively. There was no sense in getting Levi excited over nothing. "I don't have a pitch for you in the middle of the night, if that's what you're asking."

Levi held up his hands. "Hey, you're the brains, Felman. If you don't want me to pry, then by all means, let it stew, you know?" He paused, then added, "But you do think you'll keep it up after this?"

David sighed. "If I'm lucky."

A wide, crooked grin split Levi's face; he seemed to be taking that as a definitive *yes.* "That's the spirit."

David rested one hand on the writing desk, and Levi's eyes

dropped to the manila folder in the tray. Curiosity lit his gaze, and he reached a hand toward it. "Oh, hello. What do you have—"

David's heart leapt to his throat. Hastily, he smacked Levi's hand away, snatching up the folder. "That's not more panels."

Levi didn't seem offended. "What is it? Research? Girl's pics you're afraid I'll judge you on? Hey, don't forget I used to work with Talon Press, and they published that horrid *Fanny Follies* magazine. Probably a dozen copies under a dozen teenage boys beds in this very building. I'm not gonna lecture you."

"It's something from my time before," David replied, gripping the folder so tightly it was beginning to crease.

If anything, Levi's expression brightened even further, and his voice quickened. "What, is it classified or something? You sticking your nose where you don't belong, is that it? What're you up to?"

"Levi—"

"Wait, don't tell me," Levi said. "The less I know, the better, right?" He flashed David an exaggerated wink. "I knew it the first time I met you, Felman. You've got chutzpah coming out of—"

"Levi," David interrupted, "while you're here, there's something I've been meaning to ask you."

He'd been hoping to redirect Levi's attention away from Margie's folder, and it worked—for a man who had to juggle a dozen different magazines and twice as many writers, not to mention David's comic, his editor was easily distractible. Levi clapped him on the shoulder. "What can I do for you?"

"Have you had any luck getting that radio interview together?" For a few weeks now, David had been pushing Levi to line up a spot for him on one of the local stations to promote the next issue of the comic. Given the sensitive nature of his finale, David wanted to drum up as many readers as he could possibly manage. *The Coated Crusader* was popular, but its last issue needed to make waves outside of its normal readership, or this was all for nothing.

Levi's fingers tightened on his shoulder. "*Oy,* Felman. We've been over this. Small press doesn't get on the radio."

"I just thought that maybe, if we put in a few calls—"

"I've already put in half a dozen calls to every station in Manhattan." Levi sighed, releasing David. "It doesn't work like that. You're a big fish stuck in a tiny, tiny pond now. Your old publisher might've been able to get you an interview, but it's probably not in the cards for us."

David exhaled, nodding. It had been an adjustment, moving *The Coated Crusader* to Freedom Press. Levi was the only publisher he'd had so far who was willing to keep the comic in print despite the constant pressure and thinly-veiled threats from representatives of the FIB. Or, more exactly, the Blackwing Program—a not-so-public division inside the Flighter Investigation Bureau. In fact, the warnings seemed to galvanize Levi—Freedom Press was an outlet that prided itself on the controversy it managed to stir up. But as with all things in this city, the autonomy Levi offered came with a price. A small, independent publisher didn't have the same budget and connections as the larger companies, which would have had no trouble landing David a radio or newspaper interview.

"We can do flyers," Levi offered. "Big poster on the storefront. Real splashy."

David nodded, trying and failing to look enthusiastic. "That'll be great."

"It sure will." For the first time since Levi had arrived, there was a pause—a long one, in which the editor regarded David with an almost concerned frown. "Are you all right, Felman?"

"I'm fine."

"You seem jumpy. Don't get me wrong, you're always a little—" He whistled twice and shook his hand back and forth.

"I'm *fine,* Levi."

"I don't know what you've gotten yourself into," Levi said, "but whatever you're gonna put in that final issue, it had better be worth it."

"That's the one thing you don't have to worry about."

Levi stared at him, undisguised curiosity in his gaze. As he always did, however, he let the subject drop. That was one of the best things about Levi—as exuberant as he could be, he usually knew when to stop pushing. David had never failed to deliver on *The Coated Crusader*, and Levi seemed to trust him to stick the landing.

"You know," Levi said, switching tracks, "you've really done something with this comic book. Every time someone writes to the office, they're asking about *The Coated Crusader*. I'm kvelling, David. Never been prouder of a writer. I'm serious."

"Thank you, Levi," David said wearily. He placed a guiding hand on Levi's back to steer him toward the door. "That's nice to hear."

Levi kept talking, as if he didn't notice David ushering him out. "Think about what I said, will you? The last two issues—they don't have to be the last. At the very least, try to come up with a pitch for your next project. If you absolutely have to wrap this one up, I want to get the next one rolling as soon as—"

"I will," David assured him. "I'll tell you all about it once I have the idea locked down and ready to release." In truth, David had no plans to think about anything beyond *The Coated Crusader* until well after the last pages were in print. It was a waste of time; Freedom Press likely wouldn't be able to publish whatever he threw together in his prison cell.

Levi stepped over the threshold, turning on his heel to face David. "If you need anything, come down to the office any time. Even if it's—"

"Go home, Levi," David said, stifling a long-suffering sigh. "It's late."

"Of course, of course. That's—"

David closed the door, cutting off the rest of his editor's sentence. If he didn't eventually close the door on Levi, they'd be talking in circles until the sun rose. Which was only an hour or two away. Every once in a while, David was willing to entertain it, but not that night—not after the night he knew lay ahead.

Out of the corner of his eye, he could see the folder sitting on his drafting desk. Perhaps that was the perfect place for it. He couldn't continue his work on the comic pages until he had opened it and perused its contents. Before he told the rest of this story, he needed to know how the real one had ended.

Nonetheless, the idea of looking through Margie's folder twisted his stomach into knots. She had warned him as they sat in the car, the engine purring as the vehicle idled by the curb: "It's tough to look at, David. You might want to wait until you're in the right frame of mind."

He was never going to be in the right frame of mind. The longer he put it off, the worse it would be when he finally mustered up the energy to do it.

David turned the lock on the door, then he paced in his kitchen, working up the nerve. He stopped and rummaged in the lower cabinet for the bottle of illegal, caramel-colored moonshine, pouring himself a generous glass. The liquid trembled and sloshed as he carried it over to the coffee table.

David grabbed the manila folder and settled down onto the couch. He traced the outer edge with one finger, unsure. He took a gulp of the liquor—liquid courage, he'd heard Americans call it. *More of a painkiller*, he thought; the heat of the alcohol numbed the sting of consequence in advance.

David opened the envelope.

On top of the stack of files and photographs was a series of grainy, sepia-toned pictures of a dragoncoat's corpse, cut open, mutilated. Images of an autopsy.

But not just any dragoncoat's autopsy.

His dragoncoat's autopsy.

Black-stained lungs, shrunken, bared to the open air. Three stomachs, all of them peppered with stretched out holes like snags in wet cloth. The neighboring organs that had succumbed to the dragon's burning acid as it leaked through the cancerous lesions on the stomachs and into the body itself. Clinical notes jotted beside the photographs, pointing out the visible damage to the dragon's insides. Backscatter's eyes, lusterless and staring.

And that hit the hardest. They hadn't even had the decency to close his friend's eyes.

David swore under his breath, fighting a sudden rush of nausea. He returned the pictures and closed the envelope, setting it gingerly on the coffee table as if worried it would detonate.

He leaned back into the cushions, closing his eyes to ward off the image of his loyal friend's broken body, the insides blackened, like they had been splattered with ink. No matter how many times he blinked, he couldn't stop seeing it.

Margie had been right. He should have waited until he was more prepared. At the very least, he should have waited until he'd had a few hours of sleep.

David picked up the glass with an unsteady hand and took a long, burning drink.

CHAPTER

THREE

From the roof of Felman's apartment building, Jade and Night Armor had a decent view of Lower Manhattan, stretching around them in all directions. It was a bright day; the sun's rays seemed to sink into Night Armor's matte-black scales like he was leaching them from the air, reflecting nothing. Her partner could take the heat well enough, though. Some dragon's nests went so deep into the earth that the temperature could get to twice what a human could stand. Still, it was bad weather for hiding a Blackwing.

But decent weather for almost anything else. After losing Felman's trail last night, Jade was determined to advance her investigation.

"I don't mean to sideline you," she said to her dragoncoat. "It's just that you're going to stick out like a sore thumb, and you know the jig is up the second Felman sees a dragon—let alone a black one. Got it?"

Of course, of course, Night Armor said, fidgeting restlessly. He had seemed distracted all morning, and Jade had to stifle a flash of frustration as he went on, <u>Do you think you'll be able to get him to sign my comic book?</u>

"Night Armor, we aren't here for *fun*." Jade sighed. "This guy is our mark. We're *on-mission*."

<u>Yes, I know, but this is just like when the Coated Crusader has to infiltrate the secret laboratory to find out what the—</u>

"Focus," she chastised, and immediately, the dragoncoat's excitement deflated. He shrank down, shuffling his talons, the gleam gone from his eyes. Jade grimaced, regretting the harshness of her tone; Night Armor tended to need a lot of encouragement, and she hadn't meant to stoke her dragon's insecurities, but she needed him to stay out of sight. If he appeared at the wrong time, it was a failed mission—and the BWP didn't have a high tolerance for failure.

<u>Sorry, Jade.</u> Night Armor wandered dejectedly over to the center of the roof, which was taken up mostly by an empty, somewhat dilapidated pigeon roost that was nearly as large as the dragoncoat himself. He settled down in its shadow, though the relief from the sun barely covered half his side. The tip of his tail twitched in double agitation: the heat and being reprimanded. More guilt poured into Jade.

"Chin up," she said, walking over to lay a hand on his neck, the sun's warmth pouring through her leather glove. "I've got your comic book in my pocket. I'll see what I can do about that autograph, okay?"

Night Armor let out a low sigh, his breath stirring the ragged feathers that remained caught in the seams of the roost. <u>Okay. Thank you.</u>

"So, just to reiterate—you're going to stay up here and wait. I'm going to head down there, tell Felman I'm from the radio, and try to arrange an interview. Get my foot in the door, get into his apartment, and, if I'm lucky, get a look at that folder from last night. I'll come get you after I'm done talking to Felman." Jade didn't want to repeat herself, but she wasn't entirely sure that Night Armor had heard her the first time. "You're going to stay on this roof. Make sure no one sees you."

<u>Yes</u>, Night Armor clicked sullenly. <u>Staying on the roof. Got it.</u>

"You don't have to sound so down about it."

<u>It's not very heroic.</u>

"Well, we're not supposed to be big, flashy heroes," Jade reminded him. "This isn't a comic book, and you're a Blackwing now. No matter how it shakes out, there's no limelight in this for us."

Night Armor shuffled his wings and nodded, though Jade's words didn't seem to make him feel any better. She gave him a last, sympathetic pat on the head.

"I'll be back soon," she promised, with a look to the door down into the apartments below. She took off her gloves and started grabbing her street clothes from one of the saddle bags.

THE HALLWAYS of Felman's apartment building were drab and mildewy. The building, like so many in New York, was laid out in an inscrutable maze of narrow corridors and doors set askance, the geometry of the individual units almost impossible to visualize. Jade almost got lost twice before finally stumbling upon the one she was looking for: unit 603.

She hesitated before raising her hand to the door, smoothing out her peacoat and tucking a lock of black hair behind her ear. She had to look the part. When her job was to be unseen, three hundred feet in the air on the back of a pitch-black dragon, it didn't matter what her hair looked like. But for today, she was a talent coordinator for a radio station, and professionalism was key.

Another knock, and she stood back to wait. Some muffled

thumps came from inside the apartment, followed by a harried voice: "Hold on, hold on—I'll be right there!"

A few seconds later, the door swung open, and David Felman blinked at her, bleary eyed.

Jade had only seen Felman in photographs and from a distance. Up close, he was a surprisingly attractive man for his reputation as a shut-in. He had a sharp jawline and dark, wiry hair that clearly hadn't been touched by a barber in some time. There was a pencil tucked behind one of his ears, and ink stains along the rumpled wrists of his ill-fitting shirt. His soft brown eyes gave him a look of perpetual despondency—or maybe that was just the obvious weariness on his face. It was early, and Jade, of all people, was well aware that he hadn't gotten much sleep the night before.

Felman looked Jade up and down, his brow furrowed. When he spoke, his voice was quiet, tinged with a slight Eastern European accent that Jade couldn't place. "Can I help you?"

Jade cleared her throat, slipping into her practiced role. "Are you David Felman?"

"That depends on who's asking."

"My name is Tricia Harper," Jade said, extending a hand to shake Felman's. "I was wondering if I might be able to schedule an in-person interview to discuss the next issue of *The Coated Crusader?*"

For a few seconds, Felman stared between Jade's outstretched hand and her face, his expression befuddled. Then he said, "I'm a little confused. I just talked to my editor about this last night. He said he's spoken to every radio station in Manhattan, and none of them would agree to an interview. So unless something has changed in the last five hours—"

"Oh!" Jade laughed, trying to disguise her momentary panic. She quietly cursed herself. She and Night Armor had tried to get half a night's sleep, and they had ended up missing all of the important information. "Well—that's because I'm not from the radio. I'm an entertainment columnist for the *Gazette.*"

At long last, Felman shook her hand, though he still seemed perplexed. "An entertainment columnist? Shouldn't you be doing a write-up about something a little more consequential than a comic serial?"

"I'm told *The Coated Crusader* has a loyal following, Mr. Felman," Jade said. "Part of my job is uncovering new artists working in new mediums. I requested this interview myself."

"You've read my comic?"

"A friend of mine is a big fan." Jade's thoughts flashed to Night Armor, sulking on the roof. She hoped that he would be in better spirits by the time she was finished here.

There was still a doubtful look on Felman's face as he regarded her.

"Do you mind if I come in?" Jade asked. "We can talk about the specifics."

Felman stepped back, gesturing to the inside of his apartment. Jade smiled at him and strode over the threshold.

Felman's loft was spacious but cluttered. A stack of magazines sat precariously on a side table beside the worn, faded couch. The living room and the kitchen were conjoined, separated only by a high counter. There was an empty glass on the coffee table, next to a dark-green manila folder, which Jade zeroed in on momentarily—this was the folder she'd seen Felman carrying after his clandestine meetup the previous night. She resisted the urge to open it as she crossed the room, staring out of the large windows on the far wall.

"Sorry about the mess," Felman said. "I wasn't expecting company. Well, aside from my editor."

"It's no problem," Jade told him brightly. "It's a lovely place. Very fitting for an artist." She pointed at the drafting desk, positioned in a prime location between two of the windows. "I take it this is your studio, as well?"

"Sometimes." Felman's hands were tucked into his pockets, and he watched her with wary eyes as she approached the table, inspecting the paper on its surface. It was difficult to make out what was happening on the page; it seemed to be in an early stage of development, with faintly-sketched figures and unfinished speech bubbles.

"Where else do you work?"

"Sometimes I draw at my publisher's office," Felman said. "Sometimes I prefer to work outside."

Jade turned away from the desk. "Outside? As in—"

"My studio can be anywhere I need it to be."

"That's a good quote," Jade said, patting the pockets of her jacket as if searching for a notebook. She gave Felman a subtle once-over as she did so. It was difficult to tell if her charade was working. No matter how she tried to indicate that she was a journalist, Felman's demeanor remained funereal, his body language withdrawn. It gave Jade the off-putting impression that, somehow, he knew exactly who she was—and why she was really here.

She couldn't let it deter her. Felman had no reason to suspect her, and as long as she didn't give him any new ones, she was in the clear.

"Could we discuss this proposed interview?" Felman asked, shifting his weight. "It feels as though you are already conducting it. I would rather—"

"Of course," Jade said quickly. "Is there somewhere we could sit down?"

Felman nodded, leading her over to a small table off to the right of the kitchen. "I apologize for the poor welcome. Would you like anything to drink? Coffee? Or perhaps...." He hesitated for a moment, scratching the back of his neck. "Coffee? Sorry. That's all I have at the moment."

26

"Well, with options like those, how can I refuse?" Jade smiled, sitting down at the table. "I'd love a coffee. Thank you."

Felman busied himself in his small kitchen, rummaging around in the cabinets for a mug. Jade watched, bemused, as he knocked over a stack of bowls at the front of the cupboard, swearing under his breath in what sounded like another language. He was every bit as... *peculiar* as her initial briefing had indicated. Most of the Coat Wardens Jade knew were meticulous, diligent people, with a strict comportment and sense of order. Jade never would've suspected that Felman was a former Coat Warden if she hadn't already known. He seemed disheveled, and his apartment was a far cry from the pristine quarters that Jade inhabited. Scraps of paper covered the small dining table, many of them bearing little graphite doodles. In fact, there wasn't a surface in the entire apartment that wasn't covered in cheap, high-pulp sketching paper. Perhaps he'd spent enough time among artists that their carefree lifestyle was beginning to rub off on him.

After a few minutes of wrestling with his disorganized kitchen, Felman set a steaming cup of black coffee in front of Jade. "Cream? Sugar?"

"No, thank you," Jade said, mainly to spare him the effort of searching for them.

Felman sat down opposite her at the table, backlit by the steel-framed windows. "You'll have to forgive me," he said. "I'm a little out of sorts this morning. I was up late."

"Working?" Jade asked, blowing on her coffee to cool it.

"Ah... yes," Felman said. "Deadlines. And my editor paid me an unexpected visit fairly late last night."

"Your editor. That's Levi Adelman at Freedom Press, correct?" Jade took a cautious sip of the coffee, shuddering at the bitter taste. She wished that she'd taken him up on the sugar.

"Yes. That's right." Felman looked down at the table, his brow furrowed. "So, about this interview—"

"Of course," Jade said. "I'm getting ahead of myself, aren't I, Mr. Felman?"

"Please, call me David."

"Sure—whatever you'd like. This is a regular piece that I write biweekly for the *Gazette*. One part arts column, one part human interest story. Readers like these kinds of extensive interviews that give some insight into the artists themselves."

"I'd really prefer to simply talk about my comic," he said slowly. "I'm not so sure that your readers will find my life particularly interesting."

"Oh, but of course they would!" Jade set the mug back down on the table, smiling at him. "After all, the comic is only enhanced for the reader if they know more about the artist. Your work is influenced by your prior experience as a Coat Warden, isn't it?"

David's eyes widened, and Jade immediately regretted her words. "How did you know I was a Coat Warden? As far as I'm aware, that isn't public knowledge."

"I'm good at my job, Mr. Felman—David," she said. "I did my due diligence before coming over here, just to learn the basics. Have to make sure you're a good candidate for an interview. Nobody wants to waste their time on a dud."

"But I don't understand how you would have found that information," David insisted, leaning forward. He seemed agitated now, more animated than he'd been since she had arrived at his apartment. "It's not publicly available. You couldn't have found it through research."

If only you had *done your due diligence,* Jade scolded herself. *Then you wouldn't have made such an easy mistake.* She marshaled her expression into what she hoped was a charming smile. "Of course not. But your comics themselves are publicly available, aren't they? And I've interviewed enough Coat

Wardens over the course of my career to know a thing or two about dragoncoats. All of the details are spot-on in your work. You're definitely the real deal." Taking a slight risk, she shot him a coy wink. "Thanks for confirming my hunch."

To Jade's relief, David leaned back, some of the suspicion clearing from his gaze. He cleared his throat. "Well... that's an impressive thing for you to have picked up on. Yes, I used to be a Coat Warden."

"That's fantastic!"

"It is?"

"Of course! Our readers will eat that up. I'm sure you have plenty of stories of daring escapades, lots of heroics—"

"No," David interrupted, looking away. "Not particularly."

"That's fine. We don't need anything too dramatic. Just the fact that you were a Coat Warden will be enough to intrigue people."

"And is that really necessary? To be intriguing? I'm happy to answer any questions you have about the comic, but—"

"Trust me, you'll want to work the human interest angle." Jade forced herself to take another swallow of the acrid coffee. "That's the best way to ensure high readership."

"And exactly how high is your readership?"

"Decently high. Should be good publicity for your comic."

David hesitated, his fingers tapping on the paper-strewn table. After a few seconds' silence, he reached for the pencil tucked behind his ear and began to absent-mindedly sketch something on one of the blank pages. "Okay. Let's say I agree to this. What do we do, and when, and where?"

Sensing an opening, Jade said, "If you're open to it, we could do the interview here. We'd sit down, just like this, and I'd ask you all of the questions more formally. I would bring a camera, of course—for a full-page spread like this, we would need a picture."

She rocked forward in her chair, trying to get a better look at David's drawing, curious despite herself. It was a bare-bones sketch like the ones from his unfinished comic page, nothing but a few well-placed strokes and guiding lines, but it was recognizable as the beginnings of a portrait.

The tip of David's pencil paused at the incomplete nose, and he looked up at Jade. "A picture? Is that really necessary?"

"Our readers like to see a picture. It draws attention to the page." Jade couldn't fathom why David wouldn't want a picture in the article; if anything, his looks could only help with sales. Perhaps it was something to do with the notoriety. He seemed like a man who valued his privacy. But then, why was he so interested in getting a radio interview? There was a disparity there that caught at Jade's thoughts, but she didn't have time to unravel them at that moment.

"Okay," he said dubiously, continuing to draw. "You're the expert. When is your deadline?"

"We go to press in three days," Jade said. "That means I don't have much time to write this, so if it's okay with you, I'd prefer to do the actual interview today. Would that be possible?"

As David considered, staring down at his half-finished sketch, a shadow flitted in the window behind him. A stab of panic speared through Jade. Night Armor had come into view, clinging to the outside of the building like an overgrown bat, peering through the window. His claws were hooked onto the ledge, and Jade's keen hearing could pick up the quiet scratch of the sharp keratin on the concrete.

Her whole body tensed. David had the same hearing. She started shifting her feet on the wood floor and shuffling slightly in her creaking chair, praying it was enough to cover her dragon's sounds.

"Well," David said, looking up at her, "I'm supposed to get the next few pages to Levi—er, Mr. Adelman—by Friday. But I guess, if it's for publicity's sake, I could afford to take a couple of hours off from drawing. It wouldn't take much longer than that, right?"

Swallowing hard, trying to act natural, Jade shook her head. "No, no. We'll try to make it quick. I understand that you're a busy man."

"Would you like me to come to your newspaper's offices?" David asked.

"Oh, that won't be necessary. We could do it right here, if you wouldn't mind. I only need to fetch a camera and a notepad."

His forehead creased in thought, and he returned his attention to his drawing. Jade leaned to the side, glaring daggers at her dragoncoat, and made a quick, downward gesture with her hand. Night Armor's eyes shone with excitement as he spotted David through the window. He met Jade's gaze, then turned his head to one side as if asking her a silent question. Frantically, Jade shook her head and jerked her thumb to the left.

Get out of here! What's wrong with you?

The dragon seemed to realize his mistake, a sheepish look spreading across his face. He snaked his head down, ducking below the frame of the window, and sidled out of sight.

Jade barely had time to exhale in relief before David set his pencil down and got to his feet.

"I'll do it," he said.

"Really?" She shook herself, trying to focus. "That's—that's great!"

"It's no trouble." David frowned at her. "Are you all right, Ms. Harper? You look a little shaken."

"I'm fine," Jade managed, her mind buzzing with adrenaline from Night Armor's near miss. She attempted a nonchalant shrug. "I just don't usually drink coffee this strong."

"Sorry about that. Artist's habit," David said, rubbing the back of his neck.

Jade glanced back down at the table. The sketch appeared

almost finished now. Since Night Armor could hardly head over to Manhattan himself to pick up the latest issues of *The Coated Crusader,* Jade would do it for him, and she had become familiar with David's garish art style in his comics: sharp lines and bold colors, clearly designed to draw attention to the cover on the newsstands.

This portrait was similarly simplistic, with stylized features, but it had more detail than the drawings in the serial. There was light shading around the woman's jawline, a delicate sheen in her dark hair. With a start, Jade realized who David had been drawing as they spoke—it was *her.* The portrait had her high cheekbones, her short, angled haircut. She blinked, surprised and somewhat flattered.

Jade looked up at David, one eyebrow raised. The corner of his mouth twitched into a rueful smile, and pleasant warmth pooled in her at the sight of his slightly more expressive, vulnerable expression.

"That's an artist's habit, too," he said. "I apologize if you would have preferred I didn't use your likeness, Ms. Harper. I needed to give my hands something to do as we spoke."

Jade glanced back down at the portrait, then up at David. "It's okay," she said, in a slightly breathless tone that didn't sound like her at all. "I like how she looks."

Her Coat Warden hearing picked up his mumbled reply: "So do I."

CHAPTER
FOUR

The moment the door closed behind Tricia Harper, David scrambled to clean his apartment—an hour-long process that nearly had him sweating by the end.

This, he decided, was the problem with his quest for publicity. Journalists and publishers alike had no respect for the sanctity of his private space. On a whim, the entertainment editors at the *New York Gazette* could opt to send their prettiest reporter straight to his door, and she could waltz through his living room, past a coffee table cluttered with all kinds of damning evidence—both of illegal spirits, and of outright sedition.

Nonetheless, as he brought the empty moonshine glass back into his kitchen, he had to admit that the interview offer was something of a godsend. After what Levi had told him the previous night, he had been all but resigned to the limitations of *The Coated Crusader's* readership. Now, though, he had a chance. A full-page spread in the *Gazette* was a golden opportunity, perhaps even more of a platform than the comic itself could provide.

He just had to keep his wits about him. Tricia Harper's sudden appearance had caught him off-guard, and he was operating on two hours of sleep, but David was still sharp enough to be suspicious. As far as he was aware, this method of setting up an interview was unorthodox. No advance warning, no phone call, no telegram. And the paper had sent the reporter to his apartment instead of to Freedom Press, which was also strange.

Not to mention, this reporter's uncanny knowledge of his life, from his address to his buried past as a Coat Warden. It was true enough that the details in *The Coated Crusader* spoke to his experiences, but nobody had ever made the assumption before. He had never mentioned it publicly, and the records of his time with the FIB weren't readily available; the BWP would have seen to that.

David picked up the folder with the pictures of Backscatter's autopsy gingerly, as though afraid that the olive-green dye in the manila might poison him. He slipped it into the top drawer below his drafting desk, overtop of the array of pencils he kept there. This way, he wouldn't lose it, but it wouldn't be easily noticed by Tricia Harper—or anyone else.

He had put the last sketch away when there was a knock at the door. David steeled himself, heading to the door as he adjusted his crooked tie. He was certain he had tied it incorrectly—he hadn't worn a tie since his Blackwing interview years ago.

Tricia was waiting in the hallway, clutching a large, boxy case that David assumed contained the camera. She seemed out of breath from carrying it up the six flights of stairs, but otherwise looked as put-together as she had when she'd first arrived. David reached out a hand in a silent offer to take the camera case from her, and Tricia smiled at him graciously.

He felt abruptly overly hot and self-conscious, like every piece of clothing he wore was the wrong size, and all of it was suddenly made of thick and suffocating wool. He should have gelled his hair, too. He could feel the frizz on the back of his neck; he reached up to smooth it, stepping back to allow Tricia into the entranceway.

"I'm impressed," she said with a lovely little chuckle, looking around at the space. "You cleaned up fast."

"Well, there wasn't too much to do," David said. "But since I was expecting company, I couldn't leave a bunch of old sketches lying around."

Tricia's gaze flashed to the coffee table, and David tensed. She glanced back at him and said cheerfully, "Would it be all right with you if we set up for the interview in your living room?"

"That's fine." David followed her into the sitting area. He set the heavy photography equipment down on the coffee table, and Tricia opened the box, busying herself with the camera.

After a few moments, she sat down on a chair opposite the couch, gesturing for him to do the same. She flipped open her notepad. "Are you ready to start? Everything you say will be on the record, unless otherwise stated."

David nodded, sinking onto the couch. "Ask your questions."

Tricia seemed to sense his nerves, and offered him a reassuring smile. "There's no need to be so formal," she said. "Our readers want to know the real you. The more open you are with details, the more interested they'll be."

David nodded again, this time more tersely. Perhaps this had been a bad idea. The last thing he wanted was to open up to this stranger about his personal life, but if it meant higher circulation for the comic, it was worth it.

Besides, there were worse people to speak to. If he pretended that there was no invisible audience hiding behind Tricia's notepad—if he told himself that they were simply having a conversation of their own volition—then maybe this process could be painless.

Or maybe you'll be even more distracted by her, he thought to himself cynically. Here he was, about to reveal state secrets to a journalist, and he couldn't stop himself from fixating on her smile.

Tricia's beauty was striking. Her skin was the color of golden sand at the edge of a warm ocean. Her jet-black hair was styled into a flawless curtain bob, which worked in tandem with her thick brows to frame her eyes. David's hands itched for a pencil and a scrap of paper. From the moment she'd arrived in his apartment, he'd felt compelled to draw her, and the desire hadn't faded after the first sketch.

"So, let's start off with some simple questions," Tricia said. "Tell me a little about yourself. Where are you from?"

David shifted, uncertain how to answer. After a long pause, he said, "I was born in Lodz, Poland. My parents and I traveled to the United States by steamship when I was eleven years old."

Tricia nodded, jotting down a few lines at the top of her notepad. "What did you make of New York City when you first arrived here?"

"I thought it was very loud," David said shortly.

"And where did you learn to draw?"

"Ms. Harper—"

"Tricia," she insisted, setting her pencil overtop of the notepad.

"Tricia," David amended, "is there any way we can bypass some of the simpler questions? I would much prefer to talk about the comic—or even my time as a Coat Warden, as it is far more relevant."

He was expecting her to resist, but to his surprise, she merely nodded. "Of course. Let's move on. What can you tell me about your inspiration for *The Coated Crusader?*"

David's heartbeat quickened. "I started drawing *The Coated*

Crusader shortly after I was discharged as a Coat Warden. I was motivated by my dragoncoat, Backscatter."

Tricia continued to jot down notes, a small crease appearing between her eyebrows as she frowned down at the page. "I-I see. You were discharged. That must have been... difficult. If you wouldn't mind sharing the details of your time as a Coat Warden—"

"Not at all," David said, leaning forward.

"How were you discharged from the FIB? And how did your dragon inspire your work?"

"I wanted to bring some dark things to light." David's gaze drifted to the wall behind Tricia, where there were a few tacked-up drawings of a dragon in flight, the dark edges of the wings and tail stippled in white charcoal to give the illusion of silver scales. "You seem to know a thing or two about the FIB. Have you ever heard of the Blackwing Program?"

He wasn't sure what kind of reaction he was anticipating, but he certainly didn't expect Tricia to lean in, her eyes narrowed in rapt attention. "I'll know what you are willing to tell me."

"Are—are you sure?" David cleared his throat. "I'm more than happy to, but I have to let you know in advance that this information is highly classified. If I tell you—"

She waved a hand as if to brush aside the warning. "Yes. That's fine. Tell me *everything*."

Surprised by her intensity, David blinked. He settled back into the couch, wondering where to begin, then said, "The Blackwing Program is an experimental program within the FIB that selects top-performing Flighters for recruitment. It was founded for clandestine purposes. When a Flighter is selected for the project, the dragoncoat is physically altered in order to make a Flighter more effective at running espionage missions."

"Into Tsarosia?" Tricia's eyes were wide. She'd stopped taking notes; her notepad lay forgotten in her lap.

JORDAN RILEY SWAN & EZRA ZABIT

"Wherever they are needed," David replied.

"What does this have to do with the death of your dragoncoat, Mr. Felman?"

David opened his mouth, then closed it again. She seemed to have taken the news of a top-secret state operation in stride. Shaking his head, he said, "Our Flighter was chosen as test subjects for the program, along with a few other candidates. Some time after the alterations were made to Backscatter, I noticed his health starting to decline. It was just a cough, at first, but it didn't go away. That was just the beginning."

Silence settled over the room as he finished speaking. Tricia was frowning, the intensity in her gaze a jarring change from her earlier demeanor, back when their interview had been a much more casual affair.

Eventually, she spoke. "How long did it take for him to become ill after they'd replaced his scales?"

"It seemed to be going well for the first two years. After that —" David stopped himself abruptly as realization struck him.

He'd never mentioned the scales. He had only told Tricia that the dragons were altered, but he had never described *how*.

"After that?" Tricia prompted, seemingly unaware of his sudden rush of understanding.

David stared at her. "How did you know that?"

"How did I know what?"

"That the BWP replaced the scales," David said. "I never mentioned the scales."

With a heavy sigh, Tricia pursed her lips. She set the notepad to the side, as if clearing space for the conversation. "Listen, Mr. Felman—I'm sorry. I haven't exactly been forthright with you during this process."

"The very existence of the Blackwing Program is restricted knowledge," David said, unable to keep the note of accusation out of his voice. "The *nature* of its conduct, even more so. Only someone adjacent to the program would know."

"Yes, I know." Tricia looked agitated, worrying at her lower lip with her teeth. "I think, at this point, you ought to know the truth. I am not a lifestyle reporter. I am not working on a piece for the entertainment section."

"Who are you?" he demanded.

She drew herself taller. "I am an investigative journalist with the *Gazette,* and I have been chasing this story for the past two months."

"*Investigative?*" David huffed a quiet, disbelieving laugh. "You're a muckraker, are you?"

"Is that a problem for you?" She met his gaze steadily. "You *did* just tell me that you wrote your comic to bring a secret to light. You wanted to reveal classified information to me. If you're willing to continue, I see no reason to stop this interview. Clearly, you know something that I've been waiting to hear for a long while."

Involuntarily, David's gaze strayed to the top drawer of his drafting desk. He had information on his hands that had taken a significant amount of organizing to acquire, information that needed to be released to the public if he wanted the BWP to be shut down. If a prominent newspaper like the *Gazette* was willing to meet him at his front door, practically begging him to share what he knew, then he'd be a fool not to jump at the chance.

And yet, something was holding him back. As earnest as Tricia seemed, the whole affair still seemed suspicious to David. While it was true that a keen observer could intuit that he was a former Coat Warden, years of dealing with the BWP and their attempts to silence him had given him a healthy background level of skepticism. There was always the chance that Tricia Harper was not who she claimed to be. She could be there on behalf of the BWP. He wouldn't put it past them to send a spy to his door, looking to take him down for treason before the comic ever saw the light of day.

He shifted, looking away from the desk to meet Tricia's expectant gaze. "Sorry," he said. "Of course I am still willing to speak with you and tell you what I know." He had to admit that he was also relieved that someone else, someone on the outside, knew what was going on. His knowledge had isolated him from the rest of the world for a long time, and the only two people he'd been able to speak freely around had been Margie and Levi.

"That's great," Tricia said, smiling broadly. She poised her pen above her notepad as if waiting for him to begin his story.

"Ah... not *here*." David shook his head. "If we're to continue this conversation, I would prefer it were somewhere public."

"Somewhere public? Why?"

"*The Coated Crusader* has had a bit of a troubled publishing history," David explained, folding his hands in his lap. His fingers itched for a scrap of paper, something to draw with, but he forced himself to keep them still. "Threats sent to my publishers, warning them of dire consequences if they continued to print the comic—all from the BWP. So far, my work has been in the hands of five separate publishing houses. Levi Adelman is the only man in New York City willing to send *The Coated Crusader* to print."

Tricia blinked at him, nonplussed, and David suppressed a heavy sigh. He probably sounded insane to her. If he hadn't seen some of the menacing letters himself, he would think he was insane, too.

"I have enough reason to suspect that my apartment is not the most secure location for a sensitive interview like this one," he said warily. "The BWP is aware of where I live. They may be listening."

Tricia seemed miffed, but she took this development in stride, closing her notepad with a snap. "Okay. Then what would you suggest?"

"Somewhere with plenty of witnesses." He hesitated.

"There's a place across the street from the Battery, near the ferry terminal."

At that, Tricia frowned, and David folded his hands, watching her carefully. Her reaction was enough to increase his misgivings. He'd selected this location intentionally; at the southernmost tip of lower Manhattan, Battery Park was the best place to keep a close eye on the skies over the bay, where any Blackwing would have to fly from the operations base on Staten Island.

"Isn't that a little far from here?" Tricia asked. "Won't you have to—"

"I am supposed to be meeting with an old friend down-town tomorrow," David replied. "It's no trouble. I might as well make more of the trip." Time for one final test. He paused, then added, "If you wouldn't mind, it would be best for my schedule to meet in the early afternoon."

In the afternoon, the sun would be out, and no Blackwing would have the advantage of invisibility. If Tricia agreed to meet in the middle of the day, some of his doubts about this situation could be assuaged.

"Actually," Tricia said, "I'm supposed to be at the office tomorrow until five. Is there any way I could meet you at night? Say, around eight or nine?"

Eight or nine... well after sunset. With a sinking feeling in his chest, David nodded and got to his feet. Tricia beamed at him, but he didn't smile back, despite the fact that her expression was infectious. Under ordinary circumstances, he might be excited by the prospect of meeting someone like her in the late evening.

"Looking forward to it, Mr. Felman," Tricia said, reaching to shake his hand.

CHAPTER
FIVE

You didn't get it signed?

Jade had seen Night Armor crestfallen plenty of times in the past, usually while bemoaning a small mistake on his part, but something about his expression this time tugged at her. While in David's apartment, she'd gotten the sense that he was onto her—that somehow, he wasn't fooled in the slightest by her cover, despite the fact that her running amendments to her story had been as smooth as she could make them. Amidst the tension, she'd completely forgotten about Night Armor's copy of the comic book, tucked into the inside pocket of her peacoat.

She grimaced, looking up at him. "Sorry, buddy. It was a little bit of a nail-biter. It slipped my mind."

It's okay, Night Armor sniffed. It was almost always easy to tell when a dragoncoat was lying, and Night Armor was no exception. His head hung low, his yellow eyes downcast.

"I'll tell you what," Jade said, "I'm supposed to be meeting him again later tonight. I can try to get your comic signed then, okay?"

Night Armor perked up, a low purr rumbling in his throat. Okay!

After her nerve-racking interview with David, Jade had retreated to the roof of the building to wait with Night Armor until the artist left his apartment again. She'd watched him make his way down the street and hail a taxi before making her next move.

Breaking and entering hadn't been part of her official instructions, but given the kind of leeway Blackwing wardens were usually afforded, Jade was confident that it was well within her permissions. David hadn't given her much information willingly, so she'd taken the chance to seize some without his knowledge. It had taken half an hour of searching around David's cluttered studio before she managed to find the green folder, hidden in the top drawer of the artist's desk.

By the time she was finished covering her tracks, it was dark, and she had instructed Night Armor to return the pair of them to the Staten Island base for the evening. She didn't want to open the folder where the curious dragon would want to look as well. If there were damning things in it, especially about the BWP, she didn't want her far-too-honest companion spilling the beans. And they both needed rest for their mission the next day.

THE FOLLOWING MORNING, Jade walked the immaculately kept grounds of the base with Night Armor as she debated what to do next. She had left the folder in her quarters, but she wasn't sure she was going to actually turn it in.

If her superiors' overview of her assignment was any indication, the contents of the folder were sure to be treasonous, and her decision to peruse them without permission equally so. Pure curiosity alone kept her from delivering the folder straight to her direct supervisor, Sergeant Douglas. And pure curiosity meant she was probably going to find herself going through the folder anyway.

If she gave it over now, then whatever was in it—whatever information was so secret that David had gone to pick it up at three in the morning—had the potential to render Jade's mission unnecessary. If David had classified documents in his apartment, then the BWP could arrest him on charges of treason and be done with the whole affair. It would be simple, and it would probably even count as a mission success on Jade's part, another achievement on her spotless record.

Despite all of her instincts, however, something was stopping her from handing it in. David, although clearly reluctant to trust her, had at least been... earnest. Kind. More attractive than she'd been expecting, with a disarming, soft-spoken charm. She kept remembering the look in his eyes as he'd talked about his dragoncoat.

It was just a cough, at first, but it didn't go away. That was just the beginning.

As Jade made her way along the asphalt path, she shot a sideways look at Night Armor, placidly walking beside her. He caught her gaze, and his pupils narrowed to slits in alarm as he picked up on her uncertainty.

Jade? Is everything okay?

"Of course," Jade said. Her dragoncoat was always in tune with her feelings, and he had a tendency to become rattled at the smallest sign of doubt from his Coat Warden. Out of necessity, Jade had perfected the art of putting on a confident face. "Night Armor, you've been feeling okay lately, right?"

Night Armor flicked his tail in displeasure, his wings extending slightly, ruffled. Is this about the windows? I *know* I shouldn't have been near the windows. I just wanted to see—

"This isn't about the windows. It's just... a general question."

<u>Oh.</u> Mollified, Night Armor bunched up his wings, pulling them close to his body. <u>Well, in that case... yes, I'm fine. Why do you ask?</u>

"No reason." Jade hadn't yet told Night Armor all of the details of her meeting with David. It wasn't that she wanted to keep things from her dragoncoat. It was just that Night Armor was never particularly reliable with a secret, even by dragon standards.

Nothing appeared to be wrong with Night Armor, but Jade hadn't gotten the impression that David was lying. She resolved to wait before telling anyone else about the folder and, in the meantime, to stash it beneath the mattress in her quarters. There would be plenty of time to reveal it later without getting into trouble—*after* she'd had another chance to speak to David and figure out what he knew.

<u>So, what now?</u> Night Armor chirped. <u>We've got some time before you're supposed to meet David, right?</u>

"Yes, but don't worry about that," Jade told him.

Ahead, on the path, she could see Sergeant Douglas—right on schedule. Her superior officer tended to go for his daily walk around this time. He'd picked up the habit a couple of years ago. From what Jade had heard, his doctors had recommended he get more exercise. After a considerable amount of time behind a desk, the former warden had lost the fitness of his youth.

She lifted a hand to wave to Douglas, and even from her distance, she saw his expression morph into a frown.

<u>Jade?</u> Night Armor's high-pitched clicks and whistles were quieter than usual, even though Douglas was far past the age when his ears had been tuned to the full range of dragoncoat speech. <u>The Sergeant doesn't look... happy.</u>

"Don't worry about it," Jade said out of the corner of her mouth. As Douglas approached, she snapped into a salute.

"Ms. Atallah," the sergeant said, his beady gaze flicking

between Jade and her dragoncoat. "Aren't you supposed to be in Manhattan at the moment?"

"I came back to base with some minor concerns, sir."

"What sort of *concerns?*"

"I think there's something wrong with Night Armor," she lied. "He seems a little under the weather."

Jade was hoping that Douglas's face might betray a touch of worry, but his expression remained neutral as he glanced at Night Armor. "Is that so?"

<u>What?</u> Night Armor stared at Jade, his eyes wide. His claws agitated the evenly cropped grass at his feet, and he shook his head vehemently. <u>That's not true! I feel completely fine! Why are you making things up?</u>

The sergeant turned back to Jade. "What's he saying? I missed about half of that."

"He's making up excuses, sir," Jade replied. "I think he's trying to avoid a doctor's visit. He's never been a big fan of shots."

<u>Shots?</u> Night Armor's wings flared again. <u>What do you mean, *shots?* Do I have to have a shot? You didn't tell me I had to get a shot!</u>

"But he has been a bit off today," Jade continued, ignoring her dragon. "A little sluggish in the air... and I think he's developing a cough." Here, she watched Douglas carefully for any reaction. She wasn't sure if she was imagining the way the sergeant's lips pursed, his eyes narrowing at Night Armor.

"Well," Douglas said, "that does seem reason enough for a checkup—if only because the two of you are currently on-mission, and he needs to be in the best shape possible." He cleared his throat, gesturing to Night Armor, who glared balefully at his warden. "I will escort your dragoncoat to the infirmary for evaluation."

"I can join you, sir," Jade offered. "We don't have anywhere to be until this evening. It wouldn't be—"

The sergeant held up a hand to stop her, and Jade's sentence died in her throat. "That won't be necessary. Return to your quarters, Ms. Atallah. Someone will send for you when your dragoncoat's examination has finished."

<u>Jade</u>, Night Armor clicked, his expression the image of betrayal. <u>What should I do?</u>

"Do what he says, Night Armor," Jade replied, reaching up to Night Armor's shoulder to give him a reassuring touch. As much as she wanted to be with Night Armor during his evaluation, she knew better than to argue with the sergeant. "You'll be fine. A checkup now and then is good for you."

<u>If you say so.</u> Night Armor followed the sergeant, casting an uncertain glance back at Jade over his shoulder as they headed in the direction of the dragoncoats' housing.

At a loss for what to do, Jade dithered on the path for a few moments before turning back to the building. The sergeant had told her to return to her quarters; Jade took that to mean that, for the time being, her mission had been officially stalled.

JADE SPENT the next few hours sitting on her bed, debating whether or not she should open David's folder.

She wanted to maintain any plausible deniability. If David had stumbled into some classified information—more classified than the normal BWP Coat Warden level, that was—then the contents of the folder might be above her pay grade, so to speak. And protocol dictated that she should leave it well alone. But, at the same time, protocol was to have given it straight over to her handler, Sergeant Douglas. Plus, her curiosity was overwhelming.

But once she opened it, there would be no going back. What if it revealed something about the BWP that sullied her desire to work for them? Or worse, made her question the entire FIB organization? Still, any secret knowledge concerning the BWP was, in a very real sense, pertinent to her, and to Olivewing—

Night Armor.

Dang, it's been almost two years, and I keep calling him by his old name.

The folder sat on Jade's nightstand as she debated, one of the few pieces of furniture in her sparse quarters. Even by Blackwing standards, Jade had done little to decorate her living space. Some of her colleagues teased her about it, from time to time. There were no posters on her walls, no splashes of color or personality to make the space her own. The drabness was intentional. Jade didn't want to slip, to catch herself becoming too comfortable. Her quarters were provided by the BWP, in exchange for her service. They weren't her home, and at no point was she off-duty. The lack of personal adornments were a reminder of that. She had allowed herself a single token of individuality in her quarters, a group photograph of her family that sat on the writing desk. They smiled at her from the simple frame as if encouraging her, beaming in pride.

Jade looked from the photograph to the folder, weighing excuses, rationalizing each of her options. Eventually, she sighed, collapsing onto the bed. The stiff mattress provided little comfort, and she rolled over, staring at the folder on the nightstand.

Behind it, the clock displayed the time: six-thirty. In an hour and a half, she was supposed to meet David at the Battery, and she had still heard nothing about Night Armor. She felt restless, both because of the steady crawl of the minute hand around the clock's face, and also because of the thought of Night Armor, alone while he underwent his medical examination.

There hadn't seemed to be anything wrong with him, but after her conversation with David, Jade was rattled. She didn't know what she'd do if anything happened to Night Armor. Come to think of it, she wasn't entirely sure what had happened to David's dragoncoat, but she was certain that it wasn't anything good. David had been discharged from the BWP unceremoniously, so at the very least, his Flighter team had been broken apart, and he had been replaced by his second. Jade suspected from the seriousness that had weighed down David's tone that the dragoncoat's fate had been worse than that.

After a few moments of staring at the clock, Jade sat upright, taking a deep breath to steady herself. She stashed the manila folder back under her mattress. Her quarters weren't due for inspection for several weeks, so for now, it would go untouched there. Marching out of the room, Jade headed down the hall, in the direction of the BWP's administrative offices.

Sergeant Douglas was exactly where she'd expected him to be—in his office, working late, with a cigarette pinched between his meaty fingers. Douglas was even more predictable than Night Armor. He looked up as she knocked on his half-open door, adjusting the spectacles that sat low on his nose.

"Ms. Atallah," he said. "Can I help you with something?"

"My dragoncoat has been in the infirmary for quite a long time, sir. Do you have any idea of when his examinations will be over?"

Douglas frowned at her, his pallid forehead creasing. "Our doctors are the experts. Their examination will take however long they take, and you will simply have to exercise patience."

"It's not a matter of impatience," Jade assured him. "It's a matter of... eagerness, sir. I need to get back on my mission. If I'm unable to seize upon an opportunity tonight, it will be much harder for me to develop my cover with Felman."

Douglas set the still-burning cigarette in the ashtray on the corner of his desk, steepling his hands over the documents he had been perusing. "An opportunity?"

"I'm supposed to be meeting with Felman at the Battery in an hour and a half, sir."

"I see." Douglas pursed his lips.

"And without Night Armor, I'm stuck here," she added.

"You are, are you?" Douglas returned his attention to the documents on his desk, pushing his glasses back up the short bridge of his nose. He sniffed as if disinterested.

"Sir—if I'm going to make this meeting on time, I need Night Armor to be released from his examination."

"They aren't finished yet, Ms. Atallah," Douglas murmured, his watery eyes scanning a page he held before himself. He reached for the smoking cigarette at the lip of the ashtray, raising it back to his lips for a drag.

Jade forced herself to stifle the flash of frustration. She knew better than to share harsh words with the sergeant. "Let me make sure I'm understanding you correctly. Are you suggesting that I should *miss* this meeting, sir?"

Exhaling a slow cloud of smoke, Douglas lowered the paper to regard Jade. "You are on-mission. Would you consider this meeting to be part of your mission?"

"Yes, but—"

"Perhaps even *essential* to your mission?"

"Yes—"

"Then I suggest you rustle up some transport."

Jade stared at Douglas as he tapped the ash from the tip of his cigarette. "Sir, Night Armor—"

"*Night Armor,*" Douglas interrupted abruptly, his voice harsh, "is a very, *very* expensive use of taxpayer dollars, Ms. Atallah, as was your training. I'm left to assume that, since you were recommended so highly to this program and since your record reflects that recommendation, that the pair of you were not a massive waste of time and resources. However, I will admit that the past two minutes of conversation have me *confused* on that front."

Speechless, Jade gaped at the Sergeant, her mind scrambling for a response.

"You're on Staten Island, not stranded in the Yukon," Douglas snapped. "For god's sake. Take the ferry."

Jade swallowed, embarrassed. "I—yes, sir. The ferry."

"Is that all you needed?" Douglas leaned back in his chair, ditching the cigarette once more in the ashtray.

"Yes, sir." Jade dipped her head in deference, backing out of the sergeant's office with her gaze fixed upon the floor. "That's all."

SINCE HER TIME in the academy, Jade had become accustomed to the quick, convenient, and companionable transportation of dragon flight. Night Armor had never been grounded for any reason in the midst of a mission like this, and any time her dragoncoat had been unavailable for service—such as when his original copper scales had first been switched out for their black metal replacements, or his first adult molting —Jade had been put on leave alongside him. She had long since forgotten what it felt like to *wait,* and worse, to move slowly—first through the irritating line at the ferry terminal, and then on the boat itself as it cut through the choppy waters of the Upper New York Bay. The ferry took nearly half an hour to reach the Battery, and by the time it docked, the clouds that had lingered on the horizon for most of the day had finally taken their cue, dusting the city with a light drizzle.

Night Armor would've made it here in time to beat the rain, Jade thought miserably as she hurried across the street to stand under a shop's awning. *And he would've been talking non-stop the entire time.* The ferry ride had felt strangely lonely. She hadn't been able to do much but worry about Night Armor and prepare questions for David as she leaned over the railing that surrounded the top deck, staring at the dark waves.

The café David had suggested as a meeting place was on State Street, adjacent to an imposing building with large, marble columns. She could see him through the window, watching her with a slight frown as she scurried across the street. She groaned; he'd definitely been here for at least fifteen minutes. She was late, something that never happened to her.

A small bell tinkled as she opened the front door. Out of breath, she nodded at the man behind the register in brief greeting before turning to scan the dining area.

David was at a table in the corner that was adorned with a checker-patterned tablecloth and a single yellow flower in a vase, like a streetside café in Paris. He sat facing the window with his back to the wall, nursing a steaming cup of coffee. As she approached, he looked up at her, his expression unreadable.

"I'm sorry I'm late," she said before he could speak. "I got held up unexpectedly. I swear, this doesn't usually happen." She wasn't sure why she was so troubled by her unpunctuality. It wasn't as if this was a *real* interview. Still, she grimaced apologetically as David met her gaze.

"It's fine," he said. He glanced back at the window and took a sip of his coffee. "To be honest with you, I'm quite glad you're late."

There was something strange in his demeanor. He seemed even more closed-off than he had the previous day, when she'd surprised him in his apartment.

Frowning, Jade shrugged off her jacket, slipped it over the back of the chair, then sat down. "What do you mean, you're glad I'm late?"

"I saw you run over here from the ferry terminal," David said. "I'm a bit relieved you didn't fly over on a dragon." He nodded at the window, and Jade turned to follow his gaze.

From the café's vantage point, there was a view of the ferry terminal and the bay beyond it, all the way to the faint outline of Staten Island, almost obscured by the rain.

"A dragon?" Jade chuckled, trying to keep her nerves out of her voice. *It's only natural that he would suspect you,* she told herself. *But he saw you get off the ferry. Your cover is fine.* If anything, this was a stroke of serendipity—Night Armor's medical examination had protected them from David's suspicions.

"Thought you might be with the BWP," David said. "Monitoring me, or something. It makes me sound paranoid, when I put it like that, doesn't it?"

"A little bit."

David's gaze snapped away from the window, fixing upon Jade, who felt suddenly seized by the intensity in his brown eyes. "A little bit," he echoed, a strange note of irony in his voice.

"Are you feeling all right, David?" Jade asked.

"I called the newspaper," he said simply, not breaking eye contact. "You can imagine my surprise when they told me they'd never heard of a reporter by the name of 'Tricia Harper.'"

Jade froze, her mouth half open, her legs suddenly numb. "I—"

David settled back in his chair, lifting the mug back to his lips with an air of forced nonchalance. "I don't know who you are, or who you're working for," he said, "but I think I'd like you to explain yourself."

CHAPTER
SIX

"Well?" David demanded.

The woman across the table from him hesitated, the light from waking streetlamps creating shadows of raindrops across her face. When she spoke, her voice was careful, slow. "Well, what do *you* think is happening here?"

She was keeping her cards close to her chest. Fair enough. David took another sip of coffee, breathing in the earthy scent to ground himself. "Like I said, I assumed you were a Coat Warden," he said. "Probably a Blackwing, given the exact nature of this situation. I chose this café in particular so that I could keep an eye on the skies over the bay." He gestured to the rain-streaked window and the dark clouds above. "Not that it would have done me much good tonight, of course—nobody would be able to see a black dragon at this hour, particularly in this weather."

He paused for a moment, wondering if that would be enough to coax a confession out of the stranger. She was silent, her dark eyes betraying nothing.

David shrugged and continued, "But then I saw you get off the ferry. Now, I'm not sure what to think. All I know is that you aren't the person you claimed to be."

She bit her lower lip, staring down at the checkered tablecloth. "No."

"Is your name really Tricia Harper?"

Her gaze shifted to the window. "No."

"Then let's hear it," he said. "Who are you, and on whose behalf are you here?"

The woman who wasn't Tricia Harper opened her mouth to answer, but before a single word left her mouth, her entire body went rigid. She stared out of the window at Battery Park across the street, as though transfixed by something she had seen amongst the dark-leafed trees.

David cleared his throat, lifting a hand in an attempt to regain her attention. She looked back at him, the expression on her face one of sudden, unadulterated alarm.

"I'm sorry, Mr. Felman," she said, pushing away from the table. "I'm afraid I have to go." She stood and dashed toward the door, throwing it open to a cacophony of tiny bells. "Best of luck!"

David shot to his feet, taken aback. "Hey—wait!" He rushed after her, grimacing apologetically at the man behind the cash register, whose arms were raised in indignation. "I'll be right back, I promise, I'm sorry—*wait*!"

The restaurant proprietor hollered after him as David flung the door open to follow after the woman. "You owe me a nickel for that coffee!"

Ignoring him, David emerged onto the street. The gentle drizzle of rain had opened up into a steadier downpour, but he still managed to catch a glimpse of the woman a few hundred yards to his right.

"Hey!" David yelled after her, taking off down the sidewalk.

Halfway down the block, she turned sharply, disappearing into an alleyway.

David didn't slow his pace, though he knew that if she wanted to outrun him, he probably wouldn't be able to catch her. She had gotten the head start. But he had to at least try. He needed to know whether there was a new threat to add to the list, or if the Blackwing Program was simply growing more concerned about the impending comic release.

As David reached the mouth of the alleyway, he skidded to a stop, slipping on the wet concrete. Ahead, surrounded on all three sides by brick walls, was the woman—and in front of her, its gaze shifting nervously from side to side, was a dragoncoat.

Not just any dragoncoat. A dragoncoat with scales of luster-less black metal. A veritable shadow in the shape of a great, reptilian beast, bending its neck to press its snout against the woman's torso.

David hadn't been crazy, after all. On the night he had met Margie in Central Park, he had been hearing dragon clicks above the canopy of the trees. This Flighter had been tracking him for days now, and possibly far longer.

He could hear the dragoncoat's anxious whistles as it spoke rapidly to its warden. _Jade, it was awful. You wouldn't believe what they did to me. They shoved a wooden stick into my throat. They shined this horrible light into my eyes. They gave me so many shots. Three different shots! Can you believe that?_

The woman—Jade, if her dragon's anxious squeaks were anything to go by—had her hands raised to soothe him. The dragoncoat looked past her, to the mouth of the alleyway, and his lizard-like eyes landed on David.

David flinched, taking a step back, but there was sudden eagerness in the dragoncoat's expression, his plight apparently forgotten. _That's him!_ He swung his head back to Jade, who looked far less pleased to see that she'd been followed. _Did you get my comic book signed?_

~

FROM THE LOW rooftop of one of the buildings next to the alleyway, David had an impressive view over the dark water of the harbor. Under different circumstances, and with dry clothes, he might have even enjoyed it. Staten Island was visible now that the rain had ceased and the fog over the bay had begun to clear, but at this time of night, it was nothing more than a faint strip of light on the horizon. He stared out at it, turned toward the water despite the steady cold breeze that pierced his sodden jacket.

In his periphery, he could see the dragon pacing back and forth, a shadow against the gray concrete of the roof. Jade stood nearby, her arms folded.

David's shoulders still ached where Night Armor's talons had gripped him. He'd tried to run. Despite being surprised, Jade had been faster than him—with agility born from years of training, she had scaled the side of the dragon's harness and pulled herself into his saddle, crying, "Night Armor, don't let him get away!"

Night Armor had lunged at him, muttering to himself under his breath as he went: <u>And the Winged Avenger is on him in a flash of inky black!</u> Claws had closed around his shoulders —without damaging him, a neat and agile trick of its own— and lifted David into the air. Everything had become a whirl-wind of black wings and dizzying height after that. Though a dragoncoat *could* carry the weight of two people on its back for a good distance, carrying one in claws that would cramp up quickly wasn't strongly advised, so Night Armor had deposited him on the nearest rooftop. There was no need to take him far. He was trapped all the same.

David looked down at the street, six stories below. He glanced back at Jade. "You can't do this," he said, trying to keep the panic out of his voice. "I'm supposed to be meeting with my publisher tonight. He's going to wonder where I am. You can't—"

Ignoring him, Jade rounded on her dragoncoat. "Night Armor, what the hell are you doing out of medical?" she demanded.

I thought you might need some backup, the dragon chirped, holding himself taller, as though trying to seem valiant.

"Did they finish your exam? Are you cleared to fly?"

The dragoncoat ducked his head. Not exactly.

"Night Armor—"

It was *awful*, he repeated, as if she hadn't heard the first time. Poking me with cold metal, and shoving things down my throat—

"What did you do?"

The dragoncoat's claws clicked on the wet roof beneath his feet as he shuffled, ashamed. They took me outside for some other test, and I-I flew away. And now everyone's probably mad at me... and you're probably mad at me... and I'm an idiot!

"I'm not mad at you," Jade said, and David was surprised by the softness in her voice. Even with her cover in shambles and her mission a resolute failure, she obviously cared deeply about the well-being of her dragon.

Night Armor sniffed miserably. You're not?

"No." Jade reached up to his head. She had to stand on her toes to place her palm on his forehead, even though he lowered his neck to help her. "I wish you'd stayed, but it's okay to get scared sometimes."

Behind her, David cleared his throat to remind her that he was there. Both dragon and rider looked up at him abruptly—the former excited, the latter exasperated. As they all stared at each other, as if none of them were sure what to say, the sounds of the city pressed in—the roll of cars through puddles in the pitted street, the blare of angry horns.

Breaking the silence, Night Armor ventured, <u>So... did you get my comic book signed?</u>

"Comic book?" David asked.

With a sigh, Jade reached into the fold of her jacket, producing a small, bound booklet. The pages were pulpy, pressed neatly between two gloss covers. David reached out to take it, his gaze scanning the front. Volume one, issue one of *The Coated Crusader*. The cover featured the character in the earliest iteration of his silver-scaled, horned costume, standing in front of the surge of green flame that represented Blindside, his fallen dragoncoat. David thumbed through it for a moment, a twinge of regret in his stomach as he took in his old artwork, from the early days of the comic's run. The figures were less defined than his more recent works, and the pacing through the panels didn't feel quite right to him. Nonetheless, there was an adoring glow in Night Armor's eyes as David looked up at the dragoncoat.

"You've read this?"

The dragon made a quiet chuffing sound that David recognized as laughter. <u>Don't be silly! I'm a dragoncoat. I can't *read.*</u> He shook his head, composed himself, then added, <u>Jade reads them to me.</u>

"He liked the artwork on the covers," Jade said. "He wanted to hear the story."

<u>Lots of the other dragoncoats like it, too</u>, Night Armor added. <u>But I'm the biggest fan! I could tell you anything that happens in the entire run! Go ahead, ask me anything.</u>

David was taken aback, and somewhat moved. The idea of the story he'd written for Backscatter being enjoyed widely by other dragoncoats—especially Blackwing dragoncoats—would have delighted him, if it hadn't pushed against the ever-present hair-trigger of grief that sat, waiting, in the back of his mind. He thought of Jade, sitting at her dragon's side in their off-hours, reading the small print to him, holding up the pages so that he could see the pictures. That image didn't help with the grief, either.

"I see," David said. He looked between the two of them again. The dragoncoat watched him, nostrils flaring in glee, and his warden folded her arms, refusing to meet his gaze.

David rummaged in his coat pocket, producing a pen. He signed the front page of the comic, jotting down a little message below the edge of the titular character's shimmering cape. *To Night Armor, the Coated Crusader's biggest fan. David Felman.*

When he held the book back out to Jade, she frowned at him in confusion before taking it. "Why did you do that?" she demanded.

"What do you mean?"

"Why did you sign the comic? We're..." She paused to take a breath, a resigned look on her face. "We're here to keep tabs on you for the BWP. You're definitely aware of that much. So why—"

"Everyone should be able to have their dying wish. Even dragons," he said sadly, cutting her off.

Her eyes widened in shock, but before she could say anything else, David turned away once more, peering toward the harbor.

The sadness mixed with impotent anger that had shot through him faded as quickly as it had come. The anger, at any rate. Sadness was always there, like a low chill that never went away, even when he fed it bouts of hot anger. There was little point in being annoyed with Jade. In time, she would understand exactly where his bitterness had come from. It sounded as though she had sent her dragoncoat for a medical exam, and the black scales were pressing at the seams of normalcy already. It wouldn't be long until she was in the exact same position as he was, and that made her an impossible target for his frustration.

"I want to talk to you," she said. "I want the truth."

"Blackwing Flighters," he responded slowly, turning on his heel to face her, "don't get the truth."

"Why not? If you know something I don't know—"

"I think you do know it," David said. He nodded at Night Armor, who looked utterly confused. "Your dragoncoat just had a checkup, didn't he? Was that routine, or did you request it after our last conversation?"

"I requested it." Jade's olive skin tone and the shadowy roof muted the flush of pink across the bridge of her nose, but they couldn't hide it entirely. "You said some things that I found... concerning."

"I'm sure."

"I want to know the whole truth. I need you to tell me what happened."

David scowled at her, shaking his head. "You've just told me that you were assigned to spy on me. You just snatched me off the street. Why would I tell you anything?"

"Because I need to know," she said. "Please, Felman. I won't report it back to the BWP. I won't tell them anything about our interview from yesterday."

David glanced behind him at the street again. "And you'll let me come down from here?"

"Yes," Jade said, exhaling. "Of course."

"Fine." He couldn't see the harm in telling her. He would give anything now to have been given the answers to all of his questions back in the day, when he had been a Coat Warden facing down his dragoncoat's decline. "But first, I want to know everything that you've been hiding from me. The whole truth. You don't get answers without giving something in return."

"Like what? You already know that I'm a Coat Warden. You know we're with the BWP." She gestured at Night Armor, with his black scales, darker than the night sky above.

"What's your name? The dragon called you Jade," David said. "But you know my last name, so it seems only fair if—"

"Atallah," Jade said, grimacing. "My full name is Jade Atallah. This"—she swept her hand to the side to indicate Night Armor, who perked up at the recognition—"is Night Armor, formerly known as Olivewing."

"Olivewing," David repeated. "I take it he was green before they added the scales?"

<u>Kind of</u>, Night Armor whistled. <u>I was a copper.</u>

"Copper." David nodded. "So it would've depended on how long it had been since your scales were replaced... and how often you'd been out in the rain."

<u>That's right.</u>

David looked between the two of them, then he reached into the inner pocket of his jacket. He produced a carton of cigarettes and flipped open the lid, holding the box out to Jade. "Want one?"

"I don't tend to smoke."

"Neither do I," David said. "But it can help to take the edge off."

After a moment's hesitation, Jade reached out to take a cigarette with a nod of thanks. David struck a match and held it out for her. She leaned forward, the tip of the cigarette glowing orange in the flame, and David was suddenly, acutely aware of the proximity between her lips and his hand.

Jade leaned back, and David felt as though he had suddenly been doused with cold water. She took a drag from the cigarette and exhaled with a couple of quiet coughs. "We were assigned to this mission and instructed to tail you," she said. "Report back to Staten Island to tell them what your plans were with the comic."

David glanced over her shoulder at Night Armor, who was nodding along with everything his Coat Warden said. For once,

David believed her, with none of the inklings of suspicion he had felt back at his apartment. She had been particularly adept at disappearing into her cover, but there had been enough loose ends that her story hadn't quite made sense. Now, though, it all added up, and the dragon's agreement confirmed it. Dragoncoats didn't tend to be competent liars, so David was relieved to have Night Armor corroborating his warden's story.

"We were keeping an eye on you from the sky the other night," Jade confessed, "and I made up the interview to try and figure out what you knew."

"There's just one thing I don't understand," he said. "What could you possibly need to hear from me? Weren't you debriefed on all of the details before your mission?"

"I didn't know *what* you knew, only that you knew *some-thing*—something classified, something that the BWP didn't want getting out." A gust of wind from the bay stirred Jade's rain-slick black hair into her face, and she brushed it away from her eyes. "I think they're worried that you had enough hard proof to go public with it. They seem to think that you're going to blow the whistle using your comic as a platform."

The news that the BWP knew what he was planning wasn't a huge shock. They had followed David from publisher to publisher, forcing him out of print at each one. It was clear that they didn't want the comic published, regardless of how much he knew and what proof he had. Still, the confirmation was eye-opening. Somehow, the BWP must have found out that the comic was nearing the end of its run—probably by keeping tabs on Freedom Press—and the impending finale had them worried. Worried enough, it seemed, to devote further resources to the subtle dance of shutting him down.

Either his pause or the expression on his face must have given him away, for Jade's brows lifted. "Oh my god—you are, aren't you?"

"That's not—" David began hastily, but Jade interrupted him.

"That's what this is about. You're going to put the truth in the last issue of *The Coated Crusader*."

David took a deep breath to steady himself. "That's neither here nor there," he said. "What have you told your superiors?"

"Nothing, yet," Jade said. "I wanted to test my handler's reaction before I did—make sure that nothing was wrong with Night Armor. I said that he'd been coughing, and the sergeant carted him off for a medical inspection."

"The sergeant," David echoed, frowning. "Barry Douglas?"

"That's him."

"He was my handler, too." David pictured the portly man, with his thick mustache and permanent scowl. "When I was with the BWP."

"Small world," Jade said, her tone clipped. She flicked a speck of ash from the tip of her cigarette, a delicate and endearing gesture that made his stomach turn over pleasantly.

Stop it, he told himself, casting about for the thread of the conversation he'd briefly lost.

"So you made Douglas nervous, did you?" David huffed a dry laugh. "Told him that your dragoncoat had a bit of a cold, and he overreacted?"

"He did. Which is exactly why I wanted to talk to you." Her eyes narrowed. "You told me that your dragon became ill after the scale replacement. That wasn't the whole story, was it?"

"No." Earlier in the day, before coming to the Battery, David had spent some time preparing himself for the inevitability: he was going to have to divulge every horrible detail. The truth was wretched—corrosive. It sat inside of him like a poison, burning him from within, yet every bit as painful to purge as it had been to ingest. Despite everything that had changed, David felt no more ready for it than he had been in the café.

64

Jade stared at him with the same intensity as before, but David thought that her gaze had softened somehow. He leaned against the low perimeter wall that surrounded the roof, settling himself to tell her everything. Everything that he could manage to say, at any rate.

"Backscatter and I were among a few candidates chosen for the BWP in its earliest days," he said heavily. "For the first two years of the program, it seemed to be a rousing success. The scales took, and he was transformed from a silver into a black dragon, just like your friend here." He nodded at Night Armor. "He was given a Flighter name, Shadow Vision. I liked to call him Shadow. I've noticed that Blackwing scales reflect very little light—the dragoncoats look like the darkest shadows, don't they?"

Jade didn't reply. She seemed faintly uneasy, as if she already knew where this tale was going and wasn't looking forward to hearing it.

"Shadow started getting sick after his first molt. We replaced the scales, as one does, and then... slowly but surely, things started to go wrong. After a few months of normalcy, he began to develop the cough. Then the fever. Eight months after the molt, we were unable to continue missions, and I was grounded rather unceremoniously." David closed his eyes at the memory, which still stung. Back then, he had only been aggrieved about the wasted time. If he'd known how bad things were going to get, he might have done things differently. Pushed harder. "They wouldn't let me see him—kept me away, fed me plenty of nonsense about why he needed to be isolated. Telling me that he had contracted a rare, contagious virus. I insisted that it was because of the scales, but of course, they ignored me. I spent months at the base, doing nothing but worrying about Shadow.

"Eventually, I tried to go over the sergeant's head.

Contacted his superiors, asked them if I could be allowed to see Backscatter, told them about my suspicions. They all denied me. Worse, I was discharged from the FIB altogether, with little explanation as to why."

By now, both Jade and Night Armor looked considerably more disturbed. Jade stepped forward as though she wanted to comfort David, but like she didn't know how. The gesture heartened him and warmed him, allowing him to go on.

David dragged the next words out. "Right after I got the discharge, I went straight to the medical wing of the base. I broke in. Forced my way past security, into the room where I knew they were keeping Backscatter. He looked like something out of a nightmare—ribs and ridges, emaciated, like he hadn't had anything to eat in weeks...."

He trailed off, glancing down. His hands had begun to shake, but he was almost finished—and determined to see it through to the end. He took a deep breath, closing his eyes again, but opening them quickly. All he could see in the darkness was the skeletal form of his dragoncoat, withered to the bone, eyes dull and glassy. Sometime in the months that David had been apart from him, his mind had fallen victim to the illness that raged through his body, and strapped down to a massive metal dragon examination wagon in the Blackwing medical ward, he had looked up at David without fully seeing him, without any spark of recognition.

The security guards had pulled David from the room before he could do much more than call out the dragon's name, but that had been enough. For an instant, Shadow had seemed to experience a burst of clarity. It had lasted just long enough for him to feebly whistle David's name before lapsing back into his mostly catatonic state.

David cleared his throat, bringing himself back to the present. He could feel tears burning at the edges of his eyelids, but he held himself together, squeezing his trembling hands into fists. "Shadow died," he said bluntly. "Six months after we were grounded from Flighter duties. That was the only information I was able to press the BWP for, and even that they were reluctant to tell me."

"I'm sorry," Jade whispered. Her voice was almost lost to the wind that rushed across the rooftop. She approached him, laying a steadying hand on his shoulder.

"Whatever the Blackwing Program is doing, it's killing the dragoncoats." David got to his feet, tugging himself slowly away from Jade's hand. As soon as he had done so, he regretted it; there was something immensely comforting about her touch, and as he had several times over the past couple of days, he found himself thinking again about the depth of her eyes and the curve of her lower lip—

He shook his head. He couldn't allow himself to be distracted by anything or anyone, let alone a Coat Warden whose assignment was to report on him to the BWP. The only thing that mattered now was exposing the truth, avenging Backscatter. Jade was pretty, and sharp, and he liked the way she had spoken to her dragoncoat, but this train of thought had to be stopped.

"It's killing the dragoncoats," David repeated, as if to remind himself of that fact. He dropped the cigarette butt he hadn't even drawn a hit from and ground it under the heel of his shoe. "And I have a responsibility to make sure everyone knows."

Silence hung between them, and David could practically hear the turmoil of thoughts turning over in Jade's head. He almost understood. There had been a time, early on, when the truth had become clear to him, but when it had taken some time to adjust to the facts, to accept them.

But right now, with his work so close to completion, he

didn't have time to wait for Jade to come to terms with everything he'd just told her. Her job was to report back on him to the BWP. She seemed horrified by what he'd told her, but she'd also put on the convincing facade of a reporter. David couldn't bring himself to believe her assurance that she wouldn't report back to Douglas. He couldn't let himself be distracted by her—not again.

David took a deep breath, looking up to face Jade. "Now, if you wouldn't mind," he said tersely, "I'd like to get back down from here. I have to stop by Freedom Press tonight. My editor is expecting me."

This wasn't strictly true, but if Jade thought that someone out there was waiting for him, she might think twice about keeping him trapped on this rooftop.

Jade nodded, seeming lost in thought. After a moment, she gestured to the black dragoncoat. "Night Armor, can you give Felman a ride back down to the street?"

"Ah—no, thank you," David said quickly. "I'll take the stairs." He gestured across the roof to a fire escape that Night Armor had been blocking access to. He didn't want to admit that the thought of riding a dragon, after all this time, sent an unpleasant flutter of nerves through his chest.

"Sure," Jade said, frowning.

"And call me David," he added. "I'm not in the military anymore. You don't have to use my last name."

"David," Jade echoed. The smallest of smiles graced her face, and David had to look away from her to avoid returning it. "Whatever you say."

David gave her a small nod, then he turned to leave the roof. Regret tugged at him, though he couldn't place why until he had cast another glance back at Jade and Night Armor. She had turned her attention to the dragon, whose head was lowered, eyes narrowed to yellow slits in delight as Jade scratched behind one of his long, twisting horns.

You don't have time for that, he told himself firmly, pushing the feeling away. *It's not in the cards, and you know it.* In a few short months, he would be in prison, and Jade would still be a Coat Warden, reporting to the men who had put him there. There was no sense in ignoring the facts—not after years spent chasing the truth.

CHAPTER
SEVEN

"What do you mean, *paused?*"

Behind his desk, Sergeant Douglas settled back in his chair, the frame beneath the leather cushions straining under his weight. He regarded Jade over steepled fingers. "I meant simply what I said: consider your mission *paused*. Consider yourself on a well-deserved *break*."

"I don't understand," Jade said, shaking her head. She had only been back on Staten Island for an hour, and already, she was itching to leave. She wanted to go back to Manhattan, march right up to David Felman's door, and stay there until she knew exactly what was going on. "Why? We were just getting somewhere. I was so close to—"

"You should be grateful. We are giving you the opportunity to take some time to yourself. On the base, of course, but off-duty. Kick back. Relax."

"But Sergeant—"

"Ms. Atallah," the sergeant said, his voice suddenly sharp, "your dragon fled from our examiners partway through his medical inspection, without warning, and against the direct demands of our doctors. Between that little display of insubor-dination, and a few anomalies in his tests, we have decided to ground your Flighter team for the time being, until your drag-oncoat's issues—both behavioral and physical—are resolved."

Jade was about to argue, but the sergeant's words echoed in her head, freezing the words before she could say them. Cold dread ran through her veins. "Wait. What do you mean, *anomalies?*"

"It's nothing to concern yourself with," the sergeant said.

"What's wrong with Night Armor?"

"Minor anomalies in his tests," the sergeant repeated. "If the medical team thought that it was necessary to inform you, they would have. As they haven't, it's nothing you need to concern yourself with." There was an edge to his voice, a warning that Jade didn't feel comfortable pushing against.

She got to her feet stiffly, firing off a salute that felt more ironic than sincere. "Yes, sir," she said, hoping that her annoy-ance didn't bleed into her tone.

If the sergeant noticed her attitude, he didn't comment on it. He merely nodded, waving a hand to dismiss her. "You may leave, Ms. Atallah."

JADE SPENT the next few days trying to take the Sergeant's advice and relax. It was a rare opportunity on any FIB base. In fact, Jade didn't think her hands had been this idle since well before her time in the academy. She spent some time with Night Armor, who had been walking with a swagger in his step ever since his encounter with David. She spent some time wandering the grounds, centering herself, weighing her options. She spent a considerable amount of time alone in her quarters.

Jade had always had trouble fitting into the social circles

she found herself enmeshed in—in her old neighborhood in Queens, where she had been an automatic outcast as the child of Syrian immigrants; at the academy, where she had been singularly focused on becoming Night Armor's first warden; in her original post as a Coat Warden; and now here, on the Blackwing base. Even her old instructors had commented that she was a notorious loner—one had gone so far as to label her a misanthrope. The truth was that Jade never felt any particular desire for the company of others, except for Night Armor. She was perfectly content to fly solo and confide solely in her dragoncoat. The perfect BWP recruit.

And yet, as she languished in her room, she found herself wishing she'd had another chance to speak to David Felman. *To get the whole story*, she told herself, *not just for his company—* though she had to admit that she wouldn't mind that either. David was soft spoken, but there had been a bite to all of his quiet words that appealed to Jade. He was sharp, but his sharp edges lined up well with hers. Something unbidden fluttered deep inside her at that idea that her edges could line up with another's. Line up with *his*. Something she had never thought possible.

Two days after their ill-fated meeting, Jade worked up the courage to open the green folder she had stolen from his apartment. She sat on her bed and opened it with methodical care, as though she was dissecting a small, delicate creature. Despite all of her carefully cultivated apathy, the report inside was enough to turn Jade's stomach. The pictures of the mutilated dragoncoat, accompanied by cold, clinical text describing his condition, were almost too much to bear. She couldn't imagine seeing the same thing and knowing that it was her friend who had gone through this kind of suffering.

Anomalies in his tests, the sergeant had said. *Nothing to concern yourself with.*

As Jade closed the folder, nauseated and upset, the words echoed in her head like an ominous refrain.

Anomalies in his tests.

A sudden, sharp knock at the door jolted Jade out of her rumination. She realized in a panic where she was—at the Staten Island base, in her FIB-assigned quarters, with an open folder of classified information spread across her lap. A folder she hadn't reported to her superior officers, full of classified information she was definitely not supposed to know.

Jade closed the folder hastily, leaping to her feet and shoving it beneath the mattress. Once she was satisfied that none of the green manila corners were visible, she cleared her throat and approached the door.

She recognized the timid-looking young man outside immediately—the sergeant's secretary. "Can I help you?" she asked, raising an eyebrow.

"Sorry to interrupt you," the secretary said. "The sergeant has requested your presence in his office."

Jade felt a quick flash of dread. Did Douglas somehow know what she'd done? That there was a folder, chock full of forbidden knowledge, hidden in her quarters?

She forced herself to be calm. The sergeant, for all of his power on this base, was far from a mind reader. Steeling herself, she nodded at the young man. "Thank you."

As she strode down the starkly lit halls toward the sergeant's office, her mind raced. Were she and Night Armor about to be put back on the job? Cynically, she had to assume that she wouldn't be so lucky. This had to be about something else—probably about Night Armor's medical tests. She paused outside the closed office door, adorned with a brass placard bearing the name BARRY DOUGLAS in imposing capital letters.

"Atallah," boomed the sergeant's voice from within, "stop dawdling outside the door and come in."

Jade flinched. Had he heard her footsteps? She entered the office, forcing her shoulders back. "Sir."

Douglas was behind his desk, half hidden by a thick, acrid cloud of smoke that almost obscured him from view. He took a last drag from his cigarette, wheezed, and stubbed out the glowing ember in the center of his ashtray.

"Would you mind explaining to me," he said, his voice slow and dangerous, "how it could be possible for your dragoncoat to have a signed copy of Felman's comic book?"

Jade blinked, taken aback. This wasn't what she'd been expecting. "I—excuse me, sir?"

"Your dragoncoat," Douglas repeated, "was found to be in possession of a copy of Felman's rag. *Signed. Addressed* to him, by name."

"*What?*"

"He was showing it off to all of the other dragoncoats, and one of the wardens came forward to tell me. I'm assuming that you know something about this."

Jade nodded, mentally cursing Night Armor's loose tongue. Of course her dragoncoat had been excited about David's autograph, but that didn't mean he had to tell all of his friends—most dragons weren't able to keep a secret, especially from their Coat Wardens.

"It would seem that Night Armor was introduced to David Felman at some point the other night," Douglas went on, "which defeats the purpose of your entire mission."

Jade swallowed, forcing herself to nod. "Yes, sir. I can explain."

"By all means, please do."

"I saw Night Armor approaching while I was in the café with Felman," Jade began. "I didn't want Felman to see a Black-wing, because, as you said, I knew that would ruin my cover. So I ran to an alleyway to draw Night Armor away, and unfortunately, Felman followed me."

"So you're telling me that your cover was blown."

"Yes, sir," Jade said, her chest tight.

Douglas cursed, his fist pounding on the corner of his desk, an ugly scowl twisting his face. He didn't reply immediately, but a low growl rumbled in his throat, the same sort of threatening sound Night Armor might make on request. Jade waited by the door, a tremor in her knees.

Eventually, the sergeant's rage seemed to simmer, and the redness in his cheeks subsided. His grimace faded into a pensive look. "Well, then," he said at last. "It looks as though we'll have to do things differently."

Jade could feel her heartbeat in her temples. Her frustration with Night Armor flared and faded quickly. She knew that, ultimately, there was little point in assigning blame to her dragon. Night Armor had been excited after meeting his hero. If Jade herself hadn't been so distracted, she might have thought to urge him to keep quiet. She knew that Night Armor always did his best to follow her instructions, and she was certain that, if she'd explained their situation more clearly to him, he would've kept his mouth shut about their run-in with David.

Perhaps she should have shared more information with Night Armor after all. Now, the whole mission was canceled, and if she wanted to hear more from David—and there were half a dozen reasons she wanted to hear more from David, ranging from the practical to the deeply personal—she would have to do things off the books. It wasn't territory that she was particularly comfortable treading, but the sergeant might leave her no choice.

Swallowing, Jade looked up at Douglas. She had to at least *try* to keep within the strictures of her orders. She had worked too hard for too long to get here, and it seemed foolish to risk throwing it all away. Perhaps the sergeant would tell her what she wanted to know if she simply asked him. She hadn't even tried to get answers the easy way.

"Sergeant Douglas, sir," she began, "I wanted to ask you about something Felman said, when I was interviewing him."

The sergeant's comportment changed instantly. He sat back as if cringing away from her, his eyes narrowed. "What?"

"Felman said that he was a Blackwing warden," Jade said. "He told me that his dragoncoat became ill—possibly as a result of the scale change."

Douglas stared at her, aghast. A prickle of uncertainty traveled down Jade's spine, but she thought of the emaciated corpse of David's dragon in the photographs and forced herself to continue. She couldn't avoid this. She knew how she would feel if Night Armor ended up the same way.

"I just wanted to find out if that was true. I wasn't sure if Night Armor—"

Sudden color flooded the Sergeant's cheeks. "Forget all of that."

"Sir?"

"It doesn't concern you," he said coldly, "so I am ordering you to forget about it. Forget you ever heard it, drop it, and never bring it up again. Do you understand me?"

"But I—"

"I said, *drop it,* Ms. Atallah."

Jade was no stranger to the frostier side of the sergeant's personality, but she'd never heard such a bite in his voice. She held her breath and nodded. "I understand, sir."

If Douglas wouldn't give her answers, there were still avenues open to her, other potential sources of the truth on this base. Even Douglas had a superior officer. The sergeant was her handler, and the handler of many Blackwing Coat Wardens, but he wasn't in charge of the program, nor was he the highest-ranking man on the base. Jade resolved to hold her tongue until she could get out of her meeting with Douglas... and head straight for his boss's office. She had never spoken one-on-one with Major Hathaway before, but when he addressed all of the Blackwing personnel at large meetings, he seemed levelheaded and sensible. She was sure he would listen to her.

"Go." Douglas waved a dismissive hand at her. "Stay on the base, where we can find you. I'll seek you out once I have further instructions for you—or once the other officers and I decide on a disciplinary course of action for your failure in this mission."

Jade nodded stiffly, firing off a sharp salute at the sergeant. By the time she turned to walk out of the door, he was no longer focused on her, scowling instead at the file on his desk.

Once she had left the sergeant's office, she made her way down the wide, main corridor of the base's first level. The major worked in the largest office on the base, past the mess hall. As she neared it, she could hear the buzz of voices, all gathered for lunch.

Don't let them stop you, she thought to herself, determined to ignore the curious eyes that tracked her movement down the hallway. She was fifty yards from the major's door when a hand landed on her shoulder.

Jade turned to see a quiff of short, gelled black hair, shaped into the year's most fashionable style for men—Margie Gibbs never allowed herself to look anything less than dapper. She wore a pinstriped suit and a snug black tie, and her leather shoes gleamed in the harsh light of the hallway. As always, Margie looked as masculine as any of the male officers milling around in the mess hall. She never wore women's clothing. When she spoke, her voice was deep and coarse.

"Where exactly are you off to, Ms. Atallah?"

Jade blinked. She was familiar with Margie—everyone was, to a certain extent—but they'd never been anything more than acquaintances. "I was just on my way to see Major Hathaway," she said slowly. "Why?"

Margie's smile was frozen on her face, and her fingers dug

into Jade's shoulder. She leaned in and whispered, "If I were you, I wouldn't. You complain too loudly, and they're going to call up the second warden for your dragoncoat. You'll be sent to cool your heels somewhere dank and dark, and I don't think that's going to do Night Armor any good, is it?"

Flustered, Jade opened her mouth to reply, but Margie shook her head sharply and held up her other hand to forestall her.

"I think," Margie said, her voice louder, "that this is the perfect opportunity for me to finally set you up on a blind date."

"For you to *what*?"

"Yes," Margie continued, steering her away from the major's office, "I've been thinking about it for a while. I've got a friend in the city who could really use a night out, and you two would be just *perfect* for each other."

"Margie, I don't need a date," Jade protested. "I need to find—"

Margie silenced her with a firm look, tilting her head to the side to indicate the mess hall. Jade's gaze darted to the tables, where more than a few inquisitive wardens were watching the two of them. "What did I tell you?" Margie muttered, almost too quietly for Jade to hear even with her Flighter ears. "Keep quiet." She raised her voice again and added, "Oh, come on, trust me. It'll be fun!"

Jade shot Margie an uncertain look, and Margie winked at her, giving her a hearty nudge.

"Work with me here, Jade," she mumbled, a meaningful glint in her eye.

Jade glanced over her shoulder at the major's door, then she heaved a sigh. "Fine. Whatever you say."

CHAPTER
EIGHT

The grass at Van Cortlandt Park, northwest of the Bronx, was beaded with drops of rainwater from an early morning shower that had, given way to feeble sunshine. David knelt in front of his dragoncoat's memorial, tucked away behind a copse of trees, a good distance away from the path. His palm was pressed against the small opening in the stone pillar, into which he had just slipped a rolled-up bundle of papers.

He straightened, turned around, and jumped at the sight of Jade, standing silently behind him with her arms wrapped around her torso.

"*Oy gevalt*—" David staggered back, laying a steadying hand on the top of the memorial and almost dislodging one of the pebbles that rested there. Once the shock wore off, heat rose in his cheeks; the Yiddish had been startled out of him. "What are you doing here?"

Jade raised an eyebrow at him. "Margie told me you would be here," she said. "Apparently, you two know each other."

David nodded, relaxing somewhat. At least Margie, who

had been one of his few friends and only confidant during those tumultuous months on Staten Island, had been the one to give Jade the information. Shadow's memorial—and his hiding place—was still safe from the BWP.

"She told me she was setting me up on a 'blind date' with a friend of hers." Jade lifted her hands to frame the term in air quotes. "I take it you weren't exactly aware of this date."

"Not exactly," David agreed, nudging the small stones back into order at the top of Shadow's memorial.

"I asked Douglas about Night Armor's health. He didn't take it well. And he didn't tell me anything."

"No, I imagine he didn't."

"And I...." She hesitated, grimacing as if steeling herself to take a dive into cold water. "I brought this back to you."

Reaching into her inside pocket, she produced the manila folder that had contained Shadow's autopsy photographs. She held it out to him, and he stared at it in distaste. He'd known that it was missing since yesterday morning, and he'd assumed that the BWP had been through his apartment, though he hadn't known whether or not Jade herself had been the one to make the sweep. The folder constituted important evidence for David's claims, but it also turned his stomach to look at it. Gingerly, as though he thought it might infect him, David took the folder from her and slid it into the slot inside the stone, hiding it away.

"I'm sorry I took it." Jade wrung her hands together, a look of discomfort on her face. "I needed to—"

"You were doing your job," David responded simply. Jade seemed to recognize the note of contempt in his tone, even though he had tried to hide it, and her frown deepened.

"Well, if it makes you feel better," she retorted, "I'm not doing my job anymore. Night Armor blundered pretty much as soon as we got back to Staten Island. Douglas told me they're planning to do things 'differently,' whatever that means."

David hummed wordlessly in response, not looking away from Backscatter's memorial. Behind him, he heard the shuffle of Jade's shoes in the grass as she came closer.

"What's this?" she asked.

With a sigh, David gestured at the cut face of the rock, where he had inexpertly carved both of his dragoncoat's names, his birth name above his Flighter name in slightly larger text. "I knew that the BWP wasn't exactly going to give Shadow a proper burial. I thought that the least I could do was honor him somehow."

"So you came all the way out here?" Jade looked around, peering at the trees, through which the pedestrian path was barely visible. "We're almost in Yonkers. Why—"

"I didn't want anyone to disturb it," he replied.

Jade nodded, then, as she had on the roof, hesitantly reached out to lay a hand on his shoulder. There was a pause before she said, "I think it was a nice thing to do. Really."

"Too little, too late," David muttered bitterly.

"You couldn't have done anything."

"Not then, I couldn't have. But if I had known what I know now...."

Jade looked at him for a long moment. Then she stooped to the ground, running her fingers through the blades of grass.

David watched her, feeling numb. "What are you doing?"

She straightened, exhaling, and held out her hand. A perfectly oval, flattened stone was nestled in the center of her palm. "May I...?"

There was a flicker of warmth in David's chest. Despite everything, he was touched by the gesture. He nodded, stepping aside so that Jade could place the rock on top of Shadow's memorial.

"I have to admit, I don't know why you do that," Jade said. "But I assumed it was for the same reason that people lay flowers."

"It is. But stones don't wither."

Jade looked up at the light sky above them, the thin layer of clouds dispersing as the morning's rain moved farther away. After a few seconds, she said, "I looked through the folder. I'm —I'm sorry about everything that happened, and I just want you to know that I believe you." She glanced back down at the crude, pebble-covered monument and added, "He didn't deserve that, and neither did you."

Her voice was thick with emotion as she spoke, and David realized how she was probably feeling—sick with terror at the thought that the same fate awaited Night Armor. He hesitated, wanting to reach out to comfort her but unable to complete the gesture. Instead, he offered her a grateful nod, hoping it held at least some of the empathy he couldn't bring himself to show more concretely.

"Where is your dragon?" he asked, half-expecting to see Night Armor stepping out of the undergrowth behind her.

She bit her lip. "He's back at the base. I couldn't figure out a way to get him without attracting notice, and Margie sort of rushed me out."

"She was probably right to. Did the sergeant tell you to stay on Staten Island?"

Jade nodded. "I definitely pushed my luck back there. Nobody has said it out loud, but I can tell that I'm on thin ice."

"So why are you here?"

"You're planning something, and the BWP is planning a counter," she said. "Things are about to get explosive, and after everything you told me, I want to help in any way I can. I feel like it may be the only way to help Night Armor."

Frowning, David regarded her, unsure whether or not he could trust her. What if this was another level to an elaborate scheme, a facade of open honesty that would allow her to continue to report his movements back to Douglas and the BWP? He wanted nothing more than to believe her, but it was entirely possible that this was another lie. Jade had all but disappeared behind her role as Trisha Harper, her confidence convincing despite his well-founded suspicions. David would have been wary of any stranger at his door, but if it had been someone other than Jade, someone who wasn't as good at their job, he might have thrown them out rather than agreeing to the interview.

The way Jade looked at him now, though, David had to admit that he was convinced all over again. There was determination in her gaze, a slight tremor in her upper lip and a set to her jaw that seemed entirely genuine.

Or, he thought cynically, *she's winning you over again, the same way she did it before.* Her looks made everything more complicated. David had never thought of himself as a man who was easily guiled by a pretty face, but that had been before he met Jade.

She shifted her weight, leaves and pine needles crunching under her thick-soled boots. "I want to help you," she repeated, and David realized that he'd been silent for several seconds.

"We should go back to my studio and discuss this." David stretched, his joints protesting from the cold. He started off in the direction of his car, which was parked at the corner of the street a few hundred meters down the pedestrian path.

"Your apartment?" Jade blinked in surprise, jogging to catch up with him. "Isn't that a bit dangerous? The BWP knows where you live, and I have no idea what they'll do next."

David shook his head. "No. Not my apartment. I haven't been back to there in a few days—not since I realized you weren't with the paper."

"What?" There was alarm in Jade's voice. "Wait—where have you been sleeping?"

David didn't answer. When they reached the car, Jade walked to the passenger-side door.

"What are you doing?" David asked.

She paused with her fingers laced into the door handle. "We're going to your studio, right?"

David smiled. The action felt unfamiliar. "No, no. You don't understand. This *is* my studio." He opened up the back of the car, hauling out a large steamer trunk with peeling corners and tarnished hinges. He swore under his breath in Yiddish, quietly enough that Jade wouldn't be able to hear him, as he heaved the box into the grass beside the road.

Jade stared at him, mystified, as he unhooked the latches on the trunk and pulled it open. A drafting desk popped up from the right side of the trunk, and a collapsible easel unfolded on the left. David carefully extracted the stool from the back of the trunk.

"You're going to draw in the park?" Jade looked around as if self-conscious. "There will be people around."

"Probably." David shrugged, laying a fresh sheet of white paper on the drafting desk. He rooted through some of the trunk's drawers, looking for a pencil. "But that's okay. I've seen plenty of artists working in the park."

"Painting the landscape," Jade said. "Not drawing comic book characters."

There was a definite note of derision in her voice as she spoke, which amused David; he'd come across the attitude plenty of times before. They viewed him as a low artist, creating cheaply printed dreck for the masses to consume. There wasn't any point in arguing.

"What are you working on, anyway?" Jade stepped over, leaning forward to look at the paper.

"I have to get my drafts to my editor for the penultimate *Crusader* comic, but there's a change I have to make first. I have to redraw the last few pages."

"What's the change?"

David produced a ruler from the drawer, then he began to carefully outline the straight edges of the panels. "There's a foiled robbery in the second half of this story. I was going to have the villain behind the plot remain mysterious, but this will be the second to last book before—" He broke off mid-sentence, clearing his throat. "Anyway. I created a character who I think will fit nicely in the plot, so I need to make corrections and add a few additional pages."

He reached down into the drawers again, looking for the concept sketches he'd done the night before. As he opened the bottom drawer, a green mask fell onto the grass—a simple, masquerade-style guise that he had crafted out of card paper. Jade's eyes went wide, and she bent to pick it up, turning it over to examine it.

Ignoring her incredulous stare, David asked, "Do you mind if I sketch you again? It's just for a warm-up."

Jade held up the mask. "Do I have to wear this?"

"No, no."

"Do *you* wear this?"

David hesitated. "Sometimes."

Jade laughed, and even though he knew she was laughing at him, David couldn't help but smile.

"It helps to get the angles right when I'm drawing a close up," David explained. "That's what the hand mirror is for."

Jade leaned against the car, watching as David did a few quick sketches on a piece of scrap paper. He set it to the side, then pulled out the previous night's concept artwork.

"Is this the new character?"

David nodded. "The Jade Jocust." As soon as the words were out of his mouth, he realized his error. Jade's eyes narrowed, and she snatched up the top page.

"Really?" She turned it around toward him, raising an eyebrow. "The *Jade Jocust*? She looks a little like me, doesn't she?"

Cringing, David looked away. The drawings had been modeled on his initial sketch of Jade, absent-minded visual notes that he had taken on her appearance—with some liberties taken on the character's form-fitting, metallic costume, colored with a sheen of emerald ink. "Yes. A little." Flustered, he lifted his chin. "She's a thief. She only steals things that are green."

Jade heaved a sigh, rolling her eyes dramatically as she looked back at the page. "Are you serious?"

"I went back to my apartment to look for that folder yesterday," David said, his face still burning in embarrassment. "And all artists draw inspiration from reality. It's not—"

Her voice took on a teasing tone. "Was this a conscious choice, or...?"

"Sort of." The first few sketches of the Jade Jocust, he had to admit, had merely been doodles of Jade—but she didn't have to know that.

Jade was silent for a moment, her eyes tracing the lines of the drawing. It was impossible to tell whether she was annoyed or amused, or something in between the two. Finally, she looked back at David and asked, "Can I keep this?"

Taken aback, David blinked at her. "I—well—why do you want it?"

"It's for Night Armor," Jade said defensively. "A David Felman original."

She's flattered. Relief, and something else, something he hadn't felt in far too long, flooded him. "Oh, of course," he replied, grinning at her. "And I'm sure that *Night Armor* will love it."

Jade scowled at him; it was her turn to be flustered. "Don't you have work to do? Isn't that the whole point of this?"

"Yes, of course." Still smiling, David turned his attention back to his drafting desk and began to sketch figures in the panels, storyboarding the Jade Jocust's introduction into the story. *She appears in the window, silhouetted by the moon. He overhears her with his heightened senses—*

David worked in silence for a few minutes with the real-life Jade observing over his shoulder. He was keenly aware of her sharp gaze, the way that she drew a quiet breath each time he made a mistake and went for his eraser. After a while, she spoke up, breaking David's focus.

"Why a comic book?"

"What?" David lowered the pencil, glancing over his shoulder at her.

"Why a comic book?" she repeated, then added, "It's a strange way to reveal this secret, don't you think?"

"Oh." David returned his attention to the page, which was coming along nicely. The flow of the action between the panels was swift and organized; the lighting was stark, the shadows dramatic. It was turning out to be some of his better work. "Well, I didn't initially intend to be a... what do you call it...."

"An informer?"

He nodded. "Sure, that works. An informer. A conspirator. Whatever you would like to call it." He picked up his pencil and continued to draw, sketching the dark lines of the Jade Jocust's eyes. "I started creating the comic for my own sake. As an outlet to manage my own feelings. For my entire life, even during my time as a Coat Warden, I found peace when I drew. Backscatter always used to love my creations, especially when I sketched dragoncoats."

Next to him, Jade stiffened. He glanced up at her, noting her stricken expression—she had probably heard the sadness in his voice and begun to think again of her own dragon. Her hair had come out of its orderly ponytail, and wisps of black hung around her face like raven's feathers.

David tapped his pencil on the side of the table, as if to demand his own attention. He turned back to the comic page. The sketches were finished, so when he leaned in close to the paper, he began to fill in the details of the characters' features.

"I didn't expect the comic book to become so popular," he

JORDAN RILEY SWAN & EZRA ZABIT

continued as he drew. "It was just a passion project. But eventually, I began to realize that I had an audience. Thousands of people read my comic, and then tens of thousands. There's a certain trust between us—between myself and my audience, that is. I have a platform now, and I intend to use it."

He paused, frowning at a smudged area of the page. The ink would take care of that, but he liked the paper to remain crisp and unblemished as he worked. Dragging his eraser across it, he added, "Margie always goes on about how important art can be in shaping people's perceptions. She's a big fan of the Surrealists. 'Art is whatever anybody needs it to be,' and all that."

"You keep talking about art," Jade said with a quiet chuckle, "but you're drawing a comic book. It's not the *Birth of Venus,* David." She held the mask up to her eyes as if to underline the absurdity.

David frowned up at her. "Art is whatever anybody needs it to be," he repeated.

Slowly, her teasing smile faded.

David's pencil hovered over the third panel; he leaned back to see it from a greater distance. Something was strange about the Jade Jocust's pose as she leaned against a doorframe, smirking at her enemy, twin strands of hair hanging over her mask.

"Would you mind doing me a favor?" David asked.

"Depends what it is," Jade replied, guarded.

"I can't get the pose right in this panel. Could you model it for me?"

After a moment's hesitation, Jade shrugged. "Sure. What do you need me to do?"

"Lean up against the back of the car, as if it's the side of a doorway."

Jade complied, her hand above her head on the car's boxy frame. "Like this?"

"Ah... not quite," David said. "Here, let me—" He stood awkwardly, almost knocking over the spindly easel. "May I...?"

A tiny smile tugged at the corners of her mouth. "Go ahead."

Gently, David laid his hand over hers, repositioning her arm so that it was lower, her stance less dramatic. He took her other hand and laid it on her hip. "Like that."

He heard Jade's soft inhale and realized just how close he had gotten to her. There was barely any space between the two of them. He met her gaze. Her lips were inches from his, and heat crept up his neck as he realized how much he liked the shape of them. He wanted to draw them—no, he wanted to *touch* them.

Stepping back, David lifted a hand to the back of his neck, ashamed of himself and worried that he had crossed some invisible boundary. He almost expected Jade to start yelling at him, or to walk away in a huff. She didn't move. And she was still smiling, which seemed like a good sign.

Taking a deep breath to calm his heart, David went back to the drafting desk. He glanced between Jade and the paper, adjusting the angle of the Jade Jocust's elbow and the position of her feet. Jade said nothing as he put the finishing touches on the drawing then quickly went over the page in ink, emphasizing the lines where the shadows fell. By the time he had finished, the sky had begun to darken. The last panel was difficult to complete for the lack of visibility, and when he was done, David looked up at the leaden clouds with a scowl.

"This is the problem with autumn," he groused. "In the summer, I could've been out here for a few more hours."

"You still have some time before your deadline, right?" Jade asked.

"Not much," David admitted. "I'll have to get them done tonight before I give them to Levi. I only have one panel left. Shouldn't take more than ten minutes." He got to his feet, carefully gathering the pages and tucking them into a folder. As he collapsed the easel and pushed the drafting desk back into the steamer trunk, he added, "I'll be driving to my publisher's office. Freedom Press—it's in midtown." He paused, sizing her up. "Do you want to come with me?"

Jade lifted her arm to check the silver watch fastened around her wrist. "I'll come with you, but I have to stay in the car. It's getting late, and someone on Staten Island might have noticed I'm gone by now. I don't want the BWP to see me with you." She looked up at him with a sheepish expression. "No offense."

"None taken." David closed the steamer trunk, fastening the brass latches. "I wouldn't want to be seen with me, either." He flashed her a wink, and she chuckled as he hoisted the steamer trunk into the car.

FREEDOM PRESS HAD A SMALL, drab office tucked into a small, drab building in Midtown Manhattan, sandwiched between two larger storefronts. Above the glass windows, which were adorned with the name of the business in stenciled letters and backed by perpetually-drawn shutters, was Levi's apartment. David had spent the night there before, curled on his side on the too-short couch while the sounds of traffic and shouts kept him awake. David was pretty sure Levi had some kind of package deal on the rent; the payout from one successful comic and several largely unread, decidedly subversive magazines was not enough, it seemed, to grant Levi a larger printing press.

It took half an hour to drive from the park to the press. When David pulled his car up to the curb, no light filtered through the blinds on the ground level, but there was a yellow glow in one of the second-floor windows. David turned to Jade.

"Okay," he said. "I just have to run in. Won't be more than twenty minutes, I promise."

"It's fine," she replied. "I don't mind waiting. Do you know where you're going after this?"

David sighed, shrugging. "Not really. Might try to get something to eat, if you care to join me. And... I haven't been back to my apartment in a few days, but it's not like I really have anywhere else to go."

Jade pursed her lips. "I'll come with you."

"Are you sure?" David lingered by the car door. "How much longer do you think you can get away with being off-base?"

"Not sure," Jade admitted, "but hopefully longer than this. I'll stick around."

David didn't want to alarm Jade or question any of her decisions when it came to the BWP, so he turned away to disguise his worry, forcing his voice to sound nonchalant. "If you say so."

The main floor windows may have been dark, but the door was unlocked and slightly ajar when David reached it; it swung open at the merest touch. Frowning, David stepped over the threshold. Levi must be working late. His editor was prone to burning the midnight oil from time to time, a common practice in the business, what with fast-approaching deadlines and David's own last-minute changes. But usually that meant bright lights and the rolling clack and shudder of printing machines.

The front room of the office was home to the printing press itself, a steel-and-wood contraption with a sheet of paper spilling out of its narrow mouth and onto a slab table. In the back, there were a few spare offices—Levi's, as well as a workspace that David sometimes used to focus more closely on his work. The lights were off, and the door to Levi's office stood open. Through the shuttered front windows, the streetlights cast a glow over the shop, the shadows of the stenciled letters spilling across the floor.

There was a sound from the back hallway, the scuffle of footsteps and a clunking noise.

"Levi?" David said, taking a cautious step forward. The sole of his shoe touched a streak of liquid, glinting faintly blue in the light that filtered in through the blinds.

Then the smell hit him: an oily stench, like gasoline, but less pungent.

David raced to the back hallway. There, frozen with a metal drum held between them, were two men dressed entirely in black.

For a moment, the three of them stood motionless. The drum was tilted between them, and as David stared, one of the men tipped it forward. The last drops of liquid kerosene dripped to the floor. The two men tossed the drum aside; it fell with a sonorous clang, like the peal of a hollow bell.

"Who—"

Before David could speak, the intruders rushed him.

In his entire life, David had only been in two real fights. Of course, he'd sparred plenty of times in academy training; students' ambitions for partnership with a dragoncoat didn't mean that they could avoid cultivating their own combat instincts, as all military personnel were required to do. But those sparring sessions hadn't been *fights*. They had been practice. Back then, David could respond to his opponent with a clear head and no fear.

The first real fight had been a scrape between schoolboys in Lodz. He'd been nine years old, on his way home in the city center, and had come across a gang of three older Polish boys. He'd quickly given up on the fight itself, opting instead to flee for the Jewish quarter and take refuge in the back of a bakery. He could still remember the strange juxtaposition of the sweet, warm scent of bread and the pounding fear in the back of his head, the blood on his split lip.

The second fight had been in New York, a few years after he had arrived in the city with his parents—before the academy, and before Backscatter. Nobody had advised him not to get into a scrape with a mugger, and he'd drawn back a fist rather than give up his week's pay. He'd lost that fight, too, and arrived home sporting a black eye and a bruised temple, his pockets five dollars lighter.

In the absence of a wealth of experience to draw on, David's adrenaline-fueled mind resorted to instinct. He stumbled back to the main room of the office, nearly tripping over the roll of paper below the printing press. His hands rose to protect his head, and one of the intruders' blows connected with his upper arm.

He lifted a fist for a left hook, but the second trespasser caught him by the elbow and dragged him back before he could strike. The first man hit him roughly in the chest, knocking the wind from David's lungs.

He tried to imagine what his combat instructor from the academy might say. *Fight dirty,* maybe. *There's no honor in going down easy.*

David kicked out at his assailants. The heel of his right foot connected with something soft, and he heard a grunt of pain. The vise-like grip released his arm, and he took the opportunity to lunge forward, knocking the first man back.

From behind him, as if amplified, he heard the unmistakable scrape of a match. The sudden flare of light drew his gaze, and he caught a whiff of sulfur. He barely had time to react as the intruder let the match fall, the tongue of fire rippling as it dropped to the kerosene-soaked floor.

"No!" He scrambled away, shoving into the other masked intruder.

The match hit the floor, and the trail of liquid kerosene

erupted instantly into flames. The blaze traveled along its path, illuminating every corner of the darkened office. The stench of smoke made David feel lightheaded.

Over the wall of flames, he met the flickering stare of the man who had set the fire.

"Are you crazy!?" he exclaimed. "You just—"

He was interrupted by a sudden movement from the other intruder, who grabbed him from behind. David struggled to free himself, but his attacker clung to his shoulders. A thick hand closed around his throat.

David dropped to his knees, gasping for air. Between the intruder's choking hand and the dark kerosene smoke, it was almost impossible to draw a breath. He tried to pry the strong fingers from his neck, but his efforts were feeble, useless. Unfiltered panic roared inside him.

Glass shattered, the sound ringing out over the flames. Through the cloud of fumes and his rapidly tunneling vision, a figure strode forward. She wore a fitted mask of green sequins that sparkled in the light of the flames, looking all the world as if she had busted out of a panel from one of his comic books.

The lack of oxygen must be affecting my brain, he decided. Or else he had simply lost his mind under the sheer stress.

Because the Jade Jocust had arrived to save him.

CHAPTER

NINE

S moke billowed from the shattered windows of Freedom Press, cascading into the darkening sky as Jade and David stumbled into the street. His arm was slung over her shoulders, and as they escaped into the cool and relatively clear night air, he collapsed to his knees, coughing and hacking.

In the chaos of the fire, Jade hadn't recognized the two BWP goons, who had since vanished—likely through a back exit. It had been easy enough to fight off David's attacker, who had realized once his nose was broken that he would be better served escaping the blaze than trying to take them down with him.

The firm edges of the Jade Jocust's mask dug into the tops of her cheeks. She pulled it over her head, but she could still feel the soot outline on her skin, drawn across her face like one of David's draft sketches. Jade had yanked it on to hide her identity in case the fire she had seen through the outside windows had been started by the BWP. And it had been a good thing she had—she didn't know the two intruders' names, but whomever hired them from the base would be grilling them thoroughly once they heard about the fight. If they had seen her, no amount of lies or made up alibies would have saved her.

As she breathed fresh air, the adrenaline of the fight began to fade, and a searing pain flared on her upper back. Vaguely, she remembered burning debris falling from the ceiling and catching her in the shoulder.

David had finished wheezing. He looked up at the burning building with watering eyes. Glowing embers drifted through the street, where passersby had begun to gather and stare.

"Levi," David rasped.

"Levi?"

"My editor. He lives upstairs. We have to—"

He broke off at the sound of a sharp yell from the side of the burning building. A man descended the metal fire escape with rapid steps, an overstuffed folder tucked beneath one arm. He wore a cotton bathrobe and slippers, and his salt-and-pepper hair was disheveled, the tight curls strung out into frizz. Levi reached the ground and turned to the building, taking in the height of the flames, which now licked at the second-floor window. Jade expected to see a look of despair on his face, but when he glanced back at David, his expression betrayed nothing but mild annoyance.

"Felman," he said, his voice testy. "I'm gonna assume *you* didn't set my damn office on fire."

David shook his head. His voice was still hoarse as he said, "What can I say? I finally got tired of putting up with you."

A grim smile twitched the corner of Levi's mouth, but it disappeared as soon as it had come. He sighed, brushing a few flakes of smoldering ash from his shoulder; Jade thought she could see illegible print etched into the charred paper.

"There's a saying for this, eh?" Levi said dryly. "Comes with the wind—"

"—and goes up in smoke," David finished for him, nodding.

Levi looked between him and Jade. "Who's she? She have

96

anything to do with this? And why does her face look like that?" He gestured to his own cheeks and forehead, tracing the outline of the mask's soot shadow.

"Those are all complicated questions," David replied, dazed.

"Well—" Levi's gaze raked up and down the street, as if waiting for bystanders to come running along at any second. They were in the industrial part of town in the middle of the night, so a crowd hadn't started to filter out of the buildings yet, but Levi was unlikely to be the only one squatting where they worked. He ran a hand through the back of his hair, chewing on his lip. "We don't really have time for a complicated answer."

"She's with me," said David. "That's all you need to know."

Jade was grateful for the non-specificity. As casual as Levi seemed about the torching of his office, he might be less than charitable if he learned that it had been Jade's bosses who had ordered it. She also felt a strange and welcome warmth within her at David's firm declaration: *She's with me.*

David pushed himself upright, walking over to stand beside Levi. A magazine, borne aloft on flaming wings by the heat of the fire, fell the ground in front of them in a heap of charred pages. "I'm sorry, Levi," David said. "I didn't know this would happen."

Jade couldn't see Levi's face in the pause that followed, but she was taken aback again when he barked a curt laugh. "Well, you aren't exactly the brightest bulb in the box. I sure as hell did."

"What?"

"You think I haven't been getting this sort of threat from Blackwing schmucks for months now?" Levi tightened his arm against the folder and fished into the inside pocket of his bathrobe, producing a pack of cigarettes. "Why do you think I keep the most important stuff on me all the time?" he waggled the folder. "You think I don't know what 'steep consequences' means in a phone call from a shadowy government agency?" He stepped forward and stooped to light the cigarette on the smoldering magazine, straightening to take a long drag. "You don't seem surprised either, Felman. Why's that?"

David didn't say anything, but Levi seemed to take his silence as a response. He laughed again, bitterly, and said something quiet in a language that wasn't English.

David replied, equally quiet, in the same tongue. They both continued to stare at the burning building front as if mesmerized by the flames' performance. Levi took another drag from the cigarette.

Finally, driven by frustration and the pain in her shoulder, Jade broke the silence. "So... what the hell are we supposed to do now?"

They both gave a start, as if she'd interrupted some sort of spell. Levi looked between her and David, as if to say, *She's your secret, you answer her.*

"We better dodge out of here," David replied.

"Sure, sure." Levi seemed distracted. "You two ought to get out of here while you can, before the firemen arrive. This is going to be hard as hell to explain as it is."

"Whenever you're done, you should come back to my apartment," said David. "Because—"

He was interrupted by a loud crash and a shower of sparks from the building. The ceiling splintered, the second floor collapsing into the first as the fire consumed the foundations. Levi yelped, accidentally dropping his cigarette. He swore, stomping out the orange ember with the toe of his slipper.

"Just go," he said, waving David away. "I'll meet up with you later."

David turned to Jade, reaching out to her. It struck Jade that there was something almost pleading about the gesture. She realized that he was more rattled by this attack on the publishing house than he was willing to let on. He didn't want to be left alone in its aftermath.

The smoke and the stark light of the fire made the sky seem darker. Surely, by now, her absence from the base had been noticed. She wondered briefly about Night Armor, and whether he had been dragged back in for more medical testing.

She hadn't intended to stay away this long. But now, looking at David, she realized that she couldn't possibly leave him.

At any rate, she wouldn't be able to explain the wound on her shoulder to her superiors, so it was probably better to stay away until she could hide it better.

Jade nodded, taking David's hand and giving it a gentle and reassuring squeeze.

JADE WAS HALF-EXPECTING to run into a Blackwing Flighter on the way back to David's apartment, or to be interrupted on the way up the stairs by more hired mercenaries. It was only once they were inside David's apartment that she was able to somewhat relax, sinking onto the couch while he bolted both locks on the door. He went to the kitchen, rummaging around in a low cabinet. When he emerged, he set two short glasses on the wood chipped coffee table, which, like everything in David's apartment, showed clear signs of wear.

"I know things are stricter on Staten Island," David said, "but I figured that, after tonight, you might want to—"

"Yes," Jade interrupted. "That seems appropriate."

David uncapped a paper-wrapped bottle. He poured the amber liquid into one of the cups, but his hands were shaking, and a few drops of moonshine splashed onto the table.

Jade reached for the bottle. "Let me—"

"I can do it," David said. He took a breath to steady himself before pouring again. Once the glasses were full, he sank down onto the couch beside Jade. "Are we safe here? Do you think they might have followed us?"

Jade shook her head. "No. If they had anyone tailing you, they would have intervened when the fight broke out—or at least stopped me from coming inside to help you."

"What do you think? Trained operatives?"

"They didn't fight like trained operatives," Jade said stiffly. "If I had to guess, they were contractors of some sort. The BWP isn't against working with hired guns."

David's unfocused gaze became concerned as his eyes moved from the soot outline on her face to her shoulder. Instinctively, she reached up, her fingers twining into a lock of her dark hair. The strands felt brittle, and when she closed her hand, she felt them break. The burning debris must have singed her hair during their escape.

"Are you okay?" David asked.

She cleared her throat. "I'm... fine."

"It's okay if you're not," he said. "Here—let me—" He stood, disappearing back into the kitchen. When he returned, he held a few damp, folded cloths and a dark brown bottle of strong-smelling antiseptic. He sat down next to her, hesitating, an unspoken question in his eyes. She sighed and nodded, allowing him to dab the wet cloth on her face, clearing away the soot outlines of the mask.

After a few seconds, he froze, the rag hovering beside her cheek. "You're hurt," he said. "Your shoulder."

She glanced down at the wound, which she'd almost managed to forget about. The pain had dulled since they'd left the scene, and she'd been more preoccupied running through everything in her head, trying to process. Now that David pointed it out, though, she felt the searing sensation again, as strong as ever.

"It's okay," she said, trying to shift her stance to hide the burn from view. There was something about the softness in his eyes that made her nervous, and she could sense impending danger in every gentle touch. "It's not too bad."

He dropped his hands. "Jade. Let me help you."

She swallowed but didn't respond.

"You helped me," he reminded her. "You probably saved my life. This is the least I can do for you."

She couldn't argue with that. Relenting, she turned to allow David access to her shoulder. Gingerly, he pulled down the fabric covering the wound, exposing part of her upper back. Her heart leapt to her throat as he laid a steadying hand between her shoulder blades before beginning to dab the cool cloth against the burn. His eyebrows were knitted together in concentration and concern as he worked, a small crease between them. Jade gritted her teeth against the pain, which was easier to ignore than she'd expected—not least because of David's touch, firm and soothing against her spine.

"You're not alone," he said quietly, without meeting her eyes. "I know that being a Coat Warden makes you feel that way, sometimes—like the only other person in the world is your dragoncoat. But that's not true. You don't have to handle everything on your own."

Jade didn't respond. Her eyes stung, which she told herself was merely the aftereffect of the fire, or a reaction to the discomfort of her burned shoulder.

When David was done cleaning her wound, he set the cloth aside. They were close, less than two feet from each other, and Jade's breath quickened as she suddenly became aware of that proximity. Beneath the smell of charred paper and kerosene, David's hair had a fresh aroma of peppermint oil and talc. It reminded Jade of the mint tea that her mother always brewed in excess on winter days, when a frigid breeze brought white-out snow across Manhattan to bury Queens. The Atallahs had come to the city before Jade was born, and even after decades of Decembers, they had yet to adjust to the cold.

During her time at the academy, and especially at the Staten Island base, Jade had found everything about New York cold. It was a city of pure ice, of opportunity and all of its barbed claws. But being this close to David—it was like coming home, stepping out of the snowstorm.

You need to be smarter than this, she told herself. *It's one thing to save him from a burning building, but it's another thing entirely to—*

David's fingers brushed her singed hair, tucking the damaged lock behind her ear. He met her gaze. His eyes were a deep, coffee brown, heavy with unsaid things.

It was too much, the gentle touch wrapping her in desire.

Every cautious thought vanished from her mind, and she leaned toward him. His eyes widened in surprise. She paused, her fingers rising to trace his jaw, skimming over the warm skin.

Shyly, she said, "Do you—do you mind if I—"

"I've never had a supervillain steal a kiss from me before," he interrupted with a tiny smile. "Maybe it's better if I don't resist."

"*Jade Jocust* is the super villain," she replied. "*I* was the one who saved you."

"My hero," he whispered and leaned forward.

Jade smiled, closed her eyes, and pressed her lips to his. The kiss was soft and tender, and warmth radiated into her every limb, as though she was sitting at a hearth. It was David who pulled away first.

"Jade—"

She cleared her throat, suddenly self-conscious. "I'm sorry if this is all happening too fast—"

"It isn't," he assured her, his eyes glimmering, heated from behind with what she hoped was desire.

"I know this might not be a good idea. Especially now, after everything that just happened."

"If you need to get back to Staten Island, I understand." David's face fell as he spoke, and Jade's heart tightened in her chest.

"No," she said quickly, her hands landing on his forearms. "Of course not. It's just a lot to take in. I'm confused, and... scared, and I'm worried that I'm making a lot of rash decisions."

The admission of fear stuck briefly in her throat, but she forced herself to say it. David had been right; she'd been operating from the mindset of a Coat Warden, a soldier, focused only on her orders and confiding solely in Night Armor. But she *was* scared—for her dragoncoat, if not for herself. She was certain from the still-present tremor in David's hands that he was reeling from the attack on Freedom Press, but beyond that, he also must know exactly what she was going through with the Blackwing Program.

"If saving me from a fire was a rash decision," he said, with a glimmer of humor, "then I hope you continue to trust your instincts."

"That's not what I'm talking about."

"I know. But I liked *that* rash decision, too. I've liked all of your rash decisions."

Silently, Jade had to agree, though she said nothing.

"What's got you confused?" David asked.

Jade sighed, flopping back against David's worn couch cushions. "It's just... I worked my entire life to get here. I clawed my way through the academy. I sacrificed so much, just to be there." She glanced over at David, who was listening intently. "This might sound stupid to you, but... when I was in school, before the academy, I... I wanted to be an artist."

A fleeting, delighted smile flashed across his face, which made Jade's heart skip a beat. When he smiled like that, it seemed to lift the years from him, like a brief return of stolen youth. "Really?"

"Yes," Jade admitted. "I used to draw all the time. I would draw portraits of my teachers during classes. But... I had to stop when I was accepted to the academy, because from then on, it was all duty, all the time. I needed to make it. I needed to be first warden. I wasn't the only one who had made sacrifices to get me there."

"What do you mean?"

"My family came here from Syria—near Damascus—before I was born. They did it because they knew that I would have a chance to become a Coat Warden and ride a dragoncoat. It wasn't an opportunity I would've had there, and ever since I passed my first hearing tests when I was little, my parents told me that my goal was to get into an academy."

"That's a lot of pressure."

"In Syria, being bonded to a dragon is the ultimate sign of status. If I became a Coat Warden, it would mean... I don't know. That we had made it, somehow." Jade stared across the apartment, at the tall, cross-barred windows. Outside, the smog-filled sky seemed lighter than it typically would at this time of night. She wondered if the fire was still burning at Freedom Press, or if the firemen had arrived to put it out. "I *wanted* to be an artist, but I knew I *needed* to be a warden. First warden."

David nodded, closing his eyes as if in recollection. "I know what that's like."

"And after all of that work... this is how they reward me," Jade said bitterly. "With a so-called promotion that kills my dragoncoat. With a million closed doors, and with...." She trailed off, gesturing with her chin to the burn on her shoulder. In the aftermath of David's care, the throbbing pain had subsided somewhat, leaving a dull ache in its place.

"It's not meant to be a reward," David sighed. "Nor a promotion. It's Blackwing. Consider your Flighter hijacked."

If she reframed everything that way, it made much more sense. She'd felt more free as a regular Coat Warden, back before she and Night Armor had been elevated to the elite— and covert—ranks of the BWP.

"I gave up everything for Blackwing, and tonight I found out that it attacks its own citizens," Jade said. Every time she closed her eyes, she saw the flare of golden light behind the Freedom Press windows, the crackling flames swallowing the printing press and consuming the stacks of magazines. "They're so afraid of the public knowing the truth that they're willing to kill people."

"Well, they were willing to kill Levi. I get the sense that they still want to keep the scope of their problem as limited as possible."

"What did he say to you?" Jade asked, suddenly curious. "Your editor. Outside, in the street."

At that, David hesitated for a couple of seconds as if weighing his answer. Finally, he said, "Levi was born and raised in New York, but his parents were from Warsaw. He was asking me if I was reminded of the old country."

"And were you?"

David's restless fingers tapped on the armrest of the couch. "There were... certain similarities, yes."

Silence fell over the room. Despite the heat still lingering in Jade's chest and rising to her cheeks, she reached for the glass of moonshine on the coffee table. It smelled acrid, and it burned as it went down her throat. She winced, coughing, and set it back down. When she looked back up at David, he wore a small, amused smile.

"Too strong?"

"I'm not used to drinking," Jade said. "I do things by the book."

David chuckled, shaking his head. "By the book? Could've fooled me."

"What's that supposed to mean?"

"Well... since I've known you, you've gone behind the sergeant's back at least three times. You've spent the entire day with *me,* and now here you are, in my apartment...." He leaned forward again, brushing a loose lock of Jade's hair back behind her ear. Her breath threatened to leave her, as though all of the air between them had been drained from the room. "Fraternizing."

"Fraternizing?"

"That's what we're doing, no?"

"I'd use a different word," she whispered. "Something a little less clinical. A little more...." She trailed off, uncertain, unable to determine exactly what was happening between the two of them.

"I'll try to think of something," David said quietly.

Jade's hand fisted the front of David's shirt, and she closed her eyes, pulling him back down for another kiss.

Before their lips could meet, there was a loud, harsh knock at the door. A muffled voice from the hallway shouted, *"Felman!"*

Immediately, all of the tension between them vanished, cut by the sudden dose of fear that shot through Jade. She scrambled to her feet, pulling her shirt back over her burned shoulder. She didn't know what to expect, but her imagination, spurred by the excitement already buzzing through her mind, was in overdrive. Half a dozen Blackwing operatives, their dragons waiting for them on the roof the same way Night Armor had waited for her. The police, here to arrest her and David on suspicion of arson. Sergeant Douglas himself, ready to drag her back to Staten Island.

To her surprise, David just sighed, rising from the couch

with a disappointed, long-suffering air. He gestured for her to sit back down. "It's just Levi. One second."

He crossed to the door. Levi burst into the room before he could get there, apparently no longer content to wait in the hall.

As soon as he entered, he began to pace up and down behind David's couch, wringing his hands together. He still wore his soot-covered bathrobe and slippers, and the folder he'd carried down the fire escape was tucked under his arm. He gripped it with his right hand, his thumb stroking the papers as if he were soothing an injured animal. On the outside of the burning press, Jade had thought he seemed almost too calm. Now that clemency had passed, Levi looked frazzled, exactly the way Jade had originally expected him to.

"Okay, okay. Does someone wanna tell me what the hell just happened?" Levi demanded. "'Cause my apartment and my shop are a pile of rubble right now, and let me tell you—"

"Levi," David said flatly. "Sit down."

Levi didn't sit down. He pointed a finger over at David, something bordering on accusation in his gaze. "Not until you tell me everything you know."

"I know as much as you do," David replied. "You told me yourself that you weren't surprised."

"I wasn't surprised the office got torched," Levi said, an edge to his voice. "But I still want to know everything you know about it, 'cause they just burned my damn house down, so forgive me if I'm a little *jumpy*. Are we safe here?"

David glanced at Jade as if searching for confirmation. She shrugged, wishing she could summon enough confidence to reassure him. Ordinarily, it would have been easy for her to say that Blackwing would never attack a civilian's apartment, but tonight, she wasn't at all sure what Blackwing would or wouldn't do. She'd already seen them cross lines she'd thought could never be crossed.

"I hope so," David said. "But where else can we go?"

"What about your girlfriend's place?" Levi asked. He looked at Jade. "You got somewhere we can stay?"

Jade shook her head. "Probably not a good idea."

"Why not?"

"Jade is a Coat Warden," David interjected, his voice calm. "Her 'place' is the Blackwing base on Staten Island."

Levi stiffened, his eyes narrowing. "You brought one of them into—"

"Levi," David interrupted, "in case you've forgotten, *I* was a Coat Warden. Believe me, if we can trust anyone, we can trust Jade."

For a few moments, Levi continued to stare at her, as if weighing her integrity. Finally, he gave a curt nod. "Sure. Whatever you say."

"Do you want to sit down now?" David asked, a note of exasperation in his voice. The way he spoke to Levi reminded Jade of her own relationship with Night Armor—affectionate, but with a cultivated patience to mask his frustration. "Borrow something else to wear, maybe?"

Levi glanced down at his own arms, apparently realizing for the first time that he was in nightclothes—and that his sleeves were coated in a thin layer of ash. "You know what? That's a decent idea. What do you have?"

"I'll show you."

"What did you say to the firemen?" Jade asked. "They don't suspect you of starting it, do they?"

"Of course they do. It's how they approach any arson case." With a snort, Levi tossed the folder onto the coffee table. Glancing down at it, Jade saw the corners of a few *Coated Crusader* panels, outlined in thick, black ink. "But old Oscar across the street saw me run down the fire escape and said so to the firemen and the police, so I think I'm in the clear. How could I set a fire in the office from upstairs?" He paused, then added, "It took them a little too long to figure that out, though. Not exactly a bunch of philosophers. Took 'em until one in the morning to realize that I don't own the building and can't collect insurance on it. The only thing of value in there was the printing press, and she's a hunk of useless metal now."

Alarm bells rang in Jade's head at Levi's words. "Wait, sorry —one in the morning?"

Levi cocked his head to one side. "Well, yeah. And that was an hour ago, so—"

She uttered a short curse under her breath, scrambling to her feet. "I have to get back," she said to David, who was unable to keep the look of disappointment from his face. "I need to check in, and be seen on the base, or my alibi is gonna fall apart. And Night Armor—"

"I understand." He held up a hand. "There's no need to explain. Be safe, okay?"

Jade nodded. "I will be."

Her heart lodged in her throat at the thought of walking back onto the Blackwing base after what she'd seen tonight. But she had no choice. Her best friend was within those walls, his future uncertain, and she would rather die than abandon him.

CHAPTER
TEN

Between the still-present nerves that made his hands shake and the chorus of crashing sounds from his kitchen, louder and more effective than any alarm or wake-up call, David was dragged from exhausted sleep much too early the following morning.

For around a minute, he laid on his back, staring at the ceiling above his bed. The events of the previous night rushed into his head like a tidal wave; his throat was slightly sore from the sharp smoke, and he could smell a faint aroma of kerosene. He'd tried to wash his hair the previous night and was wearing different clothes, but the scent still lingered.

He closed his eyes, remembering the look on Jade's face as they'd sat in the living room, the soot outline of the jocust mask cresting her brow. Her lips had been soft, her touch perfect, as though her hands had been designed to hold him. If he was honest, he'd been imagining how it might feel to kiss her since he'd first met her, but the whole time, she had seemed so distant—so professional. Last night, as he'd cleaned the ash from her face, her mask had come off.

If Jade had any sense at all, she would know to stay away. To keep her head down and keep watch over Night Armor until everything blew over. Levi's untimely appearance had ruined their moment, and it was unlikely that they would get another one.

Levi. David's eyes flickered open, and he scowled up at the flaking paint above. He could hear the creak of the floorboards outside of his bedroom door. *This apartment is too small for a roommate,* he thought, allowing himself a moment of irritation. He had to provide a place for Levi to stay; it was his fault that Freedom Press was gone. But David had never been a wildly social person, and his capacity for conversation was particularly strained whenever he spoke to his editor.

When he emerged into the main room of his apartment, Levi was busy in the kitchen area, preparing breakfast. More accurately, he was rifling through all of David's cabinets, a frenzied look on his face as if he was searching for a bomb that was set to explode.

"Levi," David said tiredly, by way of a greeting. "What on earth are you doing?"

Levi rounded on him, wild eyed. "*Coffee.*"

"Above the sink."

Levi scrambled for the correct cabinet, knocking over a bag of flour as he snatched up the burlap pouch of coffee. Apparently oblivious to the cloud of powder settling on his borrowed clothes, he opened up the top of the little sack, inhaling the scent of the beans. "Light roast," he said appreciatively. "*Shkoy-ach,* Felman."

David's eyelid twitched. He was used to Levi's late-night antics, but at seven in the morning, after only four hours of sleep, he wasn't sure he could muster the patience.

"Hey, what's the matter?" Levi portioned out a handful of coffee beans into the grinder tucked behind the stove. "Chin up."

"Your apartment burned down last night," David said, incredulous. "How are you this cheerful?"

"Nobody's dead, and I got my photo album and a folder of your sketches on my way out. Everything else is replaceable. Coffee?"

"Please." David sat down at the counter that separated the kitchen from the rest of the living area. "The printing press is gone, Levi."

Levi hummed, turning the hand crank on the coffee grinder. The welcome smell of fresh coffee filled the kitchen. "Definitely," he said. "I saw it last night after they doused the fire. It's practically melted." He paused, glancing over his shoulder. "You got anything for us to eat?"

"There are bagels in that lower cabinet."

As Levi rummaged around for the bagels, David leaned over the counter, watching him in bemusement. Levi had always been adamant in his support of the comic book and David's right to publish it. *Come hell or high water,* he'd always said. But despite the frequent indicators of inclement weather to come, David had never seriously imagined hell or high water would arrive at Freedom Press. But the previous night had seen both. If asked to imagine a fire consuming the Lower East Side office, he certainly wouldn't have thought that Levi would whistle his way through breakfast the next morning.

"You're seriously fine with this?"

Levi shrugged, tossing a bagel at David, who fumbled to catch it. "I'd rather it hadn't happened," Levi said drily, "but they did call me more than a few times threatening property damage and bodily harm, so all things considered, I can't be too surprised. Could've been worse."

"Could've been," David echoed. He pried the bagel apart, frowning down at the two halves. It was too early for him to feel hungry, and after the previous night, it felt as though there was a pit in his stomach.

"You got cream and sugar?"

"No."

"Atta boy," Levi said. "Couple minutes on the coffee."

"So," David said, pulling the bottom half of his bagel into chunks, "I'm guessing the last comic issues aren't going to be possible anymore, right?"

Levi snorted, hopping up onto the counter and leaning back against the cabinets. "Are you kidding me? These bastards have to go down twice as hard now."

"We don't have a printing press. We can't—"

"I still have your pages," Levi said earnestly. "I know a guy in Boston who owes me a favor from back in the Great War. He'll print for us."

"What did you do for him in the Great War?"

Levi flashed him a wink. "Don't worry about it."

"He's not going to print for you. Blackwing kicked me out of every other publisher I went to," David reminded him. "What makes you think this guy will be any different?"

Apparently unconcerned, Levi took a bite out of the bagel and shrugged. "Trust me," he said through a mouthful. "He'll do it."

"If you say so." David forced himself to eat a piece of the bagel, then took the mug of coffee when Levi offered it to him. It was watery by his standards, but it was welcome nonetheless. There was no point in going back to sleep now. He might as well dedicate himself to being awake, and to working on whatever Levi needed. It might be best to start on the final issue of *The Coated Crusader*. If Levi managed to find them a press, it would likely be wise to send everything at once, before the BWP figured out what was going on.

"You got a phone I can use?" Levi asked. "I need to call my guy."

∽

LEVI SPENT most of the morning on the phone. He lingered by the tall windows, staring out at the buildings across the street. His conversations were battles, and he emerged from all of them defeated. Watching from his drafting desk, David could identify the instant in each call when his editor was forced to give up. Levi's cajoling and reminiscing soured quickly, devolving into personal attacks of a sensitive nature, which David wished he could scrub from his mind.

The fifth call, in the early afternoon, started out promising. Levi asked about his colleague's "gorgeous" family, then he seamlessly transitioned into the early days of their publishing careers, peppering in over-the-top compliments as he went. David thought that Levi's brand of flattery was paper-thin, but he often ended up surprised at its efficacy, so he did his best to stay out of his editor's way.

At the one-hour mark in Levi's most successful attempt yet, there was a sharp knock on the door.

David looked up from his drafting desk, where he'd been carefully inking the outline of the black dragon's head. Levi scowled in the direction of the noise, and he shot David a meaningful glare.

With a sigh, David stood, his spine protesting after hours spent bent over the desk. He crossed to the door.

"Who's there?"

"Sergeant Douglas," a familiar voice replied—definitely *not* the sergeant. "Open up. You're under arrest for, um, drawing."

David flung the door open, flustered. In the hallway, clad in a blonde wig and a pair of thick-rimmed glasses, stood Jade.

"What are you doing?" David hissed, glancing over his shoulder. He stepped over the threshold, closing the apartment door behind himself so as not to disturb Levi. "Are you out of your—"

"I took leave for the day." Jade lifted a hand, running her

fingers through the golden waves of her wig. "What do you think of my new look? Do you get it?"

David sighed. The wig and glasses looked just like the Jade Jocust's secret identity, which he'd drawn her wearing for a few panels in the penultimate issue. "Yes, very amusing."

"I figured that if I was going to hide my appearance, I might as well do something funny."

"You shouldn't be here," David said. "You're putting yourself in danger. What if someone followed you? What if someone from Blackwing sees you with me?"

Jade lifted a hand to her clavicle, her fingertips resting on her burned shoulder. "Don't you remember what we talked about last night?"

"Jade—"

"Everything I've given up—everything my family has given up—means absolutely nothing if I let other people make the same mistake," she said firmly. "I won't let this get any worse than it already is. And I have to protect my dragoncoat."

Relenting, David leaned back against the doorframe. "How is Night Armor?"

She pursed her lips, a crease appearing between her eyebrows. "I don't know. They wouldn't let me see him. He's under observation."

"Do you know why?"

"No. Margie promised to keep me updated, but for now, the last thing I want to do is just wait around on that base."

David nodded. He was all too familiar with the kind of restless energy that came from helplessness.

"So, here I am," Jade said with a shrug. "What have I missed?"

"Not much. Levi's been on the phone for the past six hours, trying to find someone to print the comic. I've been getting hand cramps from drawing too fast." He held up his right hand, flexing his stiff fingers. "The final *Coated Crusader* is coming along."

"You're still going to print?"

"If we can do it." David tilted his head toward the door. "Come on inside. I'll show you what I have so far."

The moment David set foot back inside the apartment, he realized that something was wrong. The phone was back in its cradle, and Levi leaned forlornly on the windowsill, rubbing his forehead as though warding off a headache.

"What happened?" David asked. "Things seemed to be going okay while I was out in the hall."

"These people flip fast," Levi muttered. He dropped his hand, looking blearily over at David. "So that's five who have said no."

"What went wrong with Boston? I thought you said that guy owed you a favor."

"Turns out he's all talk." Levi sniffed, disgruntled. "Nobody wants to deal with Blackwing, and news travels fast in the media world—everyone's squawking at each other about what happened to Freedom Press."

David's heart sank. This was exactly what he'd thought might happen. "So... is that it, then?"

For a few seconds, Levi was quiet. Then he seemed to become reanimated. "Of course not. I've still got people to call. I used to work with a fella in Philadelphia who might be able to help me out." He snatched up the phone, his finger hovering over the rotary dial, then he glanced back up at David as though seeing him—and Jade—for the first time. "Felman, what's the Blackwing girl doing back here? What did you say your name was?"

"Jade. And I'm here because I took leave for the day," Jade said at once, repeating the explanation she'd given David. "I thought I might be able to—"

Levi held up a hand. "Wait. Stop. Don't care. I have a phone call to make."

Jade fell silent, looking miffed.

"You two—get out of my office. You're gonna distract me."

David blinked at him, startled. "Your... office? You mean my apartment?"

"Yes." Levi began to dial the number, muttering to himself under his breath.

"What do you expect us to *do*?"

"What do I care?" Levi waved a hand. "Go shopping. Go to the park. Go see that damned new movie everyone's been talking about. Make it a date—oh, don't give me that look, Felman, I'm not stupid, I have *eyes*. Just leave me be!"

WITH AN AIR OF BEMUSEMENT, Jade followed David out of the apartment, down the stairs, and into the street. It was a chilly afternoon; David regretted not grabbing a scarf on his way out, but Levi probably would've yelled at him for dragging his feet.

"So," he said lightly, "a movie?"

She raised an eyebrow.

"You want to go to the theater?" Jade asked.

"I mean, I *think* Levi was joking, but..." David said. "While he's making calls, we really should stay out of his way. Plus, it's early. It'll be near-empty at the Rialto Theatre. You could catch me up on everything that's happening on Staten Island."

"I'm game. Let's do it."

David stepped toward the street, lifting a hand to hail one of the taxi cabs that filtered through the traffic like so many golden-scaled fish in a stream. When the cab pulled to the curb, he held the door open for Jade, letting her slide into the backseat first. She'd saved his life the previous day. He figured that he owed her some chivalry.

The poster outside of the Rialto depicted a strapping silver dragoncoat, posing regally behind a young woman with fiery red hair.

"*On Silver Wings I Fly*," Jade said, reading from the marquee above the doors. "Huh. I didn't know everyone was raving about a dragoncoat movie."

"I wonder if it will feel authentic."

Jade huffed a laugh. "Authentic? Nobody comes to the movies for authenticity, David. Everyone here just wants to be entertained."

He supposed that was probably true. Authenticity could have never garnered such a crowd. The line for tickets stretched into the sidewalk, and by the time David and Jade had finally secured theirs, the theater was almost full. They managed to find two adjacent seats close to the back, beneath the glowing projector.

"This must be some movie," Jade whispered. "Looks like they sold every seat."

David glanced around, taking in the full theater. *There must be something about this movie that everyone wants to see,* he mused. *It's a dragoncoat story... I wonder how they'll react to it.* Knowing how the crowd might respond to a Flighter movie might help him hit the right beats in the last issue of his comic. There might be certain things the audience expected in the narrative—things he would be remiss not to include.

As the lights went down, Jade leaned closer to David, so close that he was tempted to wrap his arm around her shoulders. He didn't; he couldn't be sure that she would want him to.

"Do you still want to stay?" she breathed in his ear, her breath tingling on his neck. "We probably won't be able to talk about much with all of these people around."

"That's okay," David said with a shrug. "We paid for the tickets. Besides, I'm curious. I want to see what people make of it—a story about a dragoncoat."

The projector fired up with a rattling sound, and light blazed across the screen. David had seen one movie in his life, and it had been a silent one, accompanied by live musicians. He was startled when, in the first scene, the actors spoke to one another, and the silver dragon let out exaggerated clicking and chirping sounds. The dragoncoat had been dubbed over so that the average viewer would be able to understand what he was saying but the underlying language and lines matched the scratchy English words someone else had recorded over him. He seemed to be enjoying his time before the camera, hamming up his performance. The great beast walked with a swagger and held his head high, like he was immensely proud of his role. David couldn't take his eyes off of him.

This silver dragoncoat looked far too much like Backscatter before they had stripped him of his silver and turned him into a shadow of his formal self.

The resemblance was so striking that David struggled to pay attention to the rest of the movie, or the audience's reactions to it. Dimly, he was aware of laughter and gasps around him, but his focus was fixed on too-familiar silver scales and the cheerful, gleaming eyes.

On screen, the dragoncoat spread its wide wings and took flight with the actress astride. As a stunning aerial shot followed the pair of them over the winding curves of a river, David dug his fingernails into the armrests of the seat, trying to keep himself grounded.

Jade's hand rested on his forearm, the callouses at the base of her fingers—he'd once had the same ones, earned by hours spent holding the leather straps of Shadow's harness—traced lines across his skin as she reacted to his tense body.

He glanced at her, saw concern in her gaze, and looked back at the screen. The dragoncoat's silver scales caught the sunlight, their glare almost blinding.

Silver scales beneath a fringe of wool, the thick sheepskin that he always tucked under Backscatter's saddle in an effort to make it more comfortable. He could feel his dragon's fear as potently as if it were his own—they had known each other for years, and each was intimately familiar with the other's subtle tells. David could glean Backscatter's emotional state from the way his head swung to the side, eyes wary, pupils narrowed to slits. Backscatter, he knew, could tell from the tension David held in his body, a subtle increase in the rate of his breath.

Ahead of them, coming over the ridge in a swarm like nothing David had ever seen: jocust beetles, in the hundreds, their carapaces glinting iridescent in the afternoon sun. The click of their mandibles filled the air with a constant, steady hum, like cicadas, but amplified from song to violent screech.

A few yards away, another Coat Warden, astride his iron-plated dragoncoat, uttered a short curse. The second Flighter team, David and Backscatter's only backup, launched itself into the sky—in the opposite direction from the swarm. They were fleeing, leaving David and his dragoncoat to fend for themselves.

<u>Should we run?</u> Backscatter asked, those needle-thin pupils landing on David.

Swallowing, David shook his head. "We can't. There's a farming village about two miles north of here. If we don't try to stop them, they're going to ruin the entire year's harvest. Or worse, get a hold of the family."

Backscatter's talons dug into the earth. <u>Hold on.</u>

The silver dragoncoat took flight. David leaned close to his lithe body, streamlining their form. In battle against jocusts, he'd learned that the most important thing for a Coat Warden to do was stay out of his dragon's way. He could smell the sharp tang of the acid that frothed in Backscatter's maw—

And suddenly, the scales beneath his hands were no longer silver. They were pitch black, like the night. The jocusts ahead were frozen in midair, and David felt a flash of panic—

This wasn't how it had gone.

He and Backscatter had fended off the jocust swarm single-handedly. He remembered the day vividly, because it had been the beginning of the end. After commendations from their immediate superiors, David had been approached by a representative from the Blackwing Program.

This rational understanding didn't seem to matter. The terrible vision took hold of David, subsuming his rational mind as quickly as the ink-black had washed over Shadow's scales.

Shadow's body shriveled beneath his hands, his healthy flesh atrophying until the straps of his saddle no longer held the equipment in place. The saddle slipped, and David was thrown loose. He felt the sensation of falling, not toward the grassy knoll above where they had fought the jocusts, but instead toward the rising peaks of tall buildings—into the busy streets of his city—

"David!"

Jade's sharp whisper cut through his reverie. David blinked rapidly, catching his breath. He became aware of more than a few judgmental stares, and a deep sense of shame overtook him as he realized what had happened. It had been a long time since he'd lost control like that.

"You're hyperventilating," Jade said, her brow furrowed. "What's the matter?"

"I—" David glanced up at the screen. The silver dragoncoat was still there, in the background of the scene as two Coat Wardens exchanged words. He couldn't stay here. Working on *The Coated Crusader* had given him enough peace to stave off this kind of flashback, but it was one thing to draw silver dragoncoats and another thing entirely to see them in the flesh.

"I can't be here," he whispered frantically. He dropped his gaze to avoid the narrowed eyes of the other audience members. "I can't deal with this."

He half expected Jade to be disappointed—surely his admission had lessened him in her eyes—but instead, she merely nodded. She took his hand and guided him out of the row of seats. Her grip was tight, and David focused on the feeling of her skin against his, the grounding pressure of her fingers.

She led him out of the theater, back onto the street. The sun was still high, and David winced, shielding his eyes from the sudden brightness.

"I'm sorry," he muttered. "If you want to go back in—"

"No," she interrupted, frowning. "It's okay. I wasn't a huge fan of that show, anyway."

David wanted to respond with something snappy, something gently teasing about Jade's taste in movies. But he couldn't think of what to say, and even if he could have, his voice was too unsteady. He didn't want her to hear a tremor in his words; it was bad enough that she could surely see his shaking hands.

What would she think of him?

That he was weak, probably. That he was frightened and unstable. That he didn't have the mettle to watch a movie, let alone handle the wrath of Blackwing.

A cold breeze picked up through the streets, goaded on by the steep, canyon-creating buildings. It toyed with the strands of Jade's blonde wig. She reached up to twine her fingers into the false hair, holding it in place before it could slip.

Tears stung in David's eyes, and he stared at the sidewalk, unable to look at her. She had risked her own personal safety to be here—to be with him—because she believed in what he was doing. Because she believed that he *could* do it, and because she believed that, once he was finished, her dragoncoat would be safe.

From experience, David knew the truth. In the aftermath of Blackwing, there was nothing but this: faltering hands and racing thoughts, the disorganization of a shattered sense of self. Even now, the lucid part of his mind was aware of the spiral. There was little he could do to fight it, to stay present.

The comic books had helped him control it to a certain degree, but they were almost over, and he dreaded how difficult things would become once he no longer had the catharsis of its story.

And whether Jade knew it or not, he was dragging her down with him, into this maelstrom of doubt and loss. She leaned over him, her hand on his shoulder like she thought she could somehow steady him, when he knew that this kind of contact could doom her, too. He could hear her voice, but he couldn't make out the words. She was trying to talk to him. To reach him.

He had the fleeting thought that he ought to stop her, before it was too late.

David felt as though the street had suddenly lurched side-ways. He sank to his knees, worried that he would lose his balance and plummet over if he tried remaining fully upright.

He was falling for her, as well, and he suspected that she might even feel the same way. But she shouldn't. She couldn't. She was a Coat Warden. At best, this would end with her losing her livelihood. At worst, she might face charges of hang-by-the-neck-until-dead treason.

And mere proximity to him was enough to spark disaster beyond just career setbacks. Hadn't that been proven just last night, with the burning of Freedom Press? Levi's home was in ashes. If he'd been slightly slower last night, he might have died. Jade had said it herself: *They're so afraid of the public knowing the truth that they're willing to kill people.*

All of this—everything he had done with Jade—could only be a terrible mistake.

CHAPTER
ELEVEN

"Are you okay? Is there something I should do?" Anxiously, Jade shook David's shoulder.

He didn't seem to hear her or register her touch. His demeanor reminded her of a teacher she'd had in the academy, a grizzled older man whose face bore the scars of a deadly confrontation with a blood-crazed dragoncoat. The former warden had taught his students everything he could about the dragoncoat language, but he refused to go anywhere near one.

Once, a practice flight had gone awry, and a would-be Flighter had crashed through his classroom's tall windows. The dragon and rider had both been unharmed, and when the dust had settled, everyone found it uproariously funny—except for the old teacher, who had taken one look at the dragoncoat's sharpened claws and hunched over in the corner of the classroom, sobbing.

Shell shock, it had been called, when soldiers returned from the Great War plagued by nightmares and terrors.

For a moment, when she'd first brought David out of the theater, he had seemed to regain his awareness. Then it had gone again, and he had receded back into the same tense panic that he had inside. He was hyperventilating as though he had just run a marathon, his eyes wide and glistening with unshed tears.

Jade had no idea what had caused this reaction. There hadn't been anything particularly troubling in the movie, just a fantastically unbelievable story about a wild girl befriending a dragoncoat. She'd seen David fight for his life in the midst of a fire the previous night, and he'd walked away from that with more confidence than he had now, after seeing fifteen minutes of a talkie. She wanted nothing more than to reassure David, to soothe him enough that he could explain himself to her.

Jade looked around at the passersby on the sidewalk. A few of them shot curious or judgmental looks in David's direction, but most of them continued on their ways without sparing them a second glance. This was Manhattan, after all; people had places to be.

Nonetheless, Jade didn't want to stay out on the street with David in this state. At any rate, it was cold, and getting colder as the afternoon wore on. Whatever David was going through, she was sure it would be easier if they were somewhere warm. She bent down in front of him, trying to catch his eye.

"Let's get you somewhere else," she suggested. "Come on. Maybe a park or something?"

David didn't respond. Jade pursed her lips, trying to hide her own nervousness.

"There's a gallery up the block," she said. "Do you want to go there? An art gallery, full of paintings. It will be plenty peaceful in there, and you'll have a chance to...." She trailed off, unsure what to say. Her first instinct had been *calm down*, but she didn't want to come across as patronizing. Finally, she settled on, "Collect your thoughts."

David looked up at her, his hands wrung together. He nodded stiffly.

Jade exhaled in relief. "Okay. Take my hand."

After a few seconds of hesitation, David complied. Jade pulled him to his feet and set off down the street, against the wind that threatened to blow away her blonde wig. The disguise, while necessary, was certainly annoying. All day, she'd been convinced that it might slip, and that someone might recognize her by her raven hair.

As soon as they stepped through the front doors of the gallery, Jade regretted her decision. Above the main gallery hall, there was a banner strung, which read in bold letters: *The Art of Dragonflight.*

Peering within, she could make out several of the paintings hanging in the silver frames. Many of the shapes and forms were abstract, but many more were not, and all were unmistakably the figures of dragons, soaring through the skies.

This had been a bad idea. If she'd known this was the current installation, she would've never brought David here. If the sight of the flying dragoncoat in the talkie had been enough to send him into a full-blown panic attack, how was he supposed to relax in a room surrounded by artwork of dragons?

"Um—David, we don't have to—" she started, reaching out to steer him away from the door. He had already begun to approach it, and her hand fell short of his shoulder.

"It's okay," he said. "This is fine."

Jade was reassured somewhat by the tone of his voice, which was much steadier and stronger than it had been in the street. She followed him into the gallery, turning in a slow circle to take in all of the artwork on the walls. The gallery had high ceilings, and its walls were washed in white, coming together in a vaulted peak above their heads. The roof was inlaid with glass, which allowed the midday sun to stream gently into the room, illuminating the polished wooden floors and the metal frames of the paintings. Dust motes danced in the sunbeams, swirling as she and David crossed the room.

"I'm sorry," Jade whispered into the silence, guilt still tugging at her for this mistake despite David's reassurance. "I didn't think this would be the installation. I just figured it would be quieter here than out on the sidewalk."

"Well, you were right about that." David gestured around them at the otherwise-empty gallery. He walked over to a low bench in the center of the room and sat down, his hands folded together as he stared at the paintings on the wall opposite.

Jade moved to stand next to him, laying a tentative hand on his shoulder, afraid that he was volatile, somehow—that any touch might set him off again. "Are you okay?"

Without taking his eyes off of the artwork, he nodded. "Sure. Fine."

His brow furrowed as he analyzed the piece directly in front of them. It was unlike the ones to its immediate left and right. As Jade scanned the room, she realized that each of the paintings was unique, as if they had all been created by different artists. *The Art of Dragonflight* had been realized by an assortment of minds.

The painting closest to the bench bore a simple, flat skyscape rendered in periwinkle, unbroken by any variations in color or texture. As Jade approached the painting to get a better look at it, she noticed the lack of brushstrokes in the background. The dragons in the scene, however, seemed to pop off the canvas with texture—thick, daubed oil paint in various jewel tones comprised their swirling forms. They were simple in form, but they seemed to writhe across the painting, their vibrant colors and gradients contrasting against the plain backdrop.

To the right, there was a painting of a golden-scaled dragoncoat as seen from above, its wings outstretched and its detailed anatomy as flawless as a live creature's. The raised oil paint seemed to give each scale a third dimension, as though the realistic dragoncoat were about to bank sharply and rise from the frame.

To the left, there was something different entirely—a cloudlike swirl of white acrylic, formless in comparison to the realism of the golden dragoncoat. It was accented with faded green and smoky gray. At first glance, Jade didn't think it looked like a dragoncoat at all, but the longer she stared at it, the more it seemed familiar to her. The painting didn't seem to hold a dragon, but it certainly evoked something she had felt many times before. She bent down to read the paper placard beneath its frame: *Flight of an Alabaster.*

Jade stepped back and looked around at the entire room once more. All of these paintings—flawless depictions of text-book-accurate dragoncoat anatomy, fully abstract displays of shape and color, and everything in between—were like flashes of memory to her. The close-up of a young copper's bright-yellow eye drew her back to her academy days with Night Armor, before the weather had given his scales their greenish patina, and the streaky lines of apricot-orange and pink in another work reminded her intimately of sunset rides in clear skies. Breathless for a moment, she wondered how many of these artists had ridden a dragoncoat. Were they working from experience, or pure imagination?

There were no black dragoncoats among the paintings, but plenty of coppers. Each one sent a pang through her heart as she thought of Night Armor, alone at the Staten Island base, waiting for her return.

I owe him a favor, being gone for this long, she thought grimly. She stared back at the deep eye of the copper dragoncoat in the painting. There was so much emotion there; the artist must have known a copper, or at least met one in person. The artwork felt like a tribute to a particular dragon. *Maybe I'll try to paint him, or get David to do it. He'd like that, wouldn't he?*

Jade glanced back at David, who was motionless on the

bench, fixated on the scene full of jewel-toned dragoncoats in mid-flight. He seemed calmer now—the razor-sharp focus had returned to his eyes.

Hesitantly, Jade asked, "So... better?"

He blinked, startled out of his reverie, and looked up at her. "Yes. Thank you." His voice was clipped, but his hands had ceased shaking, and that struck Jade as a good sign.

"If you want to talk about it..." Jade trailed off. She didn't want to embarrass David or make him feel defensive, but it felt wrong to pretend his breakdown hadn't happened.

David opened his mouth like he was about to speak, then he seemed to think better of it. He reached into the inside pocket of his jacket and withdrew a sketchbook, then rummaged around in the opposite pocket until he found a pencil. Clearing his throat, he said, "Do you mind if I just... draw for a little while?"

"Draw?" Jade repeated, surprised.

"Yes. I'm... I like this one." He gestured at the texturized, colorful dragoncoats with the end of the pencil. "There's a lot of excellent movement in it. I'd like to experiment with some... some forms."

"I see," Jade said, sitting down on the bench beside him. "Well, don't let me get in your way." She watched as he hunched over the open sketchbook. The tip of his pencil skated over the blank page, scribbling together an indecipherable outline.

After a while, David paused, a dissatisfied frown twisting his face. "Wish they'd have a more comfortable bench here," he muttered. "Or a table or something. Drawing like this is murder on the spine."

"Here—I have an idea," Jade said quickly. She shifted her position on the bench, kicking her feet up onto it. "Lean against me."

"You're sure?"

"Yeah, of course."

Uncertainly, David copied her position, resting his back against hers. She felt the movement of his shoulder blades as he took a deep breath. "That's much better," he said. "Thank you."

Leaning her head against the top of his spine, Jade smiled. "No problem. It's more comfortable for me, too."

For a few seconds, there was silence in the gallery. Then Jade heard the faint scratching sounds of David's pencil as he went back to work.

After a couple of minutes, David said, "I used to just do this for its own sake."

Jade closed her eyes, listening to his voice and enjoying the steadiness and warmth of his body against hers. "Yeah?"

"Whenever I had a little bit of downtime, or needed something to do with my hands—I would draw. Almost subconsciously. It was my first instinct." David paused, and the pencil scratches paused with him. They resumed as he continued speaking. "I drew what I knew, and from the academy onwards, that was dragoncoats."

"Makes sense," Jade said.

"Backscatter loved my artwork," he said. "Just as much as your dragoncoat seems to."

"Seems to?" A laugh escaped Jade, as light as air. "Oh, you have no idea. Night Armor is *obsessed* with your artwork. I never hear the end of it."

"That's very flattering." She could hear the smile in his voice. "If anyone's going to like what I draw, I want it to be dragoncoats. Especially the Blackwing dragoncoats. It's for them every bit as much as it's for me."

Suddenly curious, Jade twisted in her seat to get a look at David's sketchbook. The once-blank page was now adorned with the spiraling, weaving figures of dragons in flight.

"Eventually, I started doing it for a purpose," David said,

resting the tip of his pencil near the curve of a dragoncoat's wing. "I had a story to tell, and I started to tell it. But this is where it began. Just pencil sketches of dragons. Busy hands. A simple distraction for my mind."

Jade stared at the dragons on the page. Their bodies were barebones, with few specific details, but there was something about their poses that she found breathtaking.

"They're beautiful," she whispered, almost reflexively.

David turned to her, one eyebrow arched. "They're just practice sketches," he said, bemused. "I haven't even added the scales, or fixed the proportions."

Jade shrugged. "Doesn't matter. There's something about them that seems so... fluid. And you made them out of nothing."

"That's how drawing works," David said wryly.

"Oh, shut up," Jade sighed, elbowing David affectionately. "You know what I mean."

"I can't say that I do." He returned his attention to the sketchbook, stippling the tiny scales onto one dragoncoat's snout. "It's not some sort of mystical ritual. It's just a hobby. Didn't you say that you used to do it, too?"

"Yeah, I did," Jade said, "but I never could've done anything like that."

"Sure, you could. Anyone could. It takes practice, that's all."

Jade returned her gaze to the paintings on the walls, sitting to either side of the entrance. David's humility surprised her; it seemed defensive, somehow, as if he was afraid of the notion that he had made anything beautiful. Jade thought she understood. After all, wasn't that the same impulse that had driven her to downplay her own abilities?

Admitting that she enjoyed the act of creation—that she often liked the things she had made, even if the anatomy was flawed and the details were crude—was a mortifying prospect. There had to be some objectivity to the quality of art, objectivity that came into play when curators and critics delivered their verdicts. What could be worse than feeling proud of something that others disliked? Working hard on something that could never be perfect?

But what was perfect? There was a painting across the room from her that depicted a hideously distorted dragoncoat. Its claws were all different sizes, its eyes bulging, its scales half-molted. It was the ugliest thing she'd ever seen; it stirred a visceral reaction in her gut, the exact opposite feeling she got from the other, prettier works. But just like the others, it did make her feel something she'd felt before: *dread.* Horror. Revulsion. Emotions she'd felt before and knew she would feel again. It was cathartic, she thought, necessary practice for the day when circumstance roused those feelings in her once more.

She didn't like this painting, but she knew why it had been painted. She could see herself making something similar, even —a disfigured, ghastly dragoncoat, clawing itself out of its scales in desperation. *If I understand this, does that make it good?*

She swallowed, dropping her gaze to the floor. The distorted dragoncoat writhed through her mind's eye, past scores of David's lovely, unfinished dragons in full flight.

"I used to spend hours in places like this," she said. She felt David go still behind her as he paused his sketching. "Free galleries, open to the public. There are a lot of them in the city. On weekends, or school holidays, I used to go downtown."

"From Queens? That's a long walk."

"Hours," Jade agreed. "But when I was eleven years old, I got my hands on an old bicycle, and that cut down the time significantly. Over the winter holidays, I had a lot of time on my hands. My family didn't celebrate Christmas, so there was nothing to do except trek all the way to Manhattan with my brothers."

"Where did you go?"

"There were pop-up galleries all over the place," Jade

said. "There was the museum, too, but that was harder to sneak into, and we'd get chased out all the time." She smiled at the memories. "So much free artwork... We'd spend hours here, and come home late enough to make my mother furious."

"I'm sure," David said. He resumed his quick, deft strokes. "And in the cold, too. It's a miracle you never froze to death."

"You sound just like her," Jade replied, grinning.

"She sounds like a wise woman."

Jade shook her head. "She never understood. Where my parents come from, dragoncoats were the property of nobles. They knew that here, if I worked hard, I could attain a new level of status. But they didn't realize that it wasn't just dragons."

She turned to David, a building sense of euphoria making her chest feel light. He stopped sketching once more and met her gaze with trepidation. For a long moment, they looked at each other, as if each of them was searching for something in the other's eyes.

"Watching you draw," she said, "is like seeing someone spin straw into gold. Even if it's just a hobby to you, it might as well be magic to me."

"Ah." David sounded nervous, and for a moment, Jade worried that she'd somehow managed to offend him. Then he said, "That's the most beautiful compliment anyone's ever given me."

He's not nervous, Jade realized. *He's* flustered.

"But I'm not a magician," he added. "You could do it, too. I'm certain."

For the first time, Jade noticed how close she had gotten to him—close enough to see the way the sunlight permeated his brown eyes. Close enough to see the way his pupils dilated.

Rather than allow the self-consciousness to settle in, Jade leaned even closer and pressed her lips against his. Her eyes slid closed, and her hand found the back of his neck, her thumb

JORDAN RILEY SWAN & EZRA ZABIT

grazing his jawline. There was a clattering sound—David's pencil falling to the floor.

"Hey!"

A shrill voice, sharp with authority, broke through the haze. Jade withdrew from David quickly, guiltily, and shot to her feet.

A security guard stood in the doorway to the gallery, his hands on his hips. "What the hell do you two think you're doing?"

Jade glanced at David, who wore a dazed half smile on his face. He shook himself, then said, "We're appreciating the artwork, sir."

The security guard rolled his eyes. "Good grief. *Go home.* Get out of here. No loitering in the gallery, no *necking* in the gallery, and no cheesy, half-baked chat-up lines in the gallery!"

Sheepishly, Jade turned to David, offering her hand. She helped him to his feet. He snatched up his sketchbook and pencil, returning them to his coat pocket. With his hand in hers, they headed for the exit. As they brushed past the irritated security guard, Jade heard him mutter something derisive about *young people these days.*

But as she and David emerged onto the busy street, not even the embarrassment of being thrown out of the gallery could dampen her spirits.

—

To Jade's surprise, the apartment was quiet when they returned. She had expected to walk in on Levi, midway through yet another phone call, shouting full-volume at some hapless secretary. Instead, David's apartment seemed empty.

"Looks like he left a note," David said, picking up a scrap of paper from the kitchen counter. He passed it over to her, and she read:

FOUND someone who'll get the job done. I'm taking the pages over to them right now. Felman—finish the last issue. We have to get this done ASAP. Oh, and behave yourselves.

- Levi

"WELL, at least he didn't hire a babysitter," she said dryly, looking up at David.

He snorted a laugh. "Oh, please. If anyone needs supervision, it's him."

"*He* didn't just get kicked out of a gallery in Midtown," Jade pointed out.

"That's true." David shrugged, wandering into the kitchen. "You want anything to drink? Coffee, tea, something a little stronger?"

"I'm okay," Jade said. She walked over to collapse onto the couch. Truthfully, alcohol was the last thing she needed right now. Since the gallery, she'd felt like a drunk even without it. She was practically giddy just from being in David's presence. "And you shouldn't, either. Don't you have a comic to finish tonight?"

"It'll get done," David said confidently. He sat down beside her on the couch, and she leaned into him readily, enjoying the solid warmth of him close by. "Eventually. You can't rush inspiration, right?"

"Whatever you say." Now that they were in the safety of David's apartment, Jade ran her fingers along the hairline of her blonde wig, carefully pulling it off. She pulled the tie from her own hair and shook her head, letting her black locks fall freely over her shoulders. The air was a cool relief on her scalp. Jade tilted her head, running her hands through her hair in an attempt to detangle it.

"About time," David commented. "Does that feel nice?"

"You have no idea," Jade sighed.

For a few moments, they sat in contented silence. Rogue thoughts drifted through Jade's head, of Night Armor and the sergeant and the talking-to she was almost certainly facing when she returned to the Staten Island base. Being close to David was enough of a distraction to drown out those worries, though, and she closed her eyes to focus on the comforting pressure of his hand on her arm.

"About earlier," he mumbled eventually, "I'm... I'm sorry that happened. It's very difficult to control, or I would have made sure that you wouldn't see it."

"What are you talking about?" Jade straightened, frowning.

"In the theater," David said, reluctance in his expression, like every word was being dragged from him. "When I...."

"Oh." Jade's eyes widened as she realized what he was talking about. After the day's events, she'd forgotten all about the incident at the movie. "David, it's fine. Really. It's no trouble at all, and you don't have to explain yourself to me— not unless you want to."

"It's something I've been struggling with for a while," David admitted. "It got much, much worse after everything that happened to Backscatter. I never know what's going to cause that kind of reaction. Since I started working on the comic, it's been easier, but it's never *over*."

"It doesn't have to be," Jade replied, laying a hand on his knee.

"I just feel terrible that you had to deal with it."

"Deal with it?" She shook her head. "I didn't have to *deal with* anything. You didn't feel comfortable where we were, and

I was more than happy to leave." She smiled, reaching up to give David a quick kiss on the cheek. "Besides, that's why we went to the gallery, and I'm so glad we did."

"Thank you," David said quietly. He leaned back against the weathered cushions of the couch, looking at the tall windows. Jade followed his gaze. A smile crossed her lips, unbidden, as she remembered seeing Night Armor hanging off of the window ledge like an overgrown bat.

"You know when we first talked?" Jade said, eager to offer David a distraction. "At that table, when I was asking to interview you?"

"Yes?"

"You didn't see him, but Night Armor was lurking in that window. I told him a million times to stay on the roof, but he wanted your autograph."

David huffed a soft laugh. "That sounds about right. And it must've been stressful."

"I was sweating bullets," Jade admitted. "I thought he was about to blow my cover."

"But he didn't blow your cover until a few days later."

"No," she said with a chuckle. "I was impressed with his restraint." She paused, looking David up and down. "And he's not the only one."

Tilting his head to one side in confusion, much like Night Armor might, David said, "What do you mean?"

"Tell me I'm not the only one who...." Jade trailed off, suddenly anxious, in the same way she'd been when she contemplated her hypothetical flawed artwork. She'd been drawn to David, simultaneously soothed and excited by him, since the moment they'd met. She had kissed him—several times, now—and had felt heat in his touch, seen passion in his gaze. What if she was *wrong*? What if she had misjudging the connection between them, seen something where there was nothing—

"You're not," David murmured, and a wave of relief crashed over her, sending tingling cascading through her. He reached up to brush a lock of her hair behind her ear, his fingers gentle. "I swear, you're not. It's just...."

"What?"

"Your dragoncoat is at the Blackwing base," David reminded her. There was a swooping sensation in Jade's stomach, as if she was in free fall. "You have to go back there eventually. And you read Levi's note. He's asking me for the final issue of the comic."

Stubbornly, Jade twined her fingers into his shirt. "Yes. So?"

"Jade," David sighed, his expression pained. "You know that when we publish this—"

Jade interrupted him with a kiss. Rather than fight to keep speaking, David melted into her, his fingers exploring under the hem of her shirt, his palms pressing against her back.

After a long moment, Jade paused for a breath. She drew back, and David brushed her loose hair away from her face again, staring up at her as if in a trace.

"You're beautiful," he said hoarsely.

She gazed down at him, unable to think of anything but being as close to him as possible. "Everything you said before... I don't care about any of it," she told him, breathless. "Not right now. You're here, and I'm here, and everything else will have to wait, all right?"

Eagerly, he nodded, pulling her back down toward him. As their lips met, his felt stronger against hers, more certain than ever.

To her surprise, he stood up abruptly, lifting her off the couch. His palms cupped the undersides of her thighs, and she felt featherlight in his arms as she wrapped herself around him, startled but unwilling to stop kissing her way up his neck.

David laid her on the bed, his hands slow and gentle, almost hesitant. She wanted more from him; every touch of his fingers felt electric, sending tingles through her entire body. She hurried him, guiding his palms to all of the places that craved him.

There was no need to be shy, but if he wanted confidence in her desire, she'd show it to him however she could think to— by steadily undoing the buttons on his shirt, one by one, and doing some of her own exploring; by letting her shuddering breath roll across his bare collarbone.

Jade wasn't new to this feeling, and neither, it seemed, was David. He was an expert, comfortable and confident now that he was sure she wanted this. For Jade, though, it had been a long time. Ever since she'd been assigned to the Blackwing Program, her days had been full from dawn until dusk, with little time for recreation—especially of a social nature.

As David's fingertips skimmed across her shoulder, his lips busy at her jaw, she realized that she didn't feel at all self-conscious. Beneath the burning feeling inside of her, she felt a rock-solid foundation of *safety,* certainty that David would never hurt her, even if he was capable of such a thing.

"Do you... do you have a—"

She didn't even need to finish her sentence before David withdrew. He took a deep breath of air, his eyes unfocused. He blinked the haze from them and nodded. "Give me a second."

He ran from the room, and Jade heard him rummaging around in the bathroom, his medicine cabinet door squeaking open and slamming shut. Jade fidgeted in anticipation, eager for him to return, desire already pooling happily within her. The moment he appeared in the doorway to the bedroom, a coin-shaped condom-filled tin box in his left hand, she jumped up to seize him by the fabric of his unbuttoned shirt and roll him onto the bed, straddling him. He let out a breathless, surprised laugh, his fingers hooking into the seam of her pants.

"Did you miss me or something?"

"Oh, you have no idea," Jade breathed, carding a hand

through his stiff, gelled hair. "Thought you were never coming back. You should've had that in a more accessible place. Shouldn't it be in your nightstand or something?"

"What, was I supposed to expect this?" David caught her hand in his, moving her palm to his lips. His kiss was soft, and his brown eyes darted up to meet hers.

"Why not?" Jade asked.

"That would've been presumptuous."

"Since the moment I met you, part of me has thought we'd end up this way," Jade told him, letting the fingertips of her free hand skate across his bare chest. "Isn't that a little presumptuous?"

"A little," David said. He reached up to her shoulders and pulled her down to him, closing the angle between their bodies. "But you were right, so I think history has vindicated you."

Jade hummed, pleased, nuzzling her face into the crook of his neck.

For the first time in many days, she allowed herself to forget completely about Blackwing, Night Armor, and the sergeant's waiting reprimand. She forgot about the forthcoming final issue of *The Coated Crusader,* about the fire destroying Freedom Press, and about all of the work that had gone into her path to Coat Warden.

Instead of fixating on the past or the future, Jade lost herself completely in the moment, in the intoxicating rush of David's touch on her skin as he peeled up the hem of her shirt, as she tugged eagerly at his belt buckle.

When she closed her eyes, she thought of the slow, precise movements of David's hand as he sketched half a dozen intricate dragoncoats.

≈

"It's raining," David whispered into the darkness of the room. His voice was heavy, his words indistinct, like he was half-asleep.

Jade already knew. The soft light of the city that streamed into the room was speckled by the shadows of raindrops, the rivulets of water running down the glass. She could hear it too, like a gentle, steady hiss.

Jade didn't respond, waiting for David's breathing to slow into the reassuring rhythm of sleep. She sat up, trying not to wake him.

She should've known she wouldn't be able to keep reality at bay for long. Worried thoughts of Night Armor swirled in her head; she'd been away from the base for a full day, far longer than she'd expected.

But that didn't worry her nearly as much as the other pressing issue, the unfortunate truth underlying everything she and David did together: he was going to publish the last comic, the one that would bring Blackwing's activities to light. Levi's note had cast everything into stark focus, and Jade could no longer pretend that the final issue of *The Coated Crusader* was something that would happen in the distant future. It was imminent.

And as soon as he published it—as soon as the truth was out—David was certainly going to jail.

Whatever was burgeoning between them, it wouldn't be able to last. The publication of the comic was a hard stop, an inevitable end to their relationship. She should have known better than to become entangled with him. She should have let him finish his warning, rather than interrupting him with a kiss.

Beyond the barrier of David's likely arrest, there were other obstacles. She had to admit, to herself if not to David, that her proximity to him posed a significant danger. Each time she returned to this apartment, she risked being followed by a stealthy Blackwing Flighter. If she knew the sergeant—and she knew him quite well—he had already assigned a Coat Warden to the task of keeping tabs on her, reporting her whereabouts. Once her superiors found out that she was spending all of her time with her former mark, the man from the case she'd been forced to drop... she'd almost certainly be dropped from Flighter duty.

Margie's warning echoed in her head: *You'll be sent to cool your heels somewhere dark and dank.* Somehow, Jade didn't doubt that this warning was literal. If Blackwing was willing to kill dragoncoats, they'd have no problem dealing with her.

David turned over in his sleep, unconsciously reaching for her. She felt a pang in her heart; he seemed so peaceful when he was asleep. She wanted nothing more than to crawl back underneath the covers and join him, to lay her head on his chest.

This is trouble, she thought wildly, a sense of panic overtaking her. *This is nothing but trouble, and it's going to be so much worse than it would've been if I hadn't done this. If I'd kept my wits about me.*

She couldn't be in love with David. Theirs was a short road that led to an abrupt dead end, a road she should have known better than to travel.

Jade swung her legs over the side of the bed and sat there for a minute, letting her head rest in her hands.

CHAPTER

TWELVE

When David awoke from a dreamless sleep—the best he'd had in months, really—he rolled over to find the opposite side of the bed empty.

His first reaction was a dull sense of disappointment. He wasn't surprised, not fully; there had been an undeniable impermanence about the entire situation. He'd tried to bring it up, tried to remind her, and she had refused to let reality ruin the evening. At the time, he had taken her stubbornness for desire, letting himself be swept up in the fantasy that they would wake up together, no swords hanging over their heads.

David sighed, collapsing back against the pillows and closing his eyes. He could still smell her perfume, soft floral notes in the sheets.

It took him a few minutes to work up the energy to drag himself out of the bed. Levi needed those comic book pages. It was almost over—he was almost finished. He couldn't afford to sink into his feelings and become trapped there.

Aimlessly, David dressed himself, paying no attention to the mismatched, rumpled clothes. He shuffled out into the main room of his apartment, blinking in the light from the large windows. The previous night's rain had ceased while he'd slept, leaving behind a bright-but-overcast sky.

David made himself a pot of coffee, brewed too strongly, and forced himself to go straight to his drafting desk. His night with Jade had set him back in his work. It had been worth it, but now, here he was—alone in his apartment once more, and with a backlog of comic book pages to draw and ink.

As David sat down and reached for the stack of blank paper beneath the desk, he froze, blinking. There was already a sheet of paper on the desk's surface, a used pencil sitting in the tray at its edge.

The paper bore a drawing, rendered in uncertain, lightly sketched strokes. It was of him, sprawled on the bed, asleep. And it was surprisingly good.

Jade had thought too little of herself as an artist. If this drawing was anything to go by, she had plenty of talent. The sketch was recognizable and detailed despite its simplicity. It had an interesting composition and a lot of personality. David sat at the desk for several minutes, staring at the miraculous piece of paper, transfixed.

He was startled by the sound of the door closing. He whirled around and prepared a slew of excuses in his head, expecting Levi to come bustling in.

It wasn't Levi. It was Jade, clad in a peacoat, with the disheveled blonde wig covering her hair. She lowered the fake glasses down the bridge of her nose and smiled at him.

"Sorry. I had to draw you," she confessed. "You were really cute while you were asleep. You frowned a lot less." She winked at him, which made his heart flutter. "I apologize if you would've preferred I didn't use your likeness, Mr. Felman."

"You drew this?" David pointed at the sketch.

"Of course I did. Who else do you think would've? Levi?"

She shook her head, amused. "No way. He would've woken you up."

"It's amazing," David told her. "I don't know why you were so humble about this yesterday. You're very talented."

She beamed, obviously delighted, but waved a hand as if to dismiss the compliment. "Oh, I bet you say that to all the girls."

"I mean it," David insisted. "I'm blown away."

Jade shrugged off her coat, draping it over the back of the couch. She ducked her head in acknowledgment. "I was lying there, thinking about what you said at the art gallery—about how I could do it, too. So I thought I'd give it a shot." A glimmer of humor entered her gaze. "You were fast asleep, so I figured that if I messed it up, I could toss it out the window before you ever saw it."

"But you liked it enough to keep it."

She grinned. "I guess so."

"Well..." He got to his feet, crossing the room to her. "I'm glad you didn't toss it out the window."

She stretched up to kiss him, her lips soft against his, cold from the brisk air outside. He smiled down at her, delighted that she was finally back in his arms.

"When you were gone this morning, I thought I might not see you again," he confessed.

She shook her head. "No, of course not. I had to go check back in at the base. If I don't make appearances frequently, the sergeant will start to assume something's up." She hesitated, and his heart sank as she muttered, "Of course, he may already have that figured out."

"What do you mean?"

With a heavy sigh, Jade gestured to the couch, leading David over to it and curling up beside him. "Well, I went back to the base because I was hoping they'd let me see Night Armor."

David's blood went cold; he knew where this was heading.

JORDAN RILEY SWAN & EZRA ZABIT

He'd been there before, for all of the terrible months that Shadow had battled his illness. "Let me guess...."

"No dice," Jade confirmed, her voice bitter. "They're icing me out. But Margie's been keeping me informed."

Good old Margie, David thought. It was comforting, despite the gravity of the situation, to know that he still had an ally on the inside.

"She says that Night Armor's actually starting to develop some symptoms now." Jade's eyes were glassy, like she was holding back tears. "Just cold-like symptoms, but they're persistent. Treatment isn't doing anything. And, of course, I know better than to think of this as a simple cold... I know exactly what's going on here."

David's stomach turned at the thought of another dragoncoat falling to the same illness that had taken Shadow. Of course, there had likely been dozens between his dragon and Jade's, dragoncoats he'd never met who had gone through the program and been killed by the scales' effects. He'd always been aware of that, and it had made him heartsick enough to push through the times when his energy for the comic had stalled. But with Night Armor, it was different. Much more personal. He'd met the dragoncoat himself, and he'd been charmed by his quirky personality.

"I tried to play it cool," Jade said, "but I couldn't stop thinking about Night Armor, and about everything you've told me...." She paused, taking a deep breath. "So I caved. I went against Margie's advice, and I spoke to my superior about my 'pet theory'"—she framed the term in air quotes—"that the scales were making Night Armor ill."

"And what did he say?" David asked, despite knowing the answer.

"That the two were unrelated," Jade replied sourly. "That I was building castles in the air, and that I should clear out and let the medics work." She affected a deep, gruff imitation of

Sergeant Douglas: "*You're making a mountain out of a molehill, Ms. Atallah. Your dragoncoat will be ready for active duty in less than a week. Now get out of my office.*" At the end of her speech, Jade pulled a face, curling her lip in disgust.

David inched closer to her, and she leaned her head on his shoulder. "I'm sorry, Jade," he murmured, stroking her hair.

"Don't be. I knew this would happen." She sighed and sat upright. "I suppose I'm just lucky he let me leave the base at all."

"What do you mean?"

"He seemed... upset," Jade said slowly. "When I brought up the scales, he about blew a gasket. I thought he was going to confine me to my quarters or something. Guess he didn't like being found out."

David felt a flicker of unease in his chest. Suspecting that he had known the truth, Blackwing and Douglas had sent a Flighter to track his movements. Apart from Jade's assignment, he'd had a hunch that there were Blackwing eyes on him for months. If Douglas knew that Jade was aware of the truth, she might be in danger.

"Do you think you ought to have stayed on the base?" David asked, trying to keep the alarm out of his voice. "If Douglas knows how much you know...."

Jade shook her head. "It's fine. They don't know I'm spending my time with you, right? It could've just been an innocent guess, and there's nothing wrong with that. They can't do anything to me unless they have proof that I'm going against my orders."

David wished he could share her confidence. He wasn't at all certain that Blackwing was planning to play by the rules. For the most part, they'd been toeing the line thus far, but their attempt to burn down Freedom Press had thrown everything up into the air. *Arson* and *attempted murder of a civilian* weren't exactly in keeping with the FIB code of conduct. The

BWP must have assumed that the crime wouldn't be pinned on them.

We don't have any evidence that it was them, David mused. *All we have is a motive and some easy speculation. That would never hold up in court.* Come to think of it, David had assumed that Blackwing had hired the perpetrators without considering any other options, though it seemed highly unlikely that anyone else would have reason to burn down Freedom Press. Well, mostly unlikely. Maybe Levi had made himself an enemy on his own time.

"Besides," Jade added, the smile returning to her face, "if I'd stayed on the base, I couldn't have told you what I wanted to tell you."

"Which is...?"

"You have to publish."

David blinked, startled. After a moment's silence, he said, "Well... that's the idea."

"You don't understand," Jade said, her voice intense. "You have to publish this thing. Don't give in to any of their intimidation. Whatever they do, however they threaten you, you have to publish it." She swallowed. "For Night Armor."

"Of course," David said gently.

"While you're at it, you might want to go to the press as well. Just to cover your bases. They could send someone to cover the story—make it a real nightmare for Douglas."

"That's a good idea." David made a mental note to mention it to Levi. Though that had sort of been his idea when he was trying to secure a radio interview in the first place.

"Did you make any progress on the final issue while I was out?"

"No." David shook his head. "But to be honest, I don't think I'm in a particularly creative mood right now. I do most of my best work at night." He gestured to the tall windows, which revealed a sky rapidly lightening to blue. "Less distraction if it seems like a beautiful day. Otherwise, I feel like I should be outside."

"So... what? You want to go somewhere?"

"I had a few ideas," David said, suddenly feeling self-conscious. He looked at the floor underneath the coffee table rather than meeting Jade's gaze. "After last night, I... I wanted to take you somewhere."

"You mean like a date?" Jade's voice was teasing, and heat rose in David's cheeks.

"If you'd like it to be," he said. "I never did get to take you to coffee, so how about we make it dinner?"

"That was supposed to be an *interview,* not a date," Jade reminded him, brushing a lock of false blonde hair over her shoulder. David found himself wishing that she didn't need to wear the disguise, thinking of the softness of her natural hair between his fingers, but he knew it was necessary, especially after her run-in with Sergeant Douglas.

"Come on, let me treat you," David offered. "Before Levi gets back, while we still have the time to just enjoy ourselves. Let's make today a nice day."

Jade appeared to deliberate for a moment, and David held his breath. After the closeness of last night, all he wanted to do was spend the day with her—spend as long with her as he possibly could, savoring her company while it was still possible.

"Fine," she said eventually, shrugging. "Can't see the harm." Although the both knew there could be all kinds of trouble if they were caught together. She smiled slightly, giving away her delight at David's suggestion. "Where do you want to go?"

"There's a string quartet that plays in a gazebo in Central Park in afternoons. Let's walk there together and enjoy some music. Then I want to take you out to dinner, if that's okay."

Jade chuckled, laying a hand on David's shoulder. "Listen,

that's real chivalrous, but I don't know how I feel about you paying for my meal when you're an *artist*."

"What's that supposed to mean?"

"I have a steady paycheck and benefits," Jade replied. "Remember working for Blackwing? And now you make all of your money from comic book sales, of all things. Let me get dinner."

David let out a sigh; it was really about the spirit of the thing, not than the materiality. He wanted to get something for Jade. He wanted to get everything for Jade.

"I don't know," he said. "We'll see." Before she could argue, he got up from the couch and offered her a hand. "We'd better get going now, if we don't want to miss the performance."

AFTER THE PREVIOUS night's rain, the air was cool but pleasantly fresh as David and Jade made their way through Manhattan. David relished walking next to Jade with his arm around her shoulders, as if the two of them were an item. With her disguise, they'd be safe this way, though David couldn't help looking over his shoulder every few minutes, half-expecting black dragoncoats to step out of the shadows of every alleyway.

They sat on a park bench and held hands as they listened to the string quartet play a series of excerpts from Bach and Beethoven. There were many other young couples in the park despite the cold weather; as winter drew near, they were probably making the most of the last few days when it was warm enough to enjoy the outdoors. As the quartet wrapped up its final melody, David and Jade joined in the polite applause from the small crowd that had gathered, then they set off back toward Lower Manhattan to find a restaurant.

Jade was still adamant that she should pay for dinner, and when the two of them stopped at a café for a cup of coffee and a bit of warmth, she found her chance to set the record straight once and for all.

In the corner of the coffee shop, there was a table with a chessboard set up on its surface. David gestured to it as they waited for their coffees. "Do you know how to play?"

Jade shook her head, biting her lower lip. "I've played a couple of times," she said, offhand, "but only when I was very little. I don't know if I'll remember how all the pieces move."

"Come on, let's have a quick game," he said. "It's still too early for dinner. We might as well."

Once they had their coffees in hand, Jade followed him over to the corner and sat down opposite him, inspecting the board with a mystified look on her face. "So, if I remember correctly," she said, "these ones can only move one square, correct?" She gestured to the row of white pawns at the front of her pieces.

"That's right. Bishops move diagonally, rooks move in straight lines—"

"The queen can move any direction," Jade said.

David nodded, taking a scalding sip of coffee. "Yes. The king can move any direction, but only one square. And the knights move in L-shapes." As he spoke, he demonstrated the movement with each piece, hoping that would help Jade understand better.

"Okay," Jade said. "I think I've got it. Let's play."

The first game lasted ten minutes, and David won with relative ease. He grimaced as he made his last move, putting Jade's king in checkmate.

"Sorry," he said. "You played very well, though, especially for your first time."

Jade studied the board, her brow furrowed in concentration. She looked up at David abruptly, waving a hand. "Let's play one more. I think I'm getting the hang of this."

"Sure." David shrugged and began to gather the pieces, redistributing them to their respective squares.

"Tell you what—let's make it interesting."

David paused in the middle of placing his king and queen. "Interesting?"

"Winner pays for dinner," she said, flashing him a mischievous smile.

"Okay," he said, laughing, "but if it's anything like last game, you'll be eating those words."

"*I'll* be eating a well-cooked meal, one that *I* paid for," Jade retorted, moving one of her knights out toward the center of the board. "Your move."

To David's dismay, the second game was far different than the first. Jade had suddenly come into a great deal of chess competence, and within six minutes, she had thoroughly trounced him. As she reached across the board to shake his hand, he hung his head in defeat.

"How on earth did you do that?"

"I've been playing chess for years," Jade said with a lofty shrug. "I'm the best on the base. You gave it a good try, though."

They left the coffee shop and arrived at a restaurant unfashionably early, missing most of the dinner crowd—*lucky us,* thought David, who had spent most of the day wishing that he and Jade were the last two people in Manhattan. Even after a miserable loss at chess, he was more transfixed by her than ever.

Jade had chosen a romantic place to have dinner, with low lights and wax candles on every table. As they finished their shared meal, she asked him a question he had never thought he would hear.

"Will you teach me?"

He looked at her over the brim of his glass of water, puzzled. "Teach you? Teach you what?"

"To draw," she said earnestly. "Like you do."

David thought of her sketch from the previous night. "You

can already draw like I do," he said. "Believe me, you've got it. You don't need me."

"That's not what I meant. I know how to *sketch*. I want to learn how to make those comic pages like you do."

"What do you mean?"

"You make the lines so smooth," she said, gesturing in the air as if drawing panels, "and the ink is so bright. And there's so *many* drawings... yet you manage to make the characters look the same on every page."

David stared at her, flattered but bemused. "That's a different tone than you had last time we spoke about my comic books," he pointed out, remembering the derision she'd shown his work when she'd first met him in the park.

"Well...." She took a sip of water, the ice cubes clinking together in the glass. "I may have, um, re-read one of the volumes on the ferry ride back from Staten Island."

"Oh?"

Jade nodded ruefully. "Yeah. And I enjoyed it, even."

"There's a refreshing change of pace," David said. "What was different this time?"

"I was thinking about how long it took me to draw you, and how difficult it was to make sure the drawing *looked like* you," Jade explained. "I probably spent close to half an hour on that one sketch. If you took that long to do everything in the comic, with all of the action and different panels, you'd probably only release two issues a year. It was so consistent on every page."

"That's very nice, but... what makes *you* want to learn how to do it?"

Jade ducked her head as if embarrassed, hiding behind the too-thick tresses of the blonde wig. "I was thinking while I was drawing you. Thinking about... things we could do together, if all goes well."

The good mood that David had been building throughout

the day began to dissipate. This conversation was headed into territory that he didn't feel comfortable traversing. "Jade—"

"I thought maybe we could work on a project together," Jade said hurriedly, rushing to cut him off. "I know you want to wrap up *The Coated Crusader* after the final issue, but if you'd let me help you, I... I think it might be fun to continue the Jade Jocust's storyline after—"

"Jade, listen," David interrupted. He reached across the table to fold her hands in his. "You know as well as I do that there is no *after*."

She stared at him, her expression stiff. The flickering candle cast shadows over her features, and her dark eyes glittered in the light.

"I'm breaking the law with that comic," David said. "I'm revealing state secrets. There are consequences for things like this, and I can't expect those consequences to pass me by. Just look at what almost happened to Levi—and that was *before* the comic was released. In all likelihood, one or both of us is going to prison."

"I know," Jade replied, her voice wooden.

"Then what's the point in fantasizing about a future that doesn't exist?"

"What's the point in doing all of *this*"—Jade gestured between them, then around to the restaurant, as if to indicate the entire evening—"if that future doesn't exist?"

"To enjoy ourselves now," David said morosely. "While we can."

"Is that why you've been putting off the last issue of your comic?" Jade sat back, folding her arms.

David winced; she had him there. "Well... maybe."

"That's foolish," she said. "What if Blackwing gets to you before you've finished it? They've already proven they're willing to harm you." She poured herself another half-glass of wine, swirling the liquid around by the stem. "You're being so pessimistic about the aftermath that you've forgotten about that danger of *right now.*"

"We know how this is likely to end," David said. "There's no sense in lying to ourselves."

"You don't have to lie to yourself," Jade countered, "but you could look beyond the worst case scenario. Say you garner public opinion on your side. Say there's a trial. You might win."

"I have to assume that I wouldn't win."

"That's my problem," she sighed. "You don't have to assume that. You just have to write your comic book and—this part's important—*hope for the best.*"

Silence descended on their table, broken only by the muted clatter of dishes from the kitchen, and the quiet conversations happening at tables around theirs.

David had to admit that his vision of his own future had been on the bleak side for years, ever since he had conceived of the ending to his comic. However, no matter how hard he tried, he couldn't foresee anything better. The future that Jade posited, the one where he was still working and making comics, seemed like a desperate pipe dream. If he didn't go to prison, he would almost certainly find himself shut out of any publishing opportunities, and he doubted that Freedom Press would be able to continue for long after its brick-and-mortar destruction. One way or another, this would ruin him.

"Last night, before I started drawing," Jade admitted in a soft voice, "I was thinking about this very thing. I was thinking that I might have made a mistake. That whatever is happening between us, it could only end in separation and regret." She shook her head, her grip tightening on his hands. "But that's a defeatist way to think, David, and I've never been one for self-fulfilling prophecy. If you want to enjoy yourself now, maybe the best way to do it is to lie to yourself a little bit. Just enough that you can move forward without dreading your next steps."

David didn't respond right away, turning her words over in

his head. Perhaps she was right. Perhaps it would be easier to finish the comic, and to enjoy this evening, if he could let go of his ever-present certainty that his path led to nowhere.

He fumbled in the inside pockets of his jacket until he produced a drawing pencil. The tablecloth was covered in a sheet of starched white paper; he pushed his empty plate and their glasses to the side, clearing a blank patch.

"Here," he said. "Let me show you."

Both of them leaned over the table, watching the graphite tip of the pencil as he sketched out the careful outlines of six, evenly-sized boxes.

"If I simply draw my characters in these," he explained, "the shapes on the page won't lend anything to the action, nor the dialogue. When you're making comics, you have to consider the whole page, not just the individual panel. So I like to storyboard each page before I start drawing, and once I sit down to sketch out my rough draft...."

LONG AFTER THE dinner rush had come and gone, David and Jade lingered at their table for two by the window, taking turns drawing on the paper table covering and stoking the ire of the wait staff. It was almost eleven o'clock by the time the host approached their table, clearing his throat.

"Excuse me, *sir* and *madam*," he said, his voice acerbic, "but the restaurant has closed. If the two of you would please vacate the premises, that would be much appreciated."

Jade met David's gaze over the table, her shoulders shaking with a barely-suppressed laugh. "Oh, damn," she said. "I didn't even realize it had gotten so late."

"You'd better be getting back, huh?" David asked, rising to his feet. He glanced at the host, then gestured down at the multitude of comic panels adorning the paper on the table. "Sorry about the mess."

The host raised an eyebrow. "If you were really sorry, you'd *leave*. We're trying to close."

Tucking his pencil into his pocket, David reached out for Jade's hand, and the two of them beat a hasty retreat from the restaurant.

"You're right. I probably should get back," Jade said with a sigh once they were outside. "I don't want to arouse any suspicions, and with any luck, they'll let me see Night Armor."

"I hope they do. If they let you in, tell him I hope he's feeling better."

"Oh, he'll lose his mind if I do that." Jade shivered, pulling her jacket around her shoulders and stepping closer to David. Without the warmth of the afternoon sun, the Manhattan streets had gotten considerably colder. "You should sign him a 'Get Well' card."

"Maybe I will," David said with a smile. "Here—you can show him this." He pressed a small scrap of paper into Jade's palm, ripped away from the table covering: a lopsided, quick sketch of a black dragoncoat, bearing David's signature. "That's a Felman original."

Jade grinned, slipping the paper into her pocket. "He's going to love that."

"Don't worry too much about Night Armor." David placed his hands on Jade's waist, gazing tenderly into her eyes. "I'm going to do everything I can to help him. If all goes well, Blackwing will be shut down in time to save him."

"Now *that's* a future I'd like to see." Jade stood on tiptoe, softly pressing her lips to his. Closing his eyes, David let himself sink into the kiss, and the sounds of the city faded away.

Then, all too soon, she pulled away. "Think about what I told you in there. And thank you for the comics lesson."

"Anytime," David said.

Jade stepped into the street, her hand outstretched to hail a cab. Before long, a boxy, dandelion-yellow taxi pulled to a stop in front of her, and she climbed inside with a wave back at David. He stood on the sidewalk, watching the taxi drive off down the street, in the direction of downtown.

Headlights flared to life at the side of the street, startling David. An unfamiliar car, painted black, swayed on its axels as it peeled away from the curb after the taxi.

At once, all of the paranoia that David had pushed aside came rushing back to him.

Jade was being *followed*.

CHAPTER
THIRTEEN

J ade shifted her weight uncomfortably from foot to foot as she waited outside of the sergeant's office, deliberating.

The last time she had spoken to Douglas, she had nearly caused a catastrophe for all of them—her, David, and Night Armor. If she wasn't careful, there were a lot of people who could be hurt by a minor slip-up in front of her superior officer. Even Margie and Levi had stuck their necks out for this comic, and for the truth about the Blackwing Program. The last thing she wanted was to endanger anyone, and since that was the case, the best option was to keep her head down and her mouth shut.

But she couldn't just abandon Night Armor. If nothing else, she needed to see him, as powerless as she might be to stop the spread of his illness.

She had loitered outside of his office for almost a full minute when the door opened on its own. A scowling Douglas glowered down at her, his expression, more than it ever had been, resembling a bulldog's.

"Can I help you, Ms. Atallah?"

"Sir." Jade swallowed, dipping her head respectfully. "I was just about to knock."

"What do you want?"

Jade took a quiet breath to steady herself, then said, "Sir, if... if possible, I would like to be allowed to pay my dragoncoat a visit in the infirmary."

Pursing his lips, the sergeant regarded her in silence. Jade didn't know whether or not to take that as a good sign.

"It's just... Night Armor can be a little sensitive," Jade ventured, trying to read the sergeant's face for any sign of danger. "I'm worried that his mental health is going to take a toll from his isolation." She cleared her throat, then added impulsively, "You know how dragoncoats can be."

The sergeant stared down at her for another few seconds, then nodded slowly. "All right," he conceded. "You may have a point."

Jade let out a quiet breath, which she hoped was imperceptible to Douglas.

"You can visit your dragoncoat in the infirmary," he continued, turning away from her with a wave of his hand. "Go on now."

Jade nodded quickly, then she turned on her heel and raced down the hallway, away from the sergeant's office, before he could change his mind.

The infirmary was separate from the rest of the facility, so that dragoncoats with infectious diseases wouldn't spread their ailments to the rest of the base's Flighters. Nominally, this was supposed to be a measure designed to contain standard illnesses: draconic influenza, acidic pneumonia, and the like. As Jade made her way through the base, she wondered if Night Armor was being isolated because the Blackwing doctors thought that the scale-related illness might be contagious, or if they simply wanted to keep him out of sight of other Coat Wardens who might begin to make unwanted connections.

A white-coated doctor met Jade at the entrance to the infir-mary. "I was informed that you would be coming to visit your dragoncoat," he said crisply, consulting his clipboard. "Night Armor, is it?"

Jade nodded, frowning. "That order traveled fast."

"Well, that's the sergeant for you." The doctor gestured to the phone on the wall and then for her to follow, and Jade fell in step behind him. "We have a few containment procedures for you to follow. Nothing serious, of course, but protocol is necessary here."

"Do you think Night Armor is contagious?"

"It's hard to say for sure," the doctor said, his tone evasive. "We don't know anything about his condition. There is no precedent."

"No precedent?" Jade allowed her voice to pitch up in alarm. "You don't know what's wrong with him?"

"We are assuming it's viral," the doctor said quickly, flip-ping over the top page of his clipboard as he spoke. "More than likely, some sort of respiratory infection. That would explain the coughing."

"Coughing? He's coughing now?" Night Armor's condition must have progressed since she'd last seen him. The crackle in his breathing had been an irregular thing, and his symptoms had been more subtle when she'd brought him back to the base —subtle enough that Jade likely wouldn't have noticed them without knowing David's story.

"Yes. I assure you, there isn't much to worry about," the doctor said. "Allowing you this visit is merely a precaution against poor morale for you partner."

He stopped short in front of an iron-lined door, inset with a rectangular window. Jade peered through the wire mesh embedded within the glass, taking in the bare, whitewashed room on the other side. There was a huge, stainless steel exami-nation table pushed up against the far wall, and Jade shivered, remembering what David had told her about Backscatter's autopsy pictures. Mercifully, the table was empty. Instead, Night Armor was curled up on a large cushion pushed into the opposite corner, his snout tucked beneath his tail, his eyes closed as if he was asleep.

The doctor fitted a mask over Jade's nose and mouth and handed her a pair of nitrile gloves, then he opened the iron door, letting her inside. She stepped into the room and was immediately overwhelmed by the sterile scent of antiseptic.

They're just throwing anything medical at him, aren't they? She turned in a slow circle, looking over the room with a critical eye. *The infection comes from the scales, and they know that. Is the antiseptic just for show, or are they just flinging ideas at the wall, hoping something sticks?*

From the outside of the room, Jade had thought that the panel of glass against one wall was a window—if Night Armor's morale was a concern, they might have brought him to a room that faced the outdoors, so that he could, at the very least, feel sunlight on his scales and watch the moon move through the sky. Now that she was inside, however, Jade realized how wrong she'd been. It wasn't a window to the outside. It was one-way glass, reflecting her own image back at her. They had put Night Armor in an observation room, and without a doubt, someone was currently watching them.

Jade didn't look at the mirrored glass, pretending that she hadn't noticed it. Instead, she approached her sleeping dragoncoat, a timid, gloved hand extended. Night Armor wasn't sleeping restfully. With each snore, Jade could hear the hiss in his struggling lungs, and his eyelids kept twitching, as if he was seconds from waking. Jade knelt beside him and laid her palm on his forehead, stroking his scales softly, the way she had taken to when they were both in the academy. Night Armor had suffered poor sleep from stress. The other dragoncoats in their year had, from time to time, taken to bullying him, as if they could smell his inferiority complex and sought to worsen it. Adolescence was as difficult a time for dragons as it was for humans.

"Hey, Olive," Jade whispered. "It's me. You wanna wake up and say hi?"

Night Armor shifted in his sleep, pressing his forehead against Jade's hand. After a few seconds, his eyes opened to yellow slits, the pupils rolling around until they had landed on Jade. Then he awoke abruptly, lifting his head and pushing it affectionately into Jade's chest.

Jade, he purred, his voice a low rumble that was almost imperceptible to even Jade's keen ears. Then, louder, I missed you so much. Where—

He was interrupted by a sudden fit of hacking coughs that shook his entire frame. It was several seconds before he managed to control his breathing again.

"I know, bud," Jade said, guilt tugging at her heart. "I know. I'm sorry I couldn't come in to see you sooner. The sergeant told me to wait."

They're saying I'm really sick now, Night Armor told her.

"Well, you were really sick before, too," she said, with a nervous glance over at the observation window. "It's just getting worse, that's all. That's how these things work."

Night Armor's eyes were round as he studied her, his nostrils flaring. His long, reptilian tongue snaked out from between his teeth and flickered in the air. Then his tail began to thrash in enthusiasm. Jade! You and David have mated!

Jade rocked back on her heels, sudden panic making her dizzy. "Um—what?"

Why didn't you say something? This is such good news!

"Night Armor, I don't know what you're—"

I can scent it on you! Night Armor whistled gleefully, ignoring Jade's quick, silencing gestures. Oh, this is so exciting! Did he show you any more pages from the next issue of The

Coated Crusader? Do you know what happens next? Wait, no—don't tell me, don't tell me!

"You must be confused," Jade said, her heart pounding in her temples. "You're sick—you're probably hallucinating, or—"

Behind Jade, the iron door opened, and she gritted her teeth, turning to face the doctor who had escorted her to Night Armor's room. Beside him, his face ruddy with built-up anger and his thick arms folded, stood Sergeant Douglas. Internally, Jade groaned. She'd been a fool to think that this meeting was a favor to her or her dragoncoat. Douglas would only agree to a situation that would benefit him, and he cared little for the dragons' well-being. He'd been behind the one-way glass the entire time, waiting for Night Armor to say something incriminating. She should have known that this was a setup, but her desperation to see Night Armor had made her shortsighted.

"Ms. Atallah," Douglas said, his voice dangerously quiet, "I believe a conversation is in order. If you would please accompany me to the main office, I would appreciate it." His eyes flashed as he added, "It's in your best interests to cooperate. You wouldn't want to make this any worse than it needs to be."

Reluctantly, Jade rose to her feet, lifting her chin to meet the sergeant's gaze. Night Armor watched her, the excitement fading from his expression as he seemed to realize what was happening.

Jade? Uncertainty tinged his clicking, humming voice.

"It's okay, Olive," Jade said, inhaling deeply through her nose. "You didn't do anything wrong. I'll see you soon."

The slight tightening at the corner of the sergeant's mouth as she spoke didn't bode well. But as she turned to look at Night Armor over her shoulder, she gave him a firm nod, trying to emanate a confidence she didn't feel.

∾

JADE SAT ALONE in Douglas's office, handcuffed to the chair, for at least an hour before she was joined by the sergeant. The wait didn't surprise her; it was a common enough intimidation tactic, and she was sure that Douglas and the other Blackwing officers needed to confer about how to best deal with her treachery.

She was almost grateful for the time alone. Douglas's office was quiet and still. It smelled of smoke, but also of paper—a warm scent that helped to calm Jade. The only source of light was the hanging filament bulb above the desk, which was surrounded by a bowl-shaped fixture that kept the ceiling shadowed. Jade stared into the darkened corners, taking deep breaths to center herself. She managed to slow her racing heart enough that she was only mildly startled when the door burst open, striking the file cabinet behind it with a resonant peal.

"I can't imagine you have a single decent excuse for this," Douglas snarled, slamming the door shut as he stalked into the office, "but if you do, now is the time to offer it."

Jade tried to conjure one, rolling around her few options in her head. Nothing good. Nothing that Douglas would believe, especially now. If she'd known that Night Armor would be able to sniff out her transgressions so easily, she would never have agreed to visit with him, despite her earlier desperation to see him. Still, she couldn't bring herself to regret it.

"I think fraternizing with the enemy is a significant under-statement for what you've done here," the sergeant said, his doughy face creased with anger. "Do you understand the trouble you're in? The severity of what you've—"

"Yes," Jade interrupted, lifting her chin to look him in the eye. He stopped talking at once, startled by her audacity. In the pit of her stomach, she felt a surge of something close to satis-faction.

The sergeant set his jaw. "I don't believe that you do."

"Can we dispense with the righteous disapproval," Jade

said, folding her arms defensively, "and move on to the part where you tell me what the consequences will be?"

Douglas fumed for a moment, his icy eyes narrowed, the whiskers of his moustache twitching. Despite the seriousness of her situation, Jade was calm, focused. She'd had plenty of training in the art of handling a blown cover. This time, rather than being unmasked by one of Blackwing's targets, it was her superior officer staring her down with that mixture of triumph and fury. The only difference was the scale of consequence, and as such, the consequence was all that mattered.

Blackwing could hurt her in a way that David couldn't. If she had to guess, they would send her back with a Flighter escort. After everything they had done to stop David from publishing the final comic, she assumed that this censorship, above all else, was their goal. In all likelihood, they would leverage her connection to him to halt production of *The Coated Crusader*.

"The consequences," the sergeant muttered, pacing back behind his desk. He fished in the top drawer for a cigar, lighting it. The glowing tip wobbled up and down as he took a puff, then he breathed a cloud of foul-smelling air into Jade's face. She wrinkled her nose, flinching away from him. "Got used to this pretty quick, didn't you? You're already ready to talk about the consequences."

Jade didn't respond.

He glared at her for a few seconds through the haze of cigar smoke, then snorted. "We'll see. I need to consult with a few of the other officers, and we need to deal with the artist first."

"If you're planning on sending me back to Manhattan—"

"Why on earth would we send you back to Manhattan?" Douglas interrupted, a sudden look of incredulity on his face. "You've proven, beyond a doubt, that you cannot be trusted around that man."

"I might be able to convince him not to publish," Jade said.

She kept her voice even, fighting the tremor that threatened to sneak into it. If Blackwing gave her the opportunity escape to Manhattan, she could tell David everything that had happened. He and Levi might be able to help her find somewhere to hide. It would be easy enough to slip her escort, and then—

"No need," Douglas grunted. He took a drag from the cigar, then he spewed the smoke toward the ceiling, where it lingered in the incandescent glow of the low-hanging light. "Convincing Felman of anything is off the table, Ms. Atallah. We're going to shut it down the old-fashioned way."

"The old-fashioned way?"

"Conspiracy to commit treason. Revealing state secrets. We are an arm of this government, lest you forget, and the happenings on this base are sacrosanct."

"Wait," Jade said, "you're going to arrest him?"

Douglas nodded, sitting down heavily at the desk. "Of course."

"But he hasn't done anything yet," Jade protested. "You can't—"

"Oh, we'll find something." Douglas leered at her, one eyebrow arched. "He hasn't done anything yet. That doesn't mean there isn't evidence of conspiracy lying around his apartment—or wherever his sneaky little editor is planning on printing that damned rag."

"You already burned down Freedom Press. I don't even know where Levi is planning on printing. How are you going to—"

"Please. The DIA has had someone on Levi Adelman for years. There are plenty of would-be subversives in New York City, but none quite so keen." Douglas tapped his cigar over the ashtray, and Jade watched the falling embers flare into gray cinders. "We can check in with one of their men and have an address within the hour."

"But—then—" Jade gripped the wooden arms of her chair,

JORDAN RILEY SWAN & EZRA ZABIT

leaning forward. "Why all the games before this? Why send threats to the publishers? Why send me to track David—er, Felman," she corrected, heat rising in her face.

"We didn't want to arrest a popular public figure," Douglas said. "Why put a spotlight on this whole mess? We'd have fueled people's speculations, made the whole situation worse —especially if he turned out to be innocent." Douglas scowled as he said the word "innocent," as if it had left a taste in his mouth somehow more acrid and unpleasant than cigar smoke. "We had to be absolutely sure that he intended to do what it seemed like he was doing, and you confirmed that for us."

A wave of fury rose inside Jade at his smug expression. "What is all this, Sergeant? There's an illness killing your drag- oncoats, and—"

"That is conspiracist talk, Ms. Atallah—"

"—all you want to do is make sure it doesn't get out. What are you afraid of? That someone's going to put their foot down? That your contemporaries at the FIB are going to find out about this?"

The sergeant's lip curled, and his grip on the cigar stiffened. He sat upright, sprinkling ash over his desk. "You're in no posi- tion to be making that sort of insinuation."

"Dragoncoats are expensive," Jade said. "You have some of the very best Flighters in the country gathered right here on Staten Island—and none of them are lasting longer than two or three years. That doesn't seem like an effective use of resources, does it, Sarge?"

She ought to have stopped there; the advanced state of the protruding vein in the sergeant's forehead was a clear sign of unsteady ground. But she couldn't help herself. Finally, there was little she could do to make the situation worse. All she had left were empty threats and clear-eyed observations.

"And if there's one thing that'll garner unwanted legal

attention, it's a waste of resources," Jade said bitterly. "All of those taxpayer dollars—"

"Enough," the sergeant spat. He blotted out the end of the cigar in the ashtray with unnecessary force. Jade noticed that his hands were shaking. At least she could take that small pleasure with her—the knowledge that, after almost two years of ducking her head and accepting his blustery orders, she had finally managed to piss him off in return. "That's enough out of you."

He got to his feet, crossing to the office door. When he opened it, two men stepped inside—soldiers, not Coat Wardens, with rifles strapped across their chests. Jade tried to stand instinctively, buzzing with useless adrenaline, but her hand caught on the cuffs. It didn't matter, either way. Without her dragoncoat, she was all but defenseless. And there was no way they'd let her see Night Armor now.

"Take her to a holding cell," Douglas demanded. "I don't want to see her face again until they bring in Felman."

CHAPTER
FOURTEEN

David stared down at his drafting desk, his eyes tracing the clean lines and bold colors of *The Coated Crusader's* final page.

The last panel remained unfinished, a single square inch of green missing from the ghostly visage of the main character's dragoncoat, Blindside. David had been staring at that lone patch of blank paper for the past ten minutes. It was an almost instantaneous fix—a few dabs of ink, and the comic he'd been working on for the past couple of years would finally be finished.

Off to the side, the page that David intended to append to the comic—a carefully-inked, no-nonsense paragraph explaining the nature of the Blackwing Program—was drying, already completed. Levi had called earlier, promising good news when he returned to the Lower East Side.

At this point, it seemed that almost nothing stood between David and the goal he had pursued relentlessly since Backscatter's death. He had the pages, he had the proof, and soon, he'd have the printing press, too.

All that was left was a minute's worth of color.

For the fifth time, David dipped his ink pen back into the open jar of green. It had gone dry.

He wasn't sure why he couldn't bring himself to finish it. Perhaps he had sat with the comic for so long that he couldn't imagine a world where he was no longer working on it. Or perhaps, more likely, he was afraid of what this final issue would do to him—and to Jade. If he had held these finished pages in his hand two months ago, he would've rushed them to the press before the ink had dried. Now, though, there was a knot in his stomach as he steeled himself, the pen hovering over the white patch in Blindside's spirit.

Before he could add the color, there was an insistent knock at the door. He swore under his breath, set the pen in the tray at the edge of the desk, and turned to look over his shoulder. "Who is it?" he called.

"Who do you think? Quit putzing around, let's get this show on the road!" The eager tension in Levi's voice drove David to his feet, and he hurried over to let his editor inside.

"Did you figure it out?"

Levi strode inside, a jaunt to his step and a slightly manic look in his eyes. "You bet I did. I solved both of our problems today. Oh, I'm good, Felman, I'm—"

"What did you do?"

"I got an old friend in Brooklyn with a press in the base-ment," Levi said. "It's an older model, smaller than the one I had at Freedom Press, but it'll do. And he—"

"Let me guess," David interrupted. "He owes you a favor."

Levi grinned. "You got it."

"Why do you have so many—you know what, forget it," David said, as Levi's grin widened. "I don't want to know. I don't care. You said *smaller*. Does that mean—"

"Oh, it'll take longer." Levi waved a hand as if to dismiss the issue. "But what's a couple sleepless nights? That's why we've got coffee, right?"

"Right," David said, with a brief, longing glance over at his closed bedroom door. "You said you solved two problems. What was the second one?"

"Found myself a cheap place to stay," Levi replied. "That way, I can stop infringing on your hospitality, my friend."

There was a knowing glint in Levi's eye, and David, suddenly embarrassed, dropped his gaze to the floor. He had to admit that this announcement was a substantial relief, but if he was being perfectly honest, he was mostly relieved out of the hope that Jade would return to Manhattan once she had finished whatever she needed to do at the Blackwing base.

Levi didn't give him time to linger on the details. He grabbed David by the sleeve and tugged him toward the door. "C'mon, let's get a wiggle on. We've gotta—"

"Slow down, wait," David protested, jerking his arm away. "I'm not actually done with it."

"You're what?" Levi gaped at him. "You're not done with it?"

"I'm almost done with it. I just need to add something." David paced back over to the drafting desk, kicking the stool aside. He stood over the final page, staring down at it for a few moments.

Levi followed him across the apartment, nearly tripping over the coffee table in his haste to reach David. "What have you been doing all day?" he cried. "I've been running around, busting my—oh." He broke off at the sight of the page. "Felman, this looks done. It looks good, too. What's your issue?"

Just do it. One last fix.

David picked up the ink pen from the tray, dipped it back in the green, and filled in the bare tip of Blindside's snout.

"*Ay-ay-ay*—artists," Levi grumbled, shaking his head. He snatched up the stack of finished, dried pages in one hand, gesturing to the freshly-inked sheet. "You take that one, and hold it out so that it dries on our way over."

"Are we really in that much of a hurry?" David asked, miffed. He'd wanted a moment to put his feet up after finishing the comic, maybe a little bit of time by himself to reflect on his work. Maybe even wait for Jade to return from the Blackwing base; he found himself craving her company even more than he did a moment alone.

"Absolutely, we're in a hurry. Are you kidding me?"

"We can't even wait for—"

Levi shot him a glare. "Is this about that woman? The Coat Warden? You've gone goofy, Felman. I got us a press across town, but you remember what happened to the last one, right?"

Right. Reluctantly, David nodded. "Just let me leave her a note. In case she stops by."

Levi groaned, but waved a hand at the drafting desk, shaking his head. "Whatever you say, lover boy. Just make it quick." As David tore a scrap of paper from a notepad and dug in his desk drawer for a pen, Levi added, "Don't tell her where we are! Don't tell her nothing you wouldn't want Blackwing to know."

"Jade wouldn't—"

"Sure," Levi said, "but even if *she* wouldn't rat you out, that doesn't mean your old boss isn't gonna send someone over here to turn the place inside out."

"Oh. I see." David thought to himself for a moment, deciding on a message. He began to scribble it down. It was unsatisfying. There wasn't enough room on the paper to say everything that he wanted to say to Jade, and he felt heavy with the realization that it might be his last correspondence to her.

He folded his finished note, staring at it glumly.

"Felman," Levi said, impatience tinging his voice. "Are you ready?"

"Ah... yes," David said, lowering the note. Then another thought occurred to him. "Actually, no. Give me a moment."

Levi grumbled something unintelligible, something about a "sense of urgency," but David wasn't listening. He crouched over the desk, flipping open the note to add a secondary message inside. Once he was finished, he tore a second sheet from the notepad, pocketed the pen, and allowed Levi to usher him toward the door.

"We've got a long night ahead of us," Levi insisted. "We gotta get these plates made." He dug in his pockets for a moment, scowling, and sucked his teeth in dismay when his search yielded nothing. "You got money for a cab? Those crooks at the flophouse really cleaned me out."

IT WAS dark by the time David arrived at Van Cortlandt Park, the original copies of his comic pages tucked under his arm. They were rolled together, bound by a sheet of protective plastic, the plates were done and Levi was finalizing the start of the run back with his friend across town. He approached Backscatter's memorial and knelt, tucking them into the alcove in the back of the roughly-hewn stone pillar.

"Almost done," he whispered. "The plates are made. I'm headed back to join Levi now, and then we'll print your comic, Shadow. It's almost over."

David straightened, looking down at the memorial. He'd hollowed out his hiding place intentionally in a fit of paranoia —a place to put all of the original copies of his comic pages, in case he ever needed them. A strange wave of emotion overcame him as he realized that this was the last time he would ever come to Shadow's memorial out of necessity. The next time he returned, if he ever got the chance to return, he wouldn't be a man on a mission. He would just be a mourner.

That, at the end of the day, was the hardest thing about finishing the comic. Once it was over, and his message was out in the world, he had to figure out what to do next. Working on the comic, figuring out clever ways to fold his experiences into the Coated Crusader's adventures, had been cathartic, comforting. He'd had a sense of direction, something he needed to do. Now there were no pages left to draw, no story left to tell —and at the end of it, he was still without his dragoncoat. Blindside's spirit had stayed with Drake, his Coat Warden, throughout the comic, empowering him. But in the real world, Backscatter was gone.

"It doesn't matter, anyway," he said aloud, speaking only to the night and the stone and the surrounding trees; he could no longer imagine that Backscatter was there to hear him, as if that last stroke of ink had severed some connection between them. He found himself longing for Jade. The last time he'd been here, she'd come to find him. He wished she would do so again.

A cold breeze rustled the trees, and David shivered, glancing around. He pulled his coat tighter about his shoulders.

"It doesn't matter," he repeated to himself. "You probably won't come back here. Whatever you do next, you're likely to do it from prison."

And Jade won't be there, either. Not if I can help it.

—

DAVID HAD BEEN EXPECTING Levi's contact to be another buddy from back in the Great War, but he turned out to be a university friend who had studied alongside him after returning from Europe. His name was Felix, and he was about a foot taller than

Levi, thin and unsmiling. He lived in a Brooklyn townhouse, which he apparently shared with two other men—of whom David and Levi had seen neither hide nor hair. Felix made his living making flyers in his cellar, using a printer that was around half the size of the one at Freedom Press. He and Levi, when in proximity with one another, had a tendency to bicker. Levi had claimed that Felix owed him a favor, but the longer he spent around the two of them together, the more certain David grew that this had been a complete lie. Whatever the nature of their relationship, Felix was acting out of the goodness of his heart, not a sense of debt.

As David descended the cobweb-strewn steps into the basement, Felix looked up from the plates of the final two issues of *The Coated Crusader* and nodded in greeting. David held up a hand.

"Oh, good, you're back," Levi said, shifting his weight from foot to foot as he lingered beside Felix at the press. "Took you long enough. Come check out the proofs—they're hot off the press. Let me know what you think."

The basement was mercifully dry and clean, but it was small, and David had to squeeze past Levi to get a good look at the pages, stacked neatly on a table beside the printing press. He tilted his head to let the light, shining from a bare, incandescent bulb hanging in the center of the room, fall upon the finished prints.

"They look good," he said, lifting up the edges to inspect them. "Very clean."

"It's turning out well, isn't it?" Levi sounded pleased. "I love this little thing. I might have to get myself one of—"

He broke off suddenly, staring up at the ceiling above their heads, and David didn't have to ask him why. Through the thin floorboards that comprised the first floor hallway of Felix's house, they'd all heard the chime of the bell that hung from the front door.

"Were you expecting anybody, Felix?" David asked, his gaze sliding down to the quiet man, who had paused midway through turning over one of the printing plates.

"You," Felix responded, his lips pursed and face tense. "No one else." He glared over at Levi and added, "You told me we wouldn't get in any—"

"Who says this is trouble?" Levi interrupted, though he kept his voice to a harsh whisper. "Just—shh. It's one of your *schlemiel* roommates."

"It's two in the morning," Felix hissed. "They're always asleep before ten."

Quietly, Levi clicked his tongue, shaking his head. "C'mon, ten at night? That's no way to live. Let me take you and the boys out for a—"

"Levi," Felix growled, "if I'm about to be—"

"*Oy,*" David interrupted, his voice low. "Shush." Both of them turned to look at him, and he pointedly held a finger to his lips, scowling up at the ceiling.

For a few minutes the three of them stood in silence, staring at the boards above as several sets of footsteps—more than two—sounded in the hall. There were voices, too, muffled and indistinct. David thought he could make out a couple of words here and there—among them, "plates," and, to his dismay, "Felman."

Then there was a sudden crash from the top of the stairs as the basement door was kicked open, and a stream of light filtered down the bare wooden steps and stone wall. A deep voice called, "Did anyone check down here yet?"

Another answered, "No, not yet."

And a third, this one harsher than the other two, yelled, "David Felman, if you're down there, come up the stairs with your hands in the air."

Contrary to heeding the order, David shrank back against the wall, shooting a frantic look at Levi.

"Let me handle this," Levi said in an undertone. He pointed at David. "You—stay. You..." He gestured for Felix to follow him, and approached the stairs.

"Who's there?" demanded the man at the top of the stairs. His tone was heavy with authority, and David assumed that he was with the police. Blackwing maintained contacts in the NYPD and would often send them to take care of raids rather than making arrests directly. David's sense of dismay grew, and he took a step deeper into the cellar, skirting behind the printing press.

"Uh, hello there, officer," Levi said, lifting a hand to shield his eyes from the light. "It's awful late for an interruption like this. If you don't mind my asking... what the hell?"

"Who're you?"

"I'm Levi Adelman, editor, and this is my good buddy, Felix Holland." Levi reached up to sling his arm around Felix's stooped shoulders. A number of emotions crossed Felix's face in quick succession, and after a brief but visible struggle, he managed to keep his expression neutral. "This is his house you're in, and his door hinges the taxpayers will be replacing."

"What are you two doing down there?" asked the cop.

"Printing," Felix replied sullenly.

Levi nodded. "Printing. Pretty sure that's legal, sir."

"Printing what?"

"Pamphlets," Felix said. "It's what I do for a living. My *friend* here"—he said the word with biting tone that Levi didn't seem to notice—"is helping me finish up this project."

"We received a tip that we might find someone here, a David Felman. We have a warrant for his arrest. Do either of you know anyone by that name?"

Both of them shook their heads, exchanging a sideways glance.

"You know, it's a felony to lie to a cop."

"Is it?" Levi asked innocently. "Well, I suppose that makes

sense, officer. You boys are the backbone of this city. Why, look at you three—out here at this ungodly hour, working hard! It's inspiring stuff, really inspiring."

Internally, David groaned, screwing his eyes shut. True to form, Levi was laying it on far too thick.

"Anyway," Levi said, "good luck looking for that fella... What'd you say his name was? Friedman?"

There was silence for a few seconds as Levi smiled up the stairs. David didn't have to see the police officer to imagine the expression on his face.

Then the cop said, "We're gonna go ahead and come down there, if it's all the same to the two of you."

"There's not a lot of room down here," Felix said quickly. "And it's a bit of a mess, what with the press and—"

"I think we'll be coming down anyway, but thank you for the warning." A leather boot landed on the top step, shaking dust and cobwebs into the cellar.

"Wait!" Levi cried, holding up his hands. "Hold on, hold on a second! You need a warrant for that!"

"I just told you, we already have one." The officer continued to descend into the basement, followed closely by one of his fellows. A flashlight beam swept over the printing press, pausing briefly on the stacked pages, then coming to rest on David. He blinked at the sudden brightness, instinctively lifting his hands to shoulder height.

"That's our man," one of the officers said. "He looks like the picture they sent."

"The picture who sent?" Levi demanded, to no response.

Blinded by the flashlight, David could only hear the officers approach by their footsteps, the metal jingling at their belts. Rough hands seized his shoulder, pulling him into the center of the room. He blinked rapidly, trying to get his bearings, as the officer forced his hands behind his back.

"Whoa, whoa, what are you doing?" Levi's voice was shrill,

indignant; there was a scuffle, and he let out a yelp. "Watch it —Hey, fellas, you can't do that! If you know what's good for you—"

"If you know what's good for you," the first officer snapped, "you'll stay out of our way. Got it?"

David felt cold steel on his wrists, uncomfortably tight. As his eyes adjusted back to the dark, he could see the shadowed outline of the third officer, the last to descend the stairs, making his way over to the printing press. "And we'll be needing these plates, too."

"You can't take those!" Levi's eyes were wild, his fingers buried in his hair. "That's this man's intellectual property, do you hear me? Hey!"

The sounds of metal plates clanking together told David that Levi's warnings had gone completely ignored. The cop with his hand on David's shoulder gave him a firm shake.

"Where are the originals?" he demanded. "We were told to collect the plates and the original copies. So where are they?"

Even if David could have responded—could have unfrozen his jaw long enough to open his mouth—he wouldn't have. He stared blankly at the officer until the man rolled his eyes, swearing under his breath.

"English," the officer said, drawing out the word as if speaking to a young child. "Do you speak English?"

For a brief moment, a flash of indignant pride loosened David's tongue. "It's not a graceful language, but I'm familiar with it, yes."

"Listen, pal—God, am I getting tired of you wise guys— where are the—"

"I don't have the originals," David said clearly, cutting him off. "They're not here."

"Well, then where are they?" When David didn't respond, the officer rounded on Levi and Felix. "Where are the originals?"

Felix, who had backed against the wall with his hands up, shrugged. Levi, meanwhile, was still raving. "You'll be hearing from my lawyers! And you'd better believe I got lawyers! The best firm in this city!"

With an irritated sigh, the officer seized David by the upper arm, forcing him toward the steps. "Forget it. We'll find them sooner or later." He nodded at the other two, who were gathering the plates into a black case. "Search this place, then we'll head to the apartment. We'll find them somewhere."

"I'll sue you into oblivion, you hear me?" Levi hollered. "I'll sue you straight outta your ugly boots, you cowardly—"

"Shut your yap!" The officer aimed a kick at Levi, who flinched away from him. "Unless you want to come along."

Levi's eyes were still blazing with anger, but he stayed quiet, which must have taken him a Herculean effort. David didn't resist as the officer led him to the stairs. As he passed by Levi, he muttered in Yiddish, "We did our best. Not your fault."

For the first time since David had met him, his editor didn't respond. David didn't look up to meet his gaze. The waves of disappointment and fury radiating from Levi were difficult enough to swallow without seeing the look on his face.

There was a warm glow in the upper windows of some surrounding townhouses as the officers brought David out to the street. The red light on top of both parked police cars were flashing; they must have roused a few of the neighbors. David could see them gawking out of the windows as he was ushered into the back of a car.

—

IT WAS no surprise to David when the police took him on a circuitous route, straight past the nearest precinct and toward the Upper Bay. He didn't bother to ask why they stopped at the edge of the Narrows, the tidal strait separating Brooklyn from Staten Island, to wait for the ferryboat's arrival. Both cops spent the rest of the ride to the Blackwing base grumbling about the unfinished tunnel project.

"They ought to just take a couple of these dragoncoats and have them get the job done," the officer behind the wheel complained. David leaned against the back window of the car, his teeth gritted against the bitter taste of disappointment and the resulting irritation. He watched the sparse, uncomfortably familiar scenery of Staten Island slide past.

He'd known it would end this way. He had simply expected that the comic would be finished by this point, in the hands of thousands, maybe tens of thousands, of readers. Apparently, that had been far too much to ask.

Perhaps someday, someone will find the originals in the park, he told himself. *They'll know how it ends, and they'll know about Blackwing.*

Unless Blackwing gets to the memorial first. David hadn't told anyone where the original copies were stashed, but Margie and Jade both knew that he commonly visited Backscatter's memorial in the Bronx park. If the sergeant pressed either of them for answers....

"True. They tunnel, right? They'd have this done a lot faster than a bunch of guys with pickaxes." The cop in the passenger seat twisted around to look at David. "Hey, you. They told us you used to be a Coat Warden."

David regarded him wearily. "Yes?"

"Do they really spit up acid? Strong enough to get through rocks?"

David nodded, and the cop turned back toward the windshield with a grimace and a shiver.

"There you go," he said. "They oughta bring a few of those things up from the mines. It's taken some heavy sugar to do things the hard way, you know?"

David bit back the instinctive retort, trying to shut out the officers' conversations. He knew that plenty of people who'd never interacted with dragoncoats saw them as little more than work animals; it was an attitude he'd tried to challenge through the story of *The Coated Crusader*. In many respects, it was a lack of attention and lack of empathy for dragons that had caused Backscatter's death in the first place.

I'm sorry, Shadow. I should've been quicker.

Eventually, after more than an hour, the police car pulled up at the front gate of the base. Douglas stood outside, two armed guards beside him. As the police vehicle rolled to a stop, he approached the car, rapping his thick knuckles on the passenger-side window.

The window rolled down, and Douglas peered into the back of the car, his eyes narrowing when he saw David. Despite years spent subverting the sergeant's authority, David hadn't come face-to-face with the man himself since he'd been discharged from active Flighter duty. Douglas had let himself go a bit in the years since David had known him, but he was still as imposing a figure as ever—well over six feet tall, his neck as wide as his head, his short-cropped, military haircut shaved into a sharp widow's peak. Rather than meet his gaze, David looked past him, at the iron gate and the entrance checkpoint.

Douglas nodded at the officers. "Good work. Thank you, gentlemen. We'll take it from here."

—

As the soldiers escorted David through the halls of the Blackwing base, he couldn't shake the subconscious feeling that the past few years had been nothing but a miserable dream.

Everything was the same as he remembered it. A few of the faces milling around in the corridors, shooting him curious looks, were familiar. They passed by a smoking room, and David caught a glimpse of Margie, sitting in a high-backed chair with her cigarette forgotten between her forefingers. She stared at them as they passed, and David grimaced, looking away from her. Her disappointment was no easier to stomach than Levi's.

He'd felt so alone after losing Backscatter that he'd never even gave thought to how many people were actually in his corner. They had hoped to see *The Coated Crusader* come to fruition almost as much as he had, and their chagrin mirrored his.

I let them down.

For the first time in months, he thought of the other members of his Flighter team—Backscatter's second and third wardens, whose potential to replace him had hung over David's head like a sword during the worst days of Shadow's illness. He wondered if they even knew what had happened, or if they had simply been discharged as unceremoniously as he had been.

I let them all down, David thought, fighting a rising sense of panic. *If I had finished this sooner—*

When the soldiers steered him through an open doorway at the end of the hall, David's train of thought veered sharply from the tracks.

He was in an interrogation room. There were three walls of bare concrete, and one with a mirrored observation window. At the center of the room, below a low-hanging light, there was a steel table. Seated at it, opposite each other, were two people:

184

THE INK DRAGON AND THE ART OF FLIGHT

on one side, a man who David recognized as Major Hathaway, the sergeant's immediate superior. The major, in contrast to Douglas, was a lean, almost gaunt man, starkly pale as though he was constantly recovering from a shock. He was older, the signs of age in the silver of his short hair, the lines that marred his forehead. On the other side of the table sat Jade, her arms drawn tightly across her chest, her face a mask of indifference.

One of the soldiers gave David a shove, and he stumbled toward Jade, whose gaze flicked over to him for only a moment, as if they had never met. David sat down next to her, unable to stop himself from shooting her frequent glances. She didn't look back at him. Perhaps she was disappointed, too. Hadn't she just told him, the other day, that he needed to print the comic?

Guilt tugged at David, dragging him further down into his own despair. She was probably furious with him. Her dragoncoat was ill, on the brink of a deadly spiral, and her only hope for him was now gone. Her mere presence in this room was an indicator that her superiors were suspicious of her.

The door slammed shut, startling David. He jumped, facing Major Hathaway and Sergeant Douglas, who had taken the empty chair beside her.

"So," the major said, his hands folded together, "I'm told there's been some... impropriety on the part of our Blackwing Coat Wardens recently."

David leaned forward. "I received a notice in the mail a long time ago that made clear I was no longer a Coat Warden, Major. And as I'm the only one guilty of improprieties—"

"Hardly," he interrupted. His narrowed eyes, emerald green and as cold as the stone itself, slid to Jade. "The sergeant tells me that he managed to confirm your little affair."

The car, David realized with an unpleasant jolt. *The car that was following Jade....*

"From the mouths of dragons," Douglas said, his voice dripping with a smugness that made David want to lunge across the table and seize him by his badge-studded lapels. "We'd had our suspicions for days, but it was the dragoncoat who confirmed it for us. Poor, stupid creature."

Jade's brow furrowed, and beneath the table, her hands closed into tight fists. But she said nothing, instead meeting the major's gaze squarely.

"So. Here's what's going to happen," Hathaway said. "Ms. Atallah, you are to leave your position with the FIB. We will cite health concerns as your reason for departure, and you will receive a general discharge, which, as far as I see it, is more than fair."

Jade had gone rigid in her seat; David knew, without asking, exactly how she felt. They were removing her from duty —removing her from her dragoncoat.

"Your second will replace you as Night Armor's Coat Warden. You will maintain your silence on the activities of this base, as Blackwing is a confidential project, and any breach of this confidentiality will be considered treason."

"No," Jade said, her voice quick and tense. "You don't have to do that. Let me—"

"If you would rather not cooperate," the major interrupted, "that discharge can be dishonorable, and you can face the same charges as Felman." He jerked his narrow chin toward David, but his eyes never left Jade. "Seditious conspiracy. Revealing state secrets. If we're lucky, we might even get the espionage charge. Under military law, all three of these are hangable offenses."

"Hold on," David said, feeling suddenly dizzy. "*Espionage?* I wrote a comic book."

"Yes, and we have the plates for your final issue," Douglas told him. "The cops still haven't found your originals, but we don't need 'em. That was quite an interesting turn of events on the last page, wasn't it? Definitely admissible evidence, I'd say. And fairly damning, too."

"Espionage?" David repeated.

"If this information were to fall into Tsarosian hands—if, say, you planned for it—"

"But I didn't."

Douglas huffed a laugh, sitting back in his chair. "You think that matters, Felman?"

Reeling, David glanced over at Jade, then back at the sergeant. "Be that as it may—you couldn't convict Jade," he said, thinking quickly. "There's no evidence of her involvement."

"Of course there is," Major Hathaway said, his voice laced with scorn. "There always is. If it's not immediately available, we'll *find* it."

"We have every legal avenue open to us." The sergeant folded his arms, his head turned toward Jade, who was silent, her gaze fixed on the table and expression unreadable. "Ms. Atallah, you have a choice here—the best choice you're going to get. You can either be sensible, or you can go down with him."

There was a moment's pause, in which Jade neither spoke nor looked up. Worried, David turned to her.

"Jade," he said quietly, "forget about this. You have to get out now, while they'll still let you."

For a few seconds, she didn't respond. Then she looked up abruptly and met his gaze. Hers was cool, impassive.

"Okay," she said.

David waited for her to say more, but she didn't. They looked at each other for a long moment, and David's stomach twisted so hard it squeezed the breath from his lungs.

It doesn't matter, he tried to tell himself, tearing his eyes away from hers. *It's more important that she doesn't go down with you.*

It was better this way—better that she walked away easily, with no remorse or regrets. Better that she walked away *now*, rather than arguing out of a sense of attachment. David had failed to do the one thing he had assured her: he hadn't saved her dragoncoat. Instead, he'd ruined her career as a Coat Warden. She had every right to clean her hands of this mess, and never look back.

And whatever was between them? He was glad it had happened, but he was not so stubborn that he would condemn her to his own fate. He couldn't. That would kill him faster than an espionage charge.

Major Hathaway exchanged a dour glance with Douglas, who hissed a low laugh, almost under his breath. "I almost feel bad, Felman," he said, fixing David with a contradictory look of absolute delight. "That's *cold*."

"Ms. Atallah, you have officially been discharged from Flighter duty," Hathaway said, his tone crisp and businesslike. "We will send a notice to your address, for your records. We expect your continued silence regarding the operations of the Blackwing Program. You are forbidden to contact your replacement Coat Warden. If you attempt to do so, we may revisit the terms of your discharge. Is that clear?"

Without emotion, Jade gave a curt nod.

"Thank you. You may leave."

She rose to her feet, walking stiffly toward the door. She paused with her hand on the doorknob, glancing back at David. He wanted to call after her; there were a million things he wanted to say to Jade, most of them pointless and confusing, and all of them ill-advised.

Before she stepped into the hallway, her eyes met his for an instant, and he could have sworn that he saw a flash of green in the depths of her irises. Then the moment was over, and she was gone, the door closing behind her.

CHAPTER

FIFTEEN

When Jade arrived at David's apartment, the door was slightly ajar, the wood splintered around the handle as though it had been kicked in by force. She brushed straight past it without pausing to examine the damage. There was no point; she knew exactly what had happened. Either Blackwing had sent their lackeys here to arrest David first, or they'd sent agents after the fact to search the place for evidence.

Judging by the apartment's state, the latter was more likely. The place had been ransacked. The living room was strewn with loose papers and old sketches, and the couch, for some reason, had been overturned.

Jade skirted past it. "Levi!" she called. "Where the hell are you?"

Outside the warehouse windows, the sky was a pale yellow. The sun was beginning to rise. Jade glanced at the clock that rested on the kitchen counter—almost seven in the morning. If Levi had spent the night here, he'd left early.

On the coffee table, amid the scattered drawings and

rejected *Coated Crusader* pages, there was a note written upon a folded scrap of lined, yellow paper, in what Jade immediately recognized as David's careful hand:

JADE—LEVI has somewhere we can print, so we're headed there now. I can't tell you where it is. Levi says it's too risky. I'll see you once we're finished. David.

JADE CURSED UNDER HER BREATH. It was probably for the best that he'd given her next to no information. Anything helpful in this note would've been more useful to Blackwing than it was to her, seeing as they'd gotten here first.

What were they looking for?

She scanned the small apartment, her brow furrowed. If the cops had seized the plates of David's comic, then he and Levi had at least made it to the printing press. They hadn't arrested him here. So why had his apartment been searched?

What had Douglas said exactly?

We have the plates for your final issue. The cops still haven't found your originals, but we don't need 'em.

The originals, Jade realized, her heart sinking. *They were looking for the originals. Of course.* Doubtless, her superiors at Blackwing hadn't trusted Levi not to publish. They couldn't arrest him, as there was no evidence that he'd been aware of David's plans to reveal Blackwing's secret, but they could put paid to *The Coated Crusader.*

A mere hour ago, on Staten Island, Douglas had admitted that the police hadn't found David's originals, so at least there was one ray of hope. And if the police hadn't found them, then David must have hidden them.

Despite the gravity of the situation, Jade had to fight the

urge to smile. David didn't know it, but his paranoid streak had thrown her a lifeline.

Jade unfolded the slip of paper, wondering if there was more to David's note. Inside, in smaller text, he had written:

P.S. If you want a number to call, just for your own peace of mind, you'll find it at the place where our mutual friend set up our first date.

OUR MUTUAL FRIEND... Jade's first thought was of the movie theater that Levi had sent them to. Then she remembered: their first *date*. Margie's ridiculous guise for arranging her meet-up with David. His memorial for Backscatter, at the park.

Excitement flooded her. When she'd met David at the park, she'd returned the green folder to him, the one that had contained his evidence against Blackwing—and *he'd hidden it inside the memorial.* He had a hiding place at the park. She glanced back down at the note, her heartbeat fast enough to make her feel breathless. Had he known this would happen? Did he hope she might find the originals?

She couldn't be sure, but either way, she had her first lead. She had to find those pages—and then she had to find Levi.

Hastily, Jade stuffed the note into her pocket. She looked around David's trashed apartment. For this to work, there were a few things she would need.

The first was her blonde wig, stuck beneath the backrest of overturned couch. Jade extricated it carefully, running her fingers through the tangled locks. She slipped it on, tucking her dark braid beneath the cap, and glanced into the cracked hand mirror on David's drafting desk. The wig was disheveled, as if she'd just had a particularly rough night, but it would have to do.

Next, she flung open the top drawer below the desk, rummaging through David's supplies. His inks and pens were in disarray, likely from Blackwing's search; Jade remembered these drawers being meticulous when she'd last gone through them, looking for a pencil to sketch David in his sleep.

She dug through David's closet for the modified trunk he'd shown her in the park, then she began to fill it with supplies. Carefully, she laid a ream of fresh paper on top of everything, then she closed and latched the trunk, lugging it behind her as she left the apartment.

BY THE TIME Jade arrived at Van Cortlandt Park, the day was in full swing. She'd been cautious on her way over, instructing the cab driver to take several wrong turns and misdirections. If the cabbie had been suspicious, he hadn't said anything. A longer drive meant a higher fare, which Jade paid in excess when he dropped her off a few blocks away from the park.

She walked briskly, the ink bottles clinking together in David's steamer trunk with each of her steps. Through the errant tendrils of blonde hair, she kept a watchful eye on the street around her and behind her. If she'd had Night Armor with her, she wouldn't have needed to worry about going unnoticed, or losing a tail; as visible as a black dragoncoat was during the early hours of the day, she still would've been able to fly, taking a much harder route to follow. Perhaps it was good that she didn't have Night Armor. Caution was key, and she would feel far more foolhardy in her Flighter team.

Her Flighter team. She wondered if they'd called up Derkins, her second, a peevish young man with whom she'd never gotten along—either in the academy or afterward. Jade suspected that they hadn't. There was little point in notifying Night Armor's second warden if they didn't expect the drag-

THE INK DRAGON AND THE ART OF FLIGHT

oncoat to survive the year. More than likely, they would replace her with Derkins on all of Night Armor's official records, but never let him know he'd been promoted. It would be easier to keep a lid on the situation if fewer people were aware of it.

Jade's hand tightened on the handle of the trunk. If that was true, it was further proof of what she'd already surmised: that Hathaway and Douglas were going off-book, drafting false reports on the realities of the Blackwing Program.

At the park, Jade took a long look at her surroundings before stepping off the path, wading through the dewy grass toward the copse of trees where David had hidden his memorial. She paused to scoop up a pebble that nudged her foot, then ducked beneath the low-hanging branches to find the stone pillar. Before she knelt beside it, she laid the small rock on top of it, beside the collection of other pebbles that David had kept there.

"Don't worry, Backscatter," she said quietly, her hand on the stone. "Everything's going to be okay. I'll make sure of it."

She crouched down to run her fingers along the stone, looking for the opening where David had stored his documents. When she found it, she pulled out all of the papers. A folded sheet of yellow paper fell out with them, fluttering to the ground.

Her heart in her throat, Jade snatched up the lined paper, unfolding it. There, in the same pen as the note he'd left at the apartment, David had written:

JADE —

IF YOU'RE READING THIS, *that means something has gone wrong—or that you're looking to find me. Call the number below and ask for Felix. He's the one helping us print.*

. . .

I wish we could have had more time together.

– David

Beneath David's signature, he had written the promised phone number and address. She folded the note carefully along its crease, tucking it into her pocket beside the other one.

Jade balanced the stack of papers on her lap. They weren't as damp as she feared they would be; all of them were still usable, protected from the elements by their hiding place. She flipped through them. There was the folder she'd stolen— David's evidence against Blackwing. She held onto it. Even if she failed, she would find a way to get this back to Margie, or even Levi. The information was far more likely to spread with *The Coated Crusader* than with an independent paper, but it needed to get out, whether she managed to print the comic or not.

Beneath the folder, to her profound relief, were pages of *The Coated Crusader*. The originals, bearing the more intricate details of David's drawings that didn't translate in the printing process. She lifted the pages to her nose and inhaled the scent of ink.

"Okay," she murmured, taking a deep breath. She glanced between the memorial and the steamer trunk, resting in the grass a few feet away from her. "Let's get this done."

—

A CALL to Felix at a payphone pointed Jade in the direction of a flophouse on the Bowery, one of several of its type. Jade caught a cab, arriving at the place just as the sun was disappearing below the buildings around her. It was a shabby, decrepit building, practically falling apart. As Jade stepped into the entryway, a cold draft floated through the hall, and a fat cockroach skittered over her foot. She suppressed a retch, a shudder shooting down her spine.

Jade found the door to Levi's rented unit—number six—and pounded on it with a closed fist. She heard a few thumps from inside, and Levi's irascible voice:

"What the hell do you want, copper?"

"Levi, it's Jade," she called back. She pounded harder on the door. "Open up! It's important!"

There were footsteps from within, and a few seconds later, Levi swung the door open. Jade blinked, taken aback at his appearance. He was even more disheveled than usual—his clothes rumpled, half of his collar flipped up, his shirt untucked. There were dark circles beneath his bloodshot eyes as he scowled at her, all of his usual vim and vigor gone. She thought she could detect the sharp, antiseptic scent of moonshine, but when she looked around the near-closet-sized room, which contained little more than a cot and a wooden chest, she couldn't see a bottle.

"Ah, it really is you," Levi said, his lip curled as though the words were bitter on his tongue. "Thought you'd be some Blackwing crony." He paused, cocking his head to one side. "Oh, wait."

"David doesn't have time for this," Jade snapped. "I need your help."

"Oh, *David*?" Levi folded his arms, leaning against the doorframe. "You seriously came here to lecture me about Felman? You've got some nerve."

"Blackwing arrested him. He's—"

"I know. I was there," Levi said slowly. Jade had never heard him speak slowly before. There was something unsettling about his tone, an undercurrent of real anger that she hadn't even heard when his apartment had burned. She didn't realize that it was directed at her until he spoke again, his tone as dry and sour as vinegar. "Do us both a favor, Coat Warden. Dry up."

Jade's grip tightened on the manila folder tucked beneath her arm. This wasn't what she'd expected. She'd thought—hoped—that she would show up at the Bowery and find Levi fired up, ready to charge into action. "Excuse me?"

"You heard me." Levi stepped back over the threshold and made to close the door. Before he could, Jade pushed a hand against it, stopping its progress.

"Will you listen to me, you stubborn son of a—"

"Get off," Levi growled, struggling to push the door shut. "*Oy*, you're strong. What do they feed you Coat Wardens? Just *get out of*—"

Jade forced her way into the room, and Levi slammed the door behind her, breathing heavily. He turned to glower, his chest heaving. Now that they were both in Levi's new quarters, the room seemed even smaller, the bare walls pressing uncomfortably close. The ceiling was higher than the room was wide. Beneath the undeniable stench of alcohol, Jade thought there was also an undercurrent of dampness and mildew.

"You've got one hell of a fitness regimen, fly girl," Levi muttered.

Jade held the folder out in front of him. His gaze didn't drop to it until she shook it slightly, demanding his attention.

"What is this?"

In answer, Jade opened the folder to show him the first page of *The Coated Crusader's* final issue. Levi swore quietly, under his breath, and closed his eyes.

"You and I are going to publish this thing," Jade told him.

"Says you," Levi scoffed.

"I've got all of the original pages." *And then some.* "We need to do this—for David's sake."

Levi shook his head, incredulous. "Are you outta your mind? You think that publishing the comic would *help* him? You're signing his death warrant—and mine! Only thing that's left is to drop this, or we both fry, and frankly I'd rather if neither of—"

"They're charging him with espionage," Jade interrupted fiercely. "Under military law. It doesn't matter what we do. You could behave yourself, and they'd still kill him. You could hide under a rock for the rest of your life, and they'd still kill him."

Levi's shoulders dropped. All of his aggression seemed to evaporate as he stared at her in disbelief. "What?"

"Espionage," Jade repeated. "And sedition. They want him to go down."

"No, they couldn't. They wouldn't dare—"

"They're daring as we speak. I was in the room when they told him," Jade said. Her heart sank when she thought of how coldly she had treated David, and the morose look he'd given her as she left. She wished she could have been honest with him, but she had needed Hathaway and Douglas to think that she was turning her back on the whole situation, or they never would have let her leave that base.

"But—but there's no evidence of espionage," Levi protested.

"They have all the evidence they need, and what they don't have, they'll just make."

Levi sank down onto the thin mattress, his expression contorting into one of despair. He was quiet for a few seconds, then muttered something in Yiddish, his head falling into his hands. Jade suddenly felt like a voyeur; she regretted telling him, even though she'd had no choice.

"But we still have a chance to help him," she said quickly.

Levi, fingers digging into his silver-dusted hair, hunched

over further. "Help him? I've killed him." He sounded hoarse, like he was parched, and his voice was unsteady. "I told him I'd publish him because I was so sure that all those threats were nothing but hot air. When they burned down Freedom Press, I thought that was as far as they would go. He asked me if we should keep printing, and I said, 'Of course, to hell with them.' And now—*zayt mir moykhl*, David. I should've stopped you, you crazy bastard."

"Please, listen to me," Jade begged. She was growing desperate; she needed Levi, or the whole plan would fall apart. "We know where he is right now. They haven't taken him off Staten Island. This might be our only chance to do something about this. You've got to trust me. Our only option is to print this."

She was expecting more questions, but Levi just sighed through his nose, leaning back against the wall. "Felix would never help me now. Not after what happened."

"Well... I need you to figure it out."

For a long moment, Levi stared at the ceiling. Jade waited for him to argue more, or to kick her back out into the hallway, but he did neither. Instead, he looked at Jade through heavy eyelids, his lips twitching into a reluctant half smile.

"Felman was so stuck on you, you know. I never saw him like that before." He huffed a soft laugh, shaking his head. "He was always just holed up with his dragoncoat sketches and his memories. I've known plenty of people like that. Too much happened to 'em, and they'd hide away from the world, like they could put a stop to it somehow. But then you came around, and all of the sudden, there's Felman. Going to the movies. Taking you out for dinner. Smiling all the time. Multiple times a day, even."

"Levi—"

"And I thought to myself, what're the chances this works out well for him? I wish it could've, you know? Felman—he was a good man, and a good friend. Weird guy, to be sure, and a bit of a *schlimazel*, but... wouldn't it be swell, if he got to be happy?"

"Levi, he's not dead."

Pursing his lips, Levi shrugged, his listless gaze fixed on the worm-eaten floor.

"Why do you think I'm here?" Jade demanded. "I'm not just going to sit back and let this happen. I'm putting up a fight, and I need you to do the same."

"A fight? What do you mean, 'a fight'? I don't know if you've noticed, but you're holding the pages for a comic book."

"David was fighting the whole time, and this comic book was his weapon." Jade sat down on the cot beside Levi, and the metal framework squeaked in protest at their combined weight. She let the folder fall open to one of David's finished pages, the ink especially bold amidst the shabbiness of the flophouse room. "He was fighting against the government, true, but he was also fighting against personal demons. He was fighting against loss and grief. He was fighting to live! And I think this will help him do that very thing."

"What do you have in mind?" Levi asked warily.

"First things first—we need a press. Give your friend Felix a call and see if you can smooth things over. And if that doesn't work, try to figure out a backup plan."

Silence settled over the boarding room, broken only by the muffled sounds of another tenant yelling from upstairs. Jade heard a tiny squeak, and she turned to see a plump mouse scuttling behind the trunk. As its tail vanished from sight, she glanced up at Levi, who raised a lethargic eyebrow at her.

"Nice place," she muttered. "Didn't know you had a roommate."

"That's Frankie," he said, with a touch of his normal spirit. "Lay off him. He's got a family to feed."

They both watched the trunk for a while, as if waiting for

Frankie to make a reappearance. Then Jade turned to face the editor, meeting his gaze.

"Come on, Levi. You've got more important things to be doing than sitting around in this slum, blaming yourself and cowering from Blackwing. That won't help anyone. So how about it?"

With a deep inhale, Levi stretched his arms above his head. He blinked rapidly, as if bringing his eyes into focus. "Okay. Fine. I hear you."

Relief flooded Jade, but at the same time, her heart spiked with a rush of urgency. They needed to act fast. Everything was out of her hands except for these comic pages. "So what do you have for me?"

"I'll give Felix a call. And I might have a few alternatives." Levi tapped his chin, his brow furrowed in thought. "Not all of them are *legal,* mind you, but at this point, I don't think that really matters."

"Great," Jade said, getting to her feet. "Whatever you get us, it just needs to be able to print thirty-eight pages."

Frowning, Levi looked up at her. "Wait, what are you talking about? The last issue only had thirty-six. I could've sworn...."

Despite the gravity of the situation, Jade couldn't help but smile. She gestured to the open folder, lying on the cot. "Why don't you go ahead and take another look?"

CHAPTER

SIXTEEN

By far, the worst aspect of being locked up on the Blackwing base, David decided, was the boredom.

The Staten Island facility featured one block of holding cells. The walls were whitewashed, and the paint flaked from the iron bars. David was alone in the cell row, and he could only amuse himself by peeling the paint away from the metal, leaving bare patches exposed. He wondered if this isolation was an intentional part of his punishment, or incidental, a byproduct of the situation that the sergeant didn't see fit to address.

As far as he could tell, he'd been locked up for the better part of two days. It was difficult to keep track of the time; there was no window in the cellblock, so he couldn't watch the sun rise and fall. He had to ask the guards for the time as they came in with food and water, hoping that they would be sympathetic enough to glance at their watches and tell him.

When the outer door opened for the fifth time since the inner cell door had locked him in, David was relieved to see a friendly face. Margie stepped into the narrow corridor, her expression grave. Her short hair, normally slicked carefully back over her scalp, was rumpled and spiky.

"Oh, it's you," David said, standing up from the cell's wire cot. "I was worried you weren't going to drop by."

Margie pursed her lips, approaching the cell. "I have something for you."

"What?"

It was only then that David noticed the booklet tucked under Margie's arm. She withdrew it, sliding it through the bars of the cell. David took it, his eyes widening in surprise at the feel of the glossy laminate on the cover.

His breath caught in his throat when he got a good look at the cover. It was the final *Coated Crusader*, printed and bound. Sure, it was a little rougher around the edges, and the paper was cheaper than ever before, but it was still whole and complete. And most importantly, it was done. He stared at it for a long moment, running his thumb along the edge of the pages.

Backscatter... we did it.

"They actually printed it," David said finally. "They printed it!"

Margie tapped the iron bars and stepped back, her chin held high. "I thought you might want something to look at. It's dull in here."

"I think it's supposed to be," David said wryly. "Are you going to get in trouble for bringing me this?"

Margie shot him a smile, a gleam in her eyes. "I don't expect so. They're scrambling out there. Distracted. They have a bit of an image problem at the moment."

An image problem.

"I just finished reading this to Night Armor," Margie continued, something akin to an actual smile playing at her lips for the first time since he'd met her. "He loved it, of course. Especially the parts with the black dragon at the end..."

The reminder of Night Armor—a still-living, still-

202

breathing Blackwing dragoncoat, whose death was not set in stone—served as a monument to the comic's ultimate purpose.

The weight of Night Armor's future loss suddenly dampened the joy he'd felt seeing the finished issue. David lifted the comic, flipping it open to the final page. There, in his own careful handwriting, was the truth. His message about Blackwing, written out in full. It explained the nature of the program, the experimentation undergone by the dragoncoats, their resulting ailments, their premature and painful deaths. He had expanded it since the burning of Freedom Press to include a detailed account of Blackwing's attempts to stop the comic's publication.

It was all there, exactly as he had planned it. And his fate was sealed.

David couldn't bring himself to feel anything but shock at the audacity of his friend, out there risking it all. *God love you, Levi.* He'd expected Blackwing's retribution, and now that the comic book was out in the world, a copy of it in his hands, he was resigned to whatever happened next.

"Thank you, Margie," David said, closing the comic. "I appreciate it."

With a firm nod, Margie reached through the bars of the cell to clap her hand awkwardly on David's shoulder. "You did good."

David opened his mouth to respond, but he couldn't find the words. Instead, he just shook his head. There was no way that he could thank Margie for everything she had done for him, and all of the personal risks she had taken to do it.

She seemed to understand. She squeezed his shoulder and gave him a fond look. "You take care of yourself, all right?"

David huffed a weak laugh. He gestured to his surroundings. "It's a little late for that."

"Ah, don't act like that," she said, withdrawing her hand

with a reproachful look on her face. "This isn't the end of the line. That beautiful girl is out there waiting for you."

"I hope not," David said. If the cold, mask-like expression Jade had worn in front of the officers was anything to go by, she was halfway across East America by now—and it was better that way.

"Don't be such a wet blanket, Felman."

With that, Margie turned to leave the cell row. She looked back over her shoulder before she left. "Oh, and you really should read all the comic," she said. "Maybe you'll get some inspiration like our mutual friend has." The cryptic words hung in the air for a second, but as he was about to comment, she shot him a quick wink. Then she was gone, and he was alone once more.

Bemused, David glanced down at the comic in his hand. He paced to the back of the cell and settled on the cot, re-tracing all of the cover's lines with his gaze—the sleek scales on the eponymous Crusader's hood, the wavering lines of Blindside's spirit as it hovered above. David's fingers itched for a pen and a scrap of paper. By his calculations, he hadn't gone this long without sketching in several years.

I hope something comes of this, old friend, he thought, as if Backscatter was as present as the dragoncoat's ghost in the comic book. *I'm sorry that neither of us got to see the results, but at least we finished what we started.*

David leaned back against the cinderblock wall. He dropped the comic in his lap and proceeded to thumb through it, wondering what Margie had meant by inspiration, when he came to a page that stopped him cold.

A page he didn't recognize.

David frowned, sitting upright. These panels—he hadn't drawn them. The style of the artwork seemed to imitate his, but they were noticeably different. The character designs were less consistent, more stylized. The penmanship was different in the speech bubbles, the letters longer and written in a lighter hand.

He snatched up the comic book to inspect it more closely. The first panel featured a voiceover from the black dragon, telling his story to the other characters in a floating, yellow box. In the scene depicted, an asphalt drive cut through a manicured lawn, leading up to a brick structure—unmistakably the Blackwing base, rendered in immaculate detail. It could only have been drawn by someone who had seen it before.

Jade.

David clutched the pages as though they were a lifeline.

She did this. Why did she do this?

In the next panel, the black dragon explained that he and his Coat Warden were imprisoned by the Black Dragon Gang, the same nefarious organization that had ambushed Blindside. The drawing showed the dragoncoat standing in the back of a cell, shadowed. Only his outline was visible, along with one gleaming, golden eye.

"They kept us separate. They thought they could prevent us from escaping if neither of us could reach the other. But I knew that base like I knew my own scales."

A new panel, in which the black dragon lunged at a white-coated medic, forcing his way into the hallway beyond his cell. The fluidity in Jade's drawing was impressive. David thought back to her sketch of him in his sleep, her doodles of Blindside on the restaurant's paper tablecloth as he had helped hone that raw talent.

"And I think we both know it's impossible to lock down a dragoncoat who doesn't want to be contained."

A harsh yell from the hallway made David look up from the comic book, his heart racing. Was Margie in trouble? He heard footsteps, but they seemed to be moving away from the cellblock, like the guards posted outside had been called away for some reason.

The next panel of Jade's addition didn't feature the black dragoncoat at all. It was a detailed, overhead map of the Blackwing base that took up half the page, a route traced out in dotted arrows. A route that led from the dragoncoat infirmary... all the way to the jail.

Oh.

From the hall, David heard the unmistakable, high-frequency sound of a dragoncoat's shriek, followed by more human yelling.

On the page, the black dragon hurtled over the heads of a row of soldiers, then turned and breathed a pool of acid onto the ceiling behind himself. The corrosive liquid ate through the concrete, and rubble fell into the hallway with an appropriately-labeled *CRASH*.

Somewhere in the corridors of the base, there was a tremendous rumble that made the cell floor vibrate, like a peal of thunder. David heard a scream, and closer to the jail, a dragoncoat's shrill cry.

No weapons can stop him! No trap can hold him! Night Armor's voice chirped and whistled through the stone.

The jail door burst open as a coal-black dragoncoat pounced on it, ripping it from its hinges. Night Armor, his tail whipping out behind him like a tendril of smoke, skidded to a halt in front of David's cell. His wingtips brushed the bars of the cells around him, too wide for the narrow corridor between them. Despite the obvious signs of his illness—the slight wheeze of his breath, a tremor in his legs—his eyes were alight with excitement, his slit pupils fixed upon David.

And with a mighty surge, the *Winged Avenger* tears through solid metal! Night Armor chirped gleefully. His talons closed around the bars, and a low growl sounded in his throat as he ripped them free from their concrete foundations. A cloud of dust descended upon the cell, and a shower of debris rained down on Night Armor, sprinkling his head with chips of cement. He didn't seem to notice. <u>Just in the nick of time, he—</u>

"Night Armor! What are you doing?"

The dragon paused his narration, swinging his head toward David and tipping it to one side. Particles of concrete fell from behind his horns. <u>What does it look like I'm doing?</u>

That, David decided, was a fair question. He stood back, pressed against the far wall, as Night Armor smashed the rest of his way into the cell, then he turned to face the cinderblock wall.

<u>No mere walls can hold him!</u> Night Armor declared. <u>It's impossible to lock down a dragoncoat who doesn't want to be</u> — He was interrupted by a sudden fit of coughing. When it subsided, he sniffed and finished, <u>contained.</u>

He blinked over at David, shuffling his talons as though self-conscious.

<u>It's the dust. You know. From the concrete.</u>

"I... of course it is." Up close, David could see that Night Armor's eyes were moist and fever-bright. His breath rasped on the intake, a phlegmy rattle in his throat. The illness was taking its toll. Night Armor was probably running on adrenaline alone.

David glanced nervously at the hole the dragoncoat had left into the main hallway. With his Flighter hearing, he could make out the sound of footsteps headed in their direction, even through the persistent blare of the alarm. "Do you have a plan to escape the rest of the way, or do we have to—"

<u>Jade does. Didn't you see the message she left me?</u>

David glanced down at the comic book, hanging open in his hand. "Yes. I saw. But—"

<u>Isn't it swell? A secret code, just for me!</u>

"How did you know those pages were a message for you?"

She's my Coat Warden, Night Armor told him. _Of course I knew._

There was a shout from the hallway. David rounded on the dragoncoat. "We have to get out of here."

Right. Night Armor turned to the outer wall and opened his maw. David recognized the familiar hissing sound that emanated from his throat. A jet of translucent, viridescent acid sprayed from Night Armor's mouth. It fizzed on the concrete, eating straight through the cinderblock. Night Armor kept up his acid breath until the opening in the wall was large enough for him to squeeze through. Wasting no time, David scrambled after him.

He tripped over the rubble and found himself outside, on his hands and knees, with the short-cropped lawn beneath his fingers. For a moment, he allowed himself to bask in the cool feeling of the grass on his skin. The sky above was gray, cloud covered, so that it was impossible to tell what time it was. He had dropped the comic book; it lay on the grass, open to Jade's pages. As he stood, he picked it up, searching the panels for her next instructions.

She'd made them clear. The last few panels featured a sequence in which the black dragon tunneled from the building to freedom using his acid breath...

And with the skies open above them, his Coat Warden climbed astride, the two of them kicking off into the air.

Oh, no. Jade, you can't be serious.

David lowered the comic book. To his dismay, Night Armor was looking at him expectantly, one wing dipped to the ground in an obvious invitation.

His heart sinking, David took a step back. "Wait. Are you sure—"

We don't have much time. Climb on.

He was right. The soldiers were in the cell row now, their

footfalls advancing. But still, David shook his head, a building sense of panic in his chest. "I can't do this."

Why not? You know how, don't you?

"Yes—but—" How could he explain it? He'd spent every waking hour of every day focused on the sensation of dragon-flight, the motions, the forms. Its thematic potential. How he could capture it safely in his work, like bottling lightning, without living through it again.

Flying with Backscatter had been the most freeing feeling in the world. But the idea of flying without him....

He met Night Armor's gaze, and the black dragoncoat blinked calmly back at him.

You're the Coated Crusader, Night Armor chirped. You'll always be able to fly.

From behind him, David heard one of the soldiers call, "This way! They broke through the wall!"

That made up his mind. Stepping onto Night Armor's outstretched wing, he climbed onto the dragoncoat's back. Night Armor's saddle was gone; David hadn't ridden a dragon bareback since he was a kid in the academy, but he didn't have much choice. He tried to find purchase on the black scales as Night Armor's wings rose on either side of him, stirring the grass below.

It was easier than he'd expected it to be. Night Armor was much smaller than Backscatter had been—Jade had mentioned that he was the runt of the litter, barely large enough to be selected for the early stages of Flighter training—but finding balance on a dragoncoat was second nature to David. It surprised him. He'd thought that the knowledge was gone, buried under years of grief.

Say the line, Night Armor said eagerly. Go on, say the line.

Through the opening in the wall, David watched the first of the soldiers step through the broken bars of the cell, his sidearm drawn. There were several others behind him. "Night Armor, please, just—"

Night Armor stomped one of his feet, his tail flicking in annoyance. <u>Don't be a killjoy! I'm not taking off until you say it!</u>

David squeezed his eyes shut, tears flush on his cheeks as he roared, "Let's fly, old chum!"

With a high-pitched, untranslatable squeal of joy, Night Armor launched himself into the air, just as the soldiers began to spill out into the lawn. David flattened himself against the dragoncoat's neck, holding on as they surged toward the sky.

Several loud blasts split the air—*gunshots*. David forced himself to look down. The soldiers below had their pistols raised, aimed at the escaping dragoncoat and his rider.

Luckily, Night Armor was one half of an elite, highly-trained Flighter team, and David could just about remember being the other half of a different one. When the black-scaled dragon swerved to the left, David was ready for it, balanced and in sync with the dragon's motion. When Night Armor went into an evasive roll, David remembered practicing a similar maneuver with Backscatter, and he managed to cling to the dragoncoat's neck. He kept his eyes tightly closed, concentrating on nothing but staying with Night Armor, thinking of nothing but the rapidly-increasing distance to the ground.

<u>See?</u> Night Armor crowed in delight. <u>You're fine. You never really forget.</u>

David's heart was in his throat, leaving him too breathless to form a cogent reply. As Night Armor's erratic flight leveled off, he sat taller, opening his wind-whipped eyes.

They were hundreds of feet in the air, probably close to a thousand. Far below, he could make out the grounds of the Blackwing base, giving way to the gray waters of the Upper Bay.

For all of his artistic focus on the motion of dragoncoats, he'd forgotten about the view from mid-flight. From up here, he could see for miles—to the ocean behind them, toward Manhattan ahead, at the fork where the two rivers split from the bay. Boats cut their way through the water below, leaving thin trails of white in their wakes. The city itself was a dense cluster of buildings, pale limestone and russet brick, tightly packed and towering, and as it always had, it promised shelter. Refuge, however temporary.

David found himself laughing into the wind, unable to stop himself. The fear had given way to sheer adrenaline, and he had to resist the urge to fling his arms out, to let the air rush through his fingers.

Night Armor turned his head. <u>What's so funny?</u>

"Nothing," David called back, raising his voice to be heard over the roar of the wind. "Head for the city. We need to get to ground before they send more Flighters after us."

Night Armor banked steeply, racing toward downtown. Toward freedom.

CHAPTER
SEVENTEEN

After hundreds of miles of endless plains, Jade had been convinced that the landscape west of the great river they'd crossed would never change from the rolling, green, windswept prairie.

But after a few days' flight, their surroundings had changed abruptly. The grasslands had been cut short by a scar of sandy-white and red stone, dropping off into steep, eroded slopes and sharp canyons. From the top of the ridge they rested upon, Jade could see for miles past the bare earth of the scar, from the lower plains below all the way to the pine-strewn foothills on the horizon. She wondered if these would eventually transform into the great mountains that she knew spanned the western edge of the Open Sky Nation, bordering Tsarosia.

She worked as she took in the view, humming to herself. She had amassed a collection of copper scraps, and she'd taken the time during Olive's molt to fashion scales from the pieces. The look wasn't entirely perfect; some of her dragoncoat's new scales were pressed pennies. But she had done her best to cut the copper plating into the aerodynamic shape of Olive's old, black scales, which now sat in a pile a few hundred yards away.

Aside from the occasional hissed complaint at the odd look of the copper scales, Olivewing wasn't paying Jade much mind. His focus was on the plain ahead of them, which was dotted with a herd of massive, slowly grazing bison.

I didn't know there were animals like that, he chirped, his pupils shifting in size as he tried to get a better look at the bison. What are they? They're neat-looking.

Jade pressed a copper piece to the exposed innerskin on Olivewing's shoulder. "They're bison, Olive."

They look like cows, but... scarier.

"Yeah, we're going to give them plenty of space. We're staying up here until you're ready to fly again."

Olivewing's tail flicked in disappointment, and the sunlight from the broad sky above glinted off the new scales. *It's strange,* Jade thought, *to see Olivewing as a copper again.* Even before Blackwing had replaced his scales, he had spent the majority of the time washed in the greenish, weathered patina that had earned him his name.

There were clouds gathering on the horizon—rains to come. Soon, the shining copper would be chemically altered once more, and Olive would look like the same dragoncoat he had been before Blackwing's intervention.

Almost. The same dragoncoat, but with the new, jaunty tilt to his head, a new confidence in his eyes. Night Armor had been the runt of the litter, all but rejected by the other two members of Jade's trangle at the academy—smaller than the other dragons, unsure of himself, slow and shy to make decisions in the field. But Olivewing, in his reappearance, had grown in his own esteem. As they'd traveled from the east, Jade had noticed the change in him.

And she suspected those ridiculous comic books were to thank.

She glanced to her right, toward the pile of discarded scales, where David was digging into the rich clay. A smile crept across her lips. He wasn't particularly efficient at the task; he'd been at it for at least twenty minutes, but the shovel kept slipping from his grasp. Despite the breeze rippling through the grass around her, Jade could still hear his muttered kvetching. The hole was barely past his knees.

As if he could feel Jade's stare, he looked up and met her gaze, tilting his head in confusion. "What?" he called, leaning on the shovel. "Something wrong?"

"No," Jade replied, raising her voice to be heard over the wind. "Just... take a break and come over here for a second."

"If you say so." He foot-pressed the edge of the shovel into to the ground, leaving it to stand on its own like a short, crooked flagpole. He dusted his hands and climbed out of the hole, striding over to her and Olivewing. He gave the dragoncoat a nod. "The copper looks good. It suits you well."

Olive blinked placidly, giving David an affectionate nudge with his forehead. You don't have to say that. It doesn't look anywhere *near* as stylish.

"No, I like it," David insisted. "Genuinely. Look how your scales shine now."

Olive ducked his head, his claws clicking together as he fought to keep his expression modest. It'll be all dull and green before long.

"Even better. When your scales become weathered, it shows that you've lived."

A trilling sound emanated from high in Olive's throat; Jade had never found an appropriate translation for the noise, but she heard it often when her dragoncoat was pleased. He lifted his head and paced away through the tall grass. When he had put some distance between himself and the humans, he turned his head to one side, watching the light shift on the copper as he flexed his wings experimentally.

214

Jade glanced at David, who was smiling after the drag-oncoat. He took a deep, contented breath, then he met her gaze.

"What?" he asked.

"What do you mean, 'what?'"

"You were staring."

"Nothing," Jade said, feeling warm despite the slight chill of the wind. She didn't want to mention how relaxed David seemed, now that Blackwing was far away from all three of them and *The Coated Crusader* was complete. It had been a slow development, and it felt premature to bring it up, like his happiness was some kind of delicate green plantlet that had only just broached the soil. "That was a nice thing you said to Olive."

He shrugged. "I meant it. I'd have liked to get Backscatter's silver back on him, and I would have liked even more to watch it tarnish at the edges."

He spoke simply, without the heaviness that begged sympathy. A wave of instinctive pity rose in Jade, but she waited for it to subside, knowing that David didn't want it. Instead, she reached out to take his hand in hers, squeezing his fingers.

After a brief period of gentle silence, David said, "What did you call me over for, anyway? I was making good progress digging over there."

"Oh, please." Jade laughed. "Let's take a look at your hands, shall we?" David didn't pull away as she flipped his palm upright, examining it closely. The skin along the base of his fingers was blistered, red and inflamed where he had gripped the shovel.

"You're right. I'm soft," David said easily. "Guilty as charged."

"Don't worry. I won't let them convict you for it."

David's hand slipped from hers, coming to rest on her cheek. His thumb brushed the side of her face. For a moment, she closed her eyes, leaning into his touch. Then she stepped forward, rising to her toes to kiss him.

"*Ikh hob dich lib*," he said, when she paused to catch her breath. "But you already know that, don't you?"

"Depends. What does that mean?"

He pulled her close again, then he leaned down to whisper the answer to her. "I love you."

"Oh. I did know that," she said. He laughed, and she interrupted him with another kiss, smiling against his lips.

When they broke apart, they spent a few seconds only inches from each other. The sunlight, unbroken by clouds for miles, illuminated David's brown irises as he gazed at her fondly, as though he'd just woken up from a good dream.

"I love you, too," she told him.

"Well, that's a relief," he said, a gleam of humor in his eyes. "You never answered my question, by the way. What did you call me over here for?"

"I wanted to show you those." Jade gestured to the plain before them. David turned and lifted a hand to his forehead, squinting to see the meandering shapes of the bison.

"That's a good sign, isn't it?"

"I think so." If there were bison herds here, they were certainly well past the East American border, deep enough into Open Sky Nation that Blackwing and the military didn't dare follow.

With any luck, Sioux Falls was within two days' travel, and the three of them would be able to seek official asylum. While he completed his molt, Olivewing was still incapable of flight; even after his innerskin had recovered and accepted the new scales, he would still travel slowly with two passengers. As they'd fled New York, he had needed frequent rests to recoup his strength, and the progress of their exodus had been staggered. Most of their journey west had involved a nerve-racking, unsanctioned ride on a cargo train, though

Olivewing had flown them across the border by his own power.

It would be a relief to reach a more permanent sanctuary, where Olivewing could recover from the lingering effects of the scales' illness. The past two weeks of his molt had done wonders to stifle the dragoncoat's fever, but Jade could tell that Olive was still wearier than usual. If she had any say in the matter—and, finally, her opinion was relevant when it came to Olivewing's well-being—he would have a long, peaceful convalescence.

"Jade," David said, his voice quiet enough that it was almost lost to the wind. His light smile was gone, replaced by an unreadable expression.

"Yeah?"

He dug in his pocket and produced two of the sharp-edged black scales. They seemed to absorb the sunlight, reflecting nothing. "We should hold on to a few of these, I think. In case we ever need proof of what happened. Or maybe someone in the Open Sky Nation will want to study them—try to figure out why they made the dragoncoats ill. Perhaps something good can come from this, after all."

Jade shuddered, wrinkling her nose, but she nodded none-theless. "That seems reasonable."

"And I think we ought to mark the spot where we bury the rest," he continued. "So that we know where to find them, if we ever need to."

"I can't imagine why we would need to."

"Nor can I, but I don't want to regret my naivete, if it can be helped." He shuffled the scales in his hand as though they were a pair of tiny playing cards. "You know I prefer to err on the side of caution."

"Of course," she said. "And a good thing, too."

"Jade, what... what now?"

"What do you mean, 'what now?'"

"When we get to Sioux Falls. What comes next? What are we supposed to do?"

Jade considered that for a moment. In truth, she hadn't thought about it beyond the rest period she'd mentally prescribed for Olivewing. She didn't know what to expect from their would-be refuge, either. She knew little about the Open Sky Nation, and she had been drawn to it mostly for the fact that it wasn't East America.

But none of that bothered her. She'd never gotten anywhere through hesitation, and she wasn't about to start now.

"Whatever we want to do," she said, leaning against him. She slipped her arm around his waist, smiling as he met her gaze. "We'll let Olive recover. And then... who knows? I expect that Olive and I will still be a Flighter team, after a fashion. However it works here, we'll adapt to it. You'll keep turning your life—and whatever adventures we have—into stories. And both of us...."

She trailed off, watching the shadow of a cloud pass over the layered sandstone ravines and the bison herd that grazed the grasses beyond. She felt the comforting pressure of David's arm as he draped it around her shoulders, and behind her, at a distance, she heard Olivewing's steady, cheerful trill as he frolicked in the grass, enjoying the shine of his new scales.

"Both of us will keep drawing dragoncoats," she said. "Does that sound about right?"

She looked back up at him. A small smile played across his face.

"Sure," he said. "I think that sounds about right."

EPILOGUE

E arly April, Margie had been told, was one of the most pleasant times of the year to visit Washington. Of course, she hadn't had much choice when it came to the date.

But as she sat on the flat, marble steps at one end of the National Mall, looking out over the vast, rippling reflecting pool as a breeze stirred its surface, she had to admit that she'd gotten lucky with the timing of the summons. A little over a decade ago, East America's capital city had been gifted three thousand cherry trees, and now that it was spring, they were in full bloom, pink petals dotting the landscape and drifting through the air. Margie had a few hours until she was to resume her testimony before Congress, and she hoped to spend them in quiet solitude, enjoying the view of the mirror-like waters and the scent of the flowers.

As she shrugged her suit jacket over her shoulders and loosened her necktie, she heard approaching footfalls on the steps behind her.

"Fancy crossing your path this far from home, fed," a familiar voice said.

So much for solitude.

Pushing down her flicker of annoyance, Margie turned away from the reflecting pool. She'd only met Levi Adelman a few times in person—most recently, as the two of them worked together to help David and Jade flee to the Open Sky Nation—but he was hardly the type of person to fade easily from one's memory.

Levi was well dressed, by his standards, in a dark, pinstriped suit. It was adequately tailored but still rumpled, like everything he wore, as though he had come off worse in a fight on his way to the National Mall. A fedora was balanced at a jaunty angle on his head, and his prematurely pewter-gray curls seeped out from beneath the brim like a fringe of steel wool, pressed together with mousse—subdued, but never fully under control. In one hand, he carried a briefcase.

"Levi," Margie said, blinking up at him neutrally. "What on earth are you doing here?"

Levi settled on the step beside Margie, resting the briefcase between his knees. "Oh, me? I'm on trial. Supreme Court hears my case tomorrow."

"Ah," she murmured, unsure how to respond. "I'm... sorry to hear that."

He waved a dismissive hand. "It's fine, it's fine. It's in the bag. Flimsy charges. My legal counsel advised me to appeal it all the way here. Freedom of the press, right?"

"I'm assuming you have a good lawyer."

"The very best," he said. He pressed his thumb to his own chest. "I'm representing myself."

"Ah," Margie repeated, nodding slowly. After a moment's pause, she added in a delicate tone, "Why?"

For a few seconds, Levi frowned out at the reflecting pool. Then he said, "Turns out legal representation is a little pricier than it oughta be. Insurance still hasn't paid out for the printing press or the office, so I don't exactly have the bees at the moment."

"Are you still living in that flophouse on the Bowery?"

"No, no," Levi said airily. "Felman left the door to his apartment unlocked, and he leaves a spare key under the—"

"Levi!" Margie exclaimed, scandalized.

"What?"

"You're living in his *apartment*?"

Levi threw his hands up, exasperated. "Well, he's not using it! What, I'm just supposed to keep living in that *hekdish*? I'm paying the utilities on Felman's place, so I don't see the issue. Besides, he owes me, you know. If I hadn't helped print that last *Crusader*—"

"Yes, you're a real hero," Margie interrupted dryly. After hearing the story from every source possible, she was almost certain that Jade had been the real impetus behind the publication of the final *Coated Crusader*, but she didn't much feel like pointing out that fact.

Levi didn't seem to notice the sarcasm, or else he chose to ignore it. "I had to pay a train fare to get here, too. I barely have the dough to make it back to New York. But," he said quickly, noticing Margie's raised eyebrows, *"me krechts, me geht veyter,* like my bubbe used to say, you know?"

Margie shook her head. "No, I don't. I have no idea what you're talking about, and I think you know that. Listen, do you need help getting back to New York?"

He shrugged, smiling to himself. "I'd take a couple clams, if you could part with 'em, but don't trouble yourself. I'll figure it out." Before Margie could say anything else, he added, "How about you, then? What're you here for?"

Margie gestured down the National Mall, toward the massive, whitewashed dome of the Capitol building. "Congress called me to testify."

"Oh, right," Levi said, a gleam in his eye. "The Blackwing hearings. I've been reading about that in the papers."

In the weeks after the publication of the final *Coated Crusader,* the public backlash against the Blackwing Program, and a few other dragoncoat-related military projects, had been swift and fierce. A slew of mass protests and the resulting pressure had led to the suspension Blackwing's operations, pending a full government investigation. The future of the program looked grim; if the hearings found evidence of malfeasance, Margie hoped that Blackwing would be shut down indefinitely.

"I should've known they'd get you on the stand," Levi said thoughtfully. "It was you giving Felman those files, wasn't it? The classified stuff he never let me look at?"

"Sure was." Secretly, Margie was gratified to learn that David hadn't let Levi look at the medical reports. She'd assumed that the Freedom Press editor had had access to all of the information she sent David's way. She should have known David would be too skittish to share the documents with someone as loose-lipped as Levi.

"And what about the dragoncoats, huh? Are they gonna switch the scales?"

"Depends," Margie said. "With any luck, yes. They're still going over the evidence, but hopefully a well-timed testimony will convince them to speed up the process. And—you're gonna like this—it's not looking great for Douglas or Hathaway."

Levi grinned. "Now that's what I like to hear."

The two of them sat in silence for a minute, which was a welcome surprise to Margie. She leaned back on the steps, flipping her tie over her shoulder, and watched as a flock of mallard ducks descended to the edge of the reflecting pool. They squabbled with each other as they landed, and a cascade of droplets sent ripples across the water's surface.

"By the way, I've got something in here that you might

want to see." Levi tapped his briefcase. "More good news, if you can believe it."

Margie glanced at him, then sighed, returning her gaze to the reflecting pool. "Why would I want to see your court documents, Levi?"

Levi snorted a laugh. "These aren't court documents. I said *good* news. This stuff is for work."

"You're still in business?" Margie asked.

"Oh, yes," Levi replied. "I smoothed things over with Felix after that whole mess with the fuzz. We've been working together on a few projects. Freedom Press is still going strong... well, it's still going, at any rate."

Curious despite herself, Margie sat up straight. "What are you printing?"

"Couple magazines. A few new comics—Felman wannabes. Felix's pamphlets." A sly smile tugged at the corner of his mouth. "And, of course, the one and only *Coated Crusader.*"

"Wait—what?" Margie's eyes widened. "Are you serious?"

In answer, Levi unlatched the buckles on his briefcase and balanced it on his lap. He rooted through the papers inside and produced a folder full of inked comic pages, which he handed to Margie.

She picked up the top page as though it were a priceless artifact, adjusting her thick-framed glasses on her face to read the print more clearly. The cover depicted the eponymous Coated Crusader, standing alongside the Jade Jocust and a pitch-black dragoncoat. The sky was wide above them, and there was a mountain range in the background with snow-capped peaks. Below the title—*The Adventures of the Coated Crusader and the Jade Jocust—Danger in the Open Sky*—the byline read, "*Written and Illustrated by David Felman and Jade Atallah.*"

"The quality's gone way up since she started helping him," Levi admitted. "I guess two heads are better than one."

Fondly, Margie smiled down at the pages as she flipped through the comic, trying to guess which elements of the artwork were Jade's and which were David's. Even though she'd known David fairly well at Blackwing, she couldn't tell where his work ended and Jade's began. It had all rolled together into its own, complete style, something wholly unique built upon the undeniable framework of the first *Coated Crusader* run.

"What do you think?" Levi asked.

"I love it," Margie said simply, handing the folder back to him. "Good for them."

"It's good stuff, right? Oughta keep the lights on at Felman's place for a while."

Out in the reflecting pool, a passerby stopped to toss ripped-up pieces of bread into the water, sending the flock of ducks into a fresh frenzy. Margie stared at them for a few seconds, then past them, to the whitewashed dome of the Capitol building. She checked her wristwatch. Two short hours remained before she was back on the stand, telling the committee everything she knew about Blackwing's experiments. From this distance, she could see the small crowd gathered on the steps—protestors, wielding signs that decried Blackwing and advocated justice for the affected dragoncoats.

David and Jade's comic pages flashed before her eyes again. Idly, she wondered what would be next. Neither of them were the sort to rest upon their laurels; soon enough, the Felman-and-Atallah comics would certainly tackle some new foe, an enemy equally as dangerous as Blackwing—and equally as corrupt. Margie had done all she could to facilitate David's art in the past, and she saw no reason to stop now.

She turned to Levi. "How do you think that trial's going to turn out? Someone needs to keep printing those comics. If you're in the big house—"

"You kidding?" He grinned. "I'm winning this thing. Mark my words."

Margie checked her watch again and sighed, adjusting her tie. She rose to her feet, drawing to eye level with Levi, and laid a hand on his shoulder.

"Listen to me," she said. "I've got a couple hours on my hands before they're expecting me on the stand. Let me take you to an attorney's office. Get you a better mouthpiece."

"I don't need a lawyer. I'm not guilty of any—"

"Let me help you, Levi."

Levi hesitated, considering. Margie could practically see the wheels turning in his head. After a long moment, he frowned at her and said, "What's it to you, anyway?"

"What do you mean?"

"I wasn't under the impression that you liked the cut of my jib," Levi said with a shrug. "You're polite to me 'cause you think Felman would want you to be, right? But—"

"I don't have to like the cut of your jib," Margie interrupted. "I like the stuff that comes off your press. It's not personal. You and I... we've got mutual interests."

"We do, do we?"

Margie gave him a firm pat on the shoulder that nearly unbalanced him. As he steadied himself, she said, "How about I put it another way? You print my favorite comic books, written by two of my favorite people. So if I have anything to say about it, Freedom Press is going to keep its doors open for as long as humanly possible."

A slow, wry smile spread across Levi's face. "Well, I gotta admit... I like the sound of that."

"Thought you might." Margie began to descend the steps, and after a few seconds' delay, Levi followed her, jogging to catch up.

The reflection of the Capitol building in the pool beside

them rippled, distorted by the ducks' wings as the entire flock, startled, rose into the air.

EZRA AND JORDAN would like to thank you for reading this Dragoncoat Chronicles novel. Sign up to our reader group to be notified for the next in the series here: JordanRileySwan-Newsletter.

If you missed book one, The Stone Dragon and the Moonshine Molly, you can find it here.

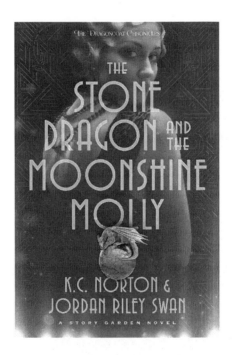

It ain't easy,
running a speakeasy,
in the dragon roaring '20s.

Argyle Galloway always follows the rules, no matter the

outcome. Without law and order to guide the Dragoncoat riders, the monsters and bugs swarming the Eastern Americas would destroy civilization. But when his dragon starts to shed its scales at the most inopportune time, he must hole up in a notorious speakeasy. The by-the-book Argyle is trying his best to keep on the straight and narrow. Yet he can't resist the beautiful barkeep who pulls him deeper and deeper into the lawless realm of gangsters and rumrunners—even though she seems more dangerous than the dragon he rides...

Molly Walker wasn't supposed to follow in her father's criminal footsteps, but when he dies suddenly, she's forced to take over his speakeasy or find herself living on the streets. She only intends to work the bar until she can find a buyer for it. Things spiral quickly out of control as clues surface, hinting that the robbery in which her father died might have been premeditated murder. Molly finds herself needing help from the stick-in-the-mud Argyle to solve the mystery, but she doesn't know which is harder to do: figure out who killed her father while running his illegal bar, or keep herself from falling in love with the stranger who thinks she's the biggest criminal of them all.

We look forward to bringing you more Dragoncoat Chronicles!

Acknowledgments

From Jordan Riley Swan:

I give my thanks to all the usual suspects: Ami and Ezra for our long bouts of plotting—I owe them so much; Diane Callahan, Story Garden's lead editor, who always puts a gun to my head and forces me to craft the best stories possible.

We have an amazing team over here at Story Garden. Thanks again to co-writer, Ezra Zabit, who was instrumental in the crafting and execution of this story. We're grateful for Angela Traficante's thorough copy editing. Our compliments also go out to the book cover chef James T. Egan of Bookfly Design, who can add *The Ink Dragon and the Art of Flight* to his extensive portfolio.

Also, we can't give enough praise to Ami Agisi for the comic panels that you found through the book (and were the inspiration to create this story in the first place).

We can't wait to share the rest of the stories in the Dragoncoat Chronicles and upcoming young adult Dragoncoat Academy and middle grade Dragoncoat Camp series. And thank you, dear reader, for reading until the very last line.

Made in the USA
Columbia, SC
06 October 2024

43742973R00140